CONSEQUENCE
OF CRIME

CONSEQUENCE
OF CRIME

ELIZABETH LININGTON

DOUBLEDAY & COMPANY, INC.
GARDEN CITY, NEW YORK

This one is for
Stephanie
on account of
the Akita-*inu*

Certainly it is the nature of extreme self-lovers, as they will set an house on fire and it were but to roast their eggs.

—FRANCIS BACON

Things and actions are what they are, and the consequences of them will be what they will be; why then should we desire to be deceived?

—FIFTEEN SERMONS, Bishop Joseph Butler

CONSEQUENCE
OF CRIME

CHAPTER 1

Maddox was a few minutes late this morning, and as he caught the light at Cahuenga and Fountain he glanced across the street a block ahead and said one unnecessary, "Damn." The new Hollywood precinct station, a present to the LAPD last year, occupied the whole block between Wilcox and Cole on Fountain, handsomely modern and pristine. Normally a hundred feet of curb space in front, red-painted, would be empty; now, of course, there were twelve cars there, nine of them nondescript unmarked sedans, three black-and-white squads.

He swung the Maserati left onto Wilcox and turned into the parking lot behind the station. D'Arcy's old tan Dodge was already there, Feinman's Chevy, Rodriguez' Ford, Sergeant Daisy Hoffman's Pontiac. It was Wednesday, Sue's day off; he had left her at home swearing at the sewing machine. They had just moved into the house in Glendale two weeks ago and he wasn't used to allowing the twenty extra minutes for the longer drive.

He came in the back door to the long hall, and into the big communal detective office. D'Arcy's lank length was bent over his typewriter; Rodriguez was reading a report; Feinman was staring into space over a cup of coffee, and Dabney, Rowan, Daisy, and George Ellis were in a little crowd of Metro men gathered around Ellis's desk.

"Traffic?" said Rodriguez uninterestedly.

Maddox sat down at his desk. "The extra ten miles—I'll get used to it eventually."

Rodriguez handed over the report, which was scrawled in Brougham's big hand: the night-watch report, short and sweet. "The ape man struck again. Laundromat on Melrose."

"Bloody hell!" said Maddox. He glanced over the page rapidly. Brougham and Donaldson, on night watch, had both gone out on it. At least this time the woman hadn't apparently been badly injured. A Linda Thorpe, address on Romaine, the hospital said to be released after treatment: forcible rape after assault, and by the little they had heard from her, it sounded like the ape man all right. "Damnation," said Maddox.

"Temper, temper," said Rodriguez, brushing his neat narrow mustache with one finger. "Sooner or later we'll have the place to ourselves again. Preserve patience, Ivor."

Maddox cast an annoyed glance at the crowd down the office. "Cockroaches," he said.

"Come again?"

"Like exterminators. Damn it, you can see the reason, but the day after they're gone, the cockroaches coming out of the woodwork again. I've got a date at the Fraud office downtown at eleven, and somebody'll have to see this woman."

"You and Daisy. I'm waiting for the witnesses to that pharmacy heist, and I think everybody else has got reports to write."

Maddox glanced at the report again and looked at his watch; it was eight-thirty. He looked up the number and dialed the hospital, the emergency wing at Hollywood Receiving; Mrs. Thorpe had been released after examination and treatment at midnight last night. "And what the hell women are thinking about," muttered Maddox, "to go wandering around alone at that time of night in this jungle—" He went down to the crowd and said, "Daisy, you can come help me talk to a victim."

The Metro men all seemed to be large and bulky and loud-voiced. Somebody had just told a joke and they were all laughing. At second count there were only five here so far; this afternoon there'd be more, and by change of shift the town would be crawling with them. And of course they were also LAPD men, and there was a good reason for them to be here, but their presence grated slightly on the Hollywood detectives.

Slim blond Daisy Hoffman, who was a grandmother but certainly didn't look it, came to join him. "The rape," she said. "You don't suppose we'll get anything new, do you?"

"Go through the motions," said Maddox. She gathered up her handbag and followed him out to the Maserati.

"I hope she'll be out of bed."

"Damn it, it's hardly the only case we've got to work."

Daisy said soothingly, "Don't let it get you down, Ivor. Just part of the job. Sue was saying she might finish those curtains today."

Maddox laughed, thrusting the key in the ignition. "No bets. You know how she hates sewing." But at least, he reflected as he backed out of the slot, that project—the acquisition of a house before prices went up any more—had turned out a good deal better than he'd thought it would. Sue and her mother had fallen in love with that house last January, and at his first look he'd thought it was the most god-awful old barracks in existence; but women did seem to know about these things, and now, this much later, it was going to be a comfortable, roomy family place. And the guardian angels on the job, minus a mortgage. After Margaret Carstairs had nearly been killed by the burglar in January, she'd been persuaded to live with them, and had sold the Hollywood house for sixty thousand; and the poor little old house on Alexandria, which poor little old Mrs. Eady had left to Sue, had been snapped up by a contractor, only for the land, for forty thousand. They'd got the house in Verdugo Woodlands in Glendale for ninety-three-five, so there had even been some cash in hand, and Maddox had put his foot down and insisted that it go to the necessary refurbishing.

"Have the pair of you killing yourselves at all the painting, and take the next six months to do it, which is damn silly when we can hire it done." Sue had argued but of course he'd had Margaret on his side, and in the end the house had got professionally painted inside and out before they moved in. The wilderness of growth in the big back yard had been cleaned up, and he had to agree that female instinct had been right: it was a gracious, old-fashioned, homey sort of house, if still rather bare of furniture.

"As a matter of fact," he said, switching on the right turn indicator, "they were going out later to look at some dogs, so the curtains—" His tone was absent-minded; he'd had a few stray thoughts about dogs lately, but hadn't said anything yet.

The address on Romaine was a middle-aged apartment building: no pool, balconies, or outside patio, just an apartment building of dirty tan brick. Linda Thorpe lived on the second floor at the back.

She was up: the door opened a crack and they saw it was on a chain. Maddox produced the badge and said, "Sergeant Maddox, Mrs. Thorpe. We'd like to talk to you about what happened last night."

"Oh." The chain was unhooked and she let them in. Maddox introduced Daisy. "I don't suppose you've got a chance of catching him," said Linda Thorpe. "But any way I can help you." She was a thin blonde about thirty-five, not a raving beauty but middling good-looking;

she clutched a blue nylon housecoat around her as if she was cold, this warm May morning. "I was just having some coffee, offer you some?"

They sat at the little table in the eating area at one end of the kitchen; she was drinking her coffee black but got out sugar and dairy creamer to put on the table. She had the start of a puffed black eye, bruises on one cheek, a cut lip, which she kept feeling tenderly. "My God," she said, "I always used to think that any woman who got herself raped probably asked for it some way, but now— That big ape just landing on me like that, I didn't have a chance—"

"Well, you were alone in the laundromat, as I understand it," said Maddox. "What time was it, rather late—"

"And smack on a main drag," said Linda Thorpe, "with the place lit up like a Christmas tree. It was about ten o'clock. Look, Sergeant. I work five days a week—I'm in Better Dresses at the Broadway—and so do a lot of other people. Saturdays and Sundays any laundromat in town is jammed, I usually have two loads at least and it takes a couple of hours even if I get a machine right away, which you never do on weekends. So I do it on a week night, and by the time I get home and fix dinner and clean up the kitchen, I'm lucky if I get there by eight o'clock. I was just taking the second load out of the dryer when that wild man came in and jumped me—" She felt her face and shuddered.

"You live alone, Mrs. Thorpe?" asked Daisy.

She nodded glumly. "Things happen, don't they? Bill and I both figured, that's it forever and ever, when we got married. It would've been. But he got rammed by a drunk driver two years back, and of course I couldn't afford the house payments. I was lucky to get this job."

"Maybe you can tell us a few more details than you gave the detectives last night. Of course you were shocked and upset. Can you add anything to your description?"

She shrugged and sighed. "I don't know—you can say that again, I don't remember exactly what I did tell them. Just, he was a wild man— like a big gorilla—a lot of hair, not a beard but long hair, and hairy arms, and he must've been six-two or three, a great big gorilla with a barrel chest. His eyes were sort of glazed—I think he could've been doped up on something—I couldn't smell any liquor on him, but his eyes were just wild, all huge and staring, kind of glassy, you know, and he never said a word—he just came in the door in a rush and fell on me, I didn't even have a chance to scream, he started punching me in the face and knocked me down in front of the line of dryers and started tearing at my clothes—" She lifted her cup in a trembling hand.

"What color was his hair?" asked Daisy. "Do you remember anything about his features? Clothes? Any scars or tattoos?"

Linda Thorpe shook her head. "He had dark brown hair—all greasy and stringy. He just looked like a wild man—I couldn't tell you if he had a crooked nose or what color his eyes were, just his size and— It was so fast. I didn't have a chance, even try to fight back—I guess I was lucky, if that doesn't sound crazy, because he knocked me right out, you know, and I don't actually remember him—raping me. Except when I came to, he'd torn my clothes off and—" She felt her mouth. "I couldn't find a dime for the phone—had an awful argument with the operator—" She poured more coffee.

"You were lucky, Mrs. Thorpe," said Daisy soberly. She exchanged a look with Maddox. This was the fourth woman who had given them that same description. All four of them had been assaulted and forcibly raped when they were alone in laundromats in the late evening. All of them had been beaten and mauled, the others injured worse than Linda Thorpe, and one of them—Cecelia Ritter—was still in the hospital ten days later, with a ruptured spleen and a broken jaw, a few other injuries. They'd all told the detectives the same thing: a big hairy wild man, probably high on something, he never said a word but just started beating them, tearing clothes off. And the description wasn't much use. The other two women, Nancy Unger and Ruth Sawyer, had done some poring over the mug shots downtown without picking any. But as they all said, it had been so fast—he could be there, they just might not be certain.

"We'd like you to look at some photographs," said Maddox. "See if you can spot him. Would you do that?"

"Mug shots," said Linda Thorpe. "Sure, I'll do that. Only when? I called in and told Mrs. Bessemer, she said take a few days off if I want. But naturally I'd get docked, I don't want to stay off too long."

"If you feel up to it, Sergeant Hoffman can take you downtown this morning."

"All right," she agreed drearily. "I'll get dressed."

"I'll come back for you in half an hour, how's that?" asked Daisy briskly. They left her rehooking the chain, and as they went down the thinly carpeted stairs Daisy added, "I don't suppose she'll make any either. Even when they only got a fast look at him, you'd think they'd spot one like that if he was on file."

"Or just maybe," said Maddox sardonically, "if he ever had his picture taken for us his hair was cut and he wasn't glassy-eyed on the foolish powder."

"Also a thought."

He dropped her in the parking lot to pick up her own car and went back into the office. The Metro men were still there; Rodriguez was talking to a middle-aged couple and taking notes; D'Arcy was on the phone; Feinman and Ellis had disappeared with Rowan and Dabney. As Maddox sat down at his desk D'Arcy put down the phone and said, "There's a new body just turned up. In a car on Yucca Street. And a little rumble going on at Hollywood High, teacher attacked."

Dick Brougham, of course, hadn't typed up an initial report on Linda Thorpe. Maddox sorted out forms and carbon and knocked one out in twenty minutes. That left him barely enough time to get downtown to headquarters. When he came up to the little blue Maserati in the parking lot, one of the Metro men was looking it over curiously and asked questions about mileage and performance; Maddox was abrupt, and slammed the door on his injured expression.

Well, there was a reason for the Metro Squad cluttering up Hollywood; but they were a damned nuisance. They'd been around for nearly three weeks now, and what they were accomplishing— Maddox had been working out of the Hollywood precinct ever since he'd made Detective, and that was seven years: and in that time, about every eighteen months the complaints stepped up, the citizens began to yell, the chief downtown got annoyed, and the Metro Squad was turned loose here to make waves.

The problem, of course, had got worse: had got bigger, in the same seven years. And any cop knew the realities of the problem. If every police officer working out of this station, in uniform and plain clothes, should forget every other case coming up to be worked and go all out just after the prostitutes and pimps, the problem would still be there. The prostitutes and pimps would still be there. Cockroaches coming out of the woodwork. But periodically something had to be done.

The chosen area, where they swarmed thickest, was Hollywood and Sunset boulevards, along the middle of town. Along the area there were still some classy shops and department stores, and up to last month the precinct had had over a hundred complaints from respectable females accosted as they were shopping in daylight hours: from store managers and personnel solicited on their jobs. The manager of the Egyptian Theater had shown up one late afternoon full of wrathful indignation and summed it up. "I know times have changed, damn it," he'd told Ellis, "but it's still supposed to be a more or less civilized country, Sergeant. When I step out for a coffee break and find this pair of—of savages making out right in front of the entrance twenty feet from all the people walking down the street, that is the end. I should think the police could do something—"

They were doing something. As before, the Metro Squad had been thrown in and was making waves in the cluttered community of prostitutes and pimps. The Metro Squad was the corps of men always on call when, for one reason or another, one of the precincts needed more manpower. As they had done before, they'd come out in force and were patrolling the indicated beats all afternoon, all night, keeping an eye out and swooping down whenever they got eyewitness evidence to make a charge: and so flagrant was that crew in picking up johns for the immediate exchange in a car or even up the nearest alley, they were hauling in dozens of them every day. Of course it was, legally, an exercise in futility: even if the charge stuck, it carried no more than thirty days in the county jail: but it was a big nuisance to the trade, for it meant making bail and time lost, and at least some of them were no sooner back on the street than they were picked up again. It was the kind of job only the Metro Squad could do: the regular detail of precinct men hadn't the time or the numbers.

But it was, all the same, an exercise in futility. It would all happen as it had before. Now, after three weeks of constant harrying, the prostitutes and pimps were going underground: at least not so visible and insolent to the respectable citizens. Possibly, as had happened before, numbers of them would drift down to Long Beach, Santa Ana, calling forth indignant comments from the lawmen in those cities. And presently the Metro Squad would go back downtown, and when the word spread that the heat was off, the cockroaches would come sneaking back again to their preferred beat. Six or eight months from now, they'd be back in full force, the citizens complaining again. It was a hell of a situation, everybody agreed, but there it was. They tried to cope the best way they could: but at the same time Hollywood, like every other precinct, had other worse things to deal with: homicides, burglaries, heist jobs, assaults, rapes, and all the assorted crime indigent to the city jungle, and they couldn't spare squad-car men and plain-clothes detectives to ride perpetual herd on the petty prostitutes and pimps.

The Metro men didn't normally clutter up the station; they hauled their catches directly to the jail. Still, they were technically working out of the precinct, their cars occupying parking space, the men patronizing the coffee and sandwich machines.

Maddox got held up in a traffic jam just after he got off the freeway downtown, and was half an hour late at headquarters. It was a joint meeting, over all those forged checks: they had turned up in Hollywood's territory, Hollenbeck's, Central, and West Hollywood—so the sheriff's boys were on it too. So far, there were just no leads at all on the bouncy checks. Maddox got to the Fraud office at Parker Center at eleven-thirty wondering what new cases might have gone down by the time he got back to Hollywood.

He was also wondering whether Sue and her mother had gone to look at those dogs, as had been casually suggested.

Linda Thorpe spent nearly three hours looking at pages of mug shots, in the Records and Identification office downtown, but didn't pick out any. She hesitated over two pictures and said, "That's not him, I can say that definitely, but it's—well, the same general type, if you see what I mean."

One was a shot of Donald Ray Hopper, who had a pedigree of heists and burglary. He was now twenty-six, male Caucasian, six-three, one-eighty, brown and blue. The other was Richard Dean Curtis, now twenty-eight, pedigree of burglary, petty theft: male Caucasian, six-two, one-ninety, brown and brown.

That wasn't much help in locating the rapist, just corroborative of the description. None of the women had seen him leave or enter a car; it was very unlikely that he'd left any prints anywhere at the laundromats. They all said he had come in fast, jumped them at once. There'd been a lab man out to dust the doors, but no clear latents had showed; Daisy supposed that Brougham would have got a lab man out last night, and eventually they'd get a report: probably more of the same.

"I'm sorry," said Linda Thorpe. "I'd sure like to help you catch him, but he's not anywhere here."

"Well, you never know until you look," said Daisy philosophically. "Thanks very much anyway, we appreciate your co-operation."

D'Arcy and Feinman had gone together to look at the body. Patrolman Percy Everard had come across it, tagging a car parked on Yucca Street. They all looked at it gloomily and D'Arcy said, "Why the hell did we ever want to make rank, Joe?"

"Ask me something easy," said Feinman. Everard, of course, would just go back on tour, and at four o'clock he could go home, at the end of Traffic shift. It was the front office boys who had to deal with the follow-up on the thankless job. Both he and D'Arcy could foresee that this one they'd probably go round and round on and never get anywhere.

The body was the body of a young woman, somewhere in the twenties. She was wearing a sleazy short blue dress, and where she sprawled in the back of the car the dress was pulled up so they could see she hadn't any underwear on. She wore an ancient pair of sandals over bare feet. She had dirty blond hair, not much make-up on. It looked as if she'd been shot in the head by a small caliber. The body was stiff.

"Last night," said D'Arcy with a sniff.

It almost spelled itself out for them. This location, the girl had probably been a prostitute. She looked the part. There'd have been an argument with her pimp, just possibly somebody else, but it was usually the pimp. She'd been holding out, or there'd been some other reason, and instead of the usual beating she'd got a bullet. They'd be lucky to get her identified.

The car was a beat-up old VW, looking to be on its last legs. It didn't carry any license plates or visible registration. They couldn't look inside until a lab team had a chance at it. At least last year when the city fathers had given them the handsome new precinct station, along with it had come two brand-new mobile lab units and the crews to man them.

They called in for one from the squad, and presently it came, with Baker and Franks. After the photographs were taken and every possible surface dusted—without conclusive result—D'Arcy looked in the glove compartment and found it empty. There was no handbag in the car and not so much as a handkerchief on the body.

"Tow it in," he said resignedly.

"And send you the engine number," said Franks with a grin. "I'd say that heap's at least twenty years old, and what do you bet that whatever dealer first sold it—anywhere from Miami to Seattle—is long out of business?"

The morgue wagon came and gathered up the body. D'Arcy and

Feinman stopped for lunch on the way back to the office. D'Arcy offered to write the report. As they came in the back door they met for of the Metro men just starting off on the afternoon's work, and Feinman stopped them.

"It'll make a little diversion for you," he said to Sergeant Conyers.

"What?" Conyers looked suspicious. He was a tall, dark, ascetic-looking fellow: in fact, he and Feinman together looked more like a pair of college teachers than cops, thought D'Arcy with an inward grin.

"Whichever ones you haul in from now on. Swing by the morgue and see if any of 'em can identify a corpse. Probably a hooker. Shot."

"What the hell?" said Conyers, annoyed. "That'll cut into our street time—all right, all right, I see it! Hell and damnation, we're not here to help the locals solve homicides!"

"Might be a short cut," said Feinman mildly.

The Metro men went off looking annoyed, and D'Arcy started to type the report. About then a memo came up from the desk, a Missing Persons report just activated from Santa Monica headquarters. It was a pair of high school kids, Peter Byron and Frances Keach, out on a date last night and expected home by eleven. Said to be good reliable kids, parents claiming not the type to run off, but these days what did parents know? There was an A.P.B. on the car, a blue Pontiac four-door registered to William Byron at a Santa Monica address.

Ten minutes after that Ellis and Rowan came in with half a dozen big louts of kids, from the rumble at Hollywood High. They'd be roping in D'Arcy and Feinman to talk to them.

As he got up, leaving the report half finished, D'Arcy cast a glance down the hall at the door to the lieutenant's office and said morosely, "Wait and see what we get in August."

"Yeah," said Feinman. "We can't be worse off."

For the last few years, the lieutenant nominally in command of the detective division had been Roy Roseman, and the powers that be had left him alone, coasting toward retirement. He hadn't pulled his weight at the daily grind for years; he had a chronic ulcer, arthritis, and all his experience had been in administrative work. He would be officially retiring in August, and the precinct would get a new lieutenant, hopefully another working hand to share the case load. They had also been promised at least three new detectives; that might or might not be helpful, for they'd be green new detectives who'd just made plainclothes rank.

The proliferating bouncy checks constituted a tedious and time-consuming job: the kind of job, reflected Maddox, to disillusion any cop who still had any lingering notion that police work was exciting. The checks went several months back into the past, for most of them purported to be checks from large department stores, chain pharmacies, and markets; it had not been until the head accounting offices of those firms began to discover discrepancies that the bundles of canceled checks were examined.

To date the Fraud office had accumulated, from the various precincts, seventy-four forged checks, and the total take added up to over twenty thousand dollars. And while a lot of diligent police work had been done, and this and that been turned up, they weren't any closer to finding out who was forging and cashing them.

"What it boils down to," Captain Lyons was neatly recapitulating to the nine men in his office, "is about the slickest little operation I've ever come across. A key point, of course, is the printing job—the damn checks look so good, a beautiful professional printing job, and of course there's just nothing to say which of five thousand print shops around might be turning them out. It could be an amateur with a press in his garage, but it's a damn good job. Apart from that, what do we know? It's got to be the same man and woman passing them. And it's all so damn low-key. They're not greedy—it's the steady long haul. They've got kosher-looking identification, it's on the cards they haven't been turned down once. It's disappointing, of course, that we reached a dead end on Standish—"

"Dead end!" muttered the sheriff's deputy to Maddox. "Stone wall! Damn sloppy system of registering people, keeping track—if we had every citizen numbered and filed in a computer—"

Maddox eyed him coldly and said, "Maybe the computers in a local KGB office?" But it was, of course, frustrating. Anybody in California could walk into a D.M.V. office and get a driver's license in any name, for the asking: pass the written and road tests, the license would be forthcoming. They had been, jointly, working on this case for the last month, and what had been turned up by all the legwork was discouraging.

Roughly half of the checks, purporting to be refund and salary checks from the May Company, the Broadway, Robinson's Department Store, Lucky Markets, Safeway Markets, Thrifty Drugs, had been made out to and endorsed by John L. Standish. In each case Standish had offered a driver's license and a VISA card as I.D. Co-operation from Sacramento had finally told them that the license had been issued at a D.M.V. office in Long Beach: a very busy office. There, the two clerks and one examiner involved barely remembered the man: they had so many people coming in. They thought he'd said something about just moving to California, losing his old license; they didn't think he'd mentioned where he came from. He'd had no trouble passing the tests; had objected to putting his thumbprint on the license, but a lot of people did that and it wasn't mandatory. They had, of course, snapped a picture of him to go on the license; but unfortunately the only copy of the license was sent to the applicant by mail, the negatives weren't retained. The mailing address had turned out to be a cheap apartment in Seal Beach, and it had been rented to John Standish for just two months, time to receive his license and VISA card through the mail.

The VISA card had dictated the name. There had been a real John Standish who owned one: a pristine VISA card routinely paid up to date. That Standish had died of a heart attack nearly six months ago; he had been a real-estate salesman with numerous acquaintances, and hundreds of people might have known that he carried a VISA card. The headquarters office of VISA had not, of course, known he was dead when they received a request by mail for a new card. The letter explained that the original card had been destroyed in a fire; when a routine check found his account in order, the headquarters office had supplied a new card, made out to the new address as he requested.

The bank, of course, had given them something there.

Maddox had seen the people at the bank—it was a Security bank on Western Avenue. The woman in charge of New Accounts and credit, a Mrs. June Lederer, had been as helpful as possible. A nice woman, placidly efficient, still rather pretty in middle age. "Well, of course, Sergeant, ordinarily anybody would do it right here at the bank—I mean, asking for a new card, or a replacement—that is, the bank where the person did business. But of course, that's why he didn't—I mean, whoever it was—because we all knew Mr. Standish was dead, he'd banked here for years. What a very funny thing—oh, terrible, of course—but I don't know that I ever heard of such a thing happening before." The local headquarters office of VISA would be listed in the phone book, naturally.

Proper records be damned, thought Maddox, nobody wanted to issue every citizen a number and I.D. card to show the Gestapo on demand, but the damn D.M.V. might keep those negatives. Take up too much space, enough paperwork now, they said. And nobody could give anything but a vague description of Standish: he seemed to be a nonentity. Middle-aged, people said doubtfully: not very tall or short, medium: either brown hair or not much hair: wore glasses: quiet and polite. What could you expect? Busy people in busy places, and all those checks cashed on Saturdays when places were even busier: also making the excuse plausible, no time to get to the bank yesterday.

The VISA card was canceled now, but that would probably make no odds. When he was just using it as I.D., not for a purchase, no clerk in a busy place was going to call the hot line, check on that number.

"As for the woman, we do have a little new information from New York," Lyons was saying. The other checks had been made out to, and endorsed by, a Rebecca Simms, who routinely offered a VISA card and a Sears Roebuck credit card as I.D., explaining to the clerks that she didn't drive. "There's been an unavoidable delay while they chased those cards down—when you think of how many'll be floating around the country, of course—"

The sheriff's deputy said disgustedly, "You'd think they'd have computers," and the pretty policewoman who was taking notes beside Lyons' desk gave Maddox another flirtatious smile. He would never know why unremarkable, thin, dark Ivor Maddox, who had just got into the force at five-nine, was apparently irresistible to so many females: a good thing Sue wasn't jealous, and his wedding ring didn't seem to mean anything to the females.

"—Information just came through that both cards were issued to an address in New York City. The VISA card goes back to 1970, but the Sears card's an oldie, first issued in 1950. Both accounts are paid up, no charges show for the last year. The New York police are checking the address, we'll see what shows on that."

Damn all, thought Maddox. New York—ten to one an anonymous apartment where neighbors didn't know each other by sight. And all anybody could tell them, vaguely, about Rebecca Simms, was that she was anywhere between thirty-five and fifty, medium height and weight, had hair more blond than dark, and was quiet and polite.

The meeting, which was largely unproductive, lasted past two o'clock, and sandwiches and coffee were sent in from the canteen. On his way back through Hollywood after leaving the freeway Maddox passed four Metro cars double-parked where the plainclothesmen had swooped down to arrest more hookers and pimps. The old Wilcox Street jail was always full these days; as soon as one batch made bail and got out, another batch was booked in.

And of course you'd never change them, but the object was to chase them decently underground, instead of flaunting themselves in front of the respectable citizens. It was bad for the tourist trade.

Back at the office, he heard about the new body. D'Arcy, Feinman, Ellis, and Rowan were still talking to the teen-age louts, about the melee at Hollywood High, a teacher stabbed and sent to emergency. By five o'clock they managed to sort out who had held the knife, and booked him into jail and notified the parents. Thankfully, no parents had descended before the end of shift. If the parents were going to come complaining about the mean cops picking on their offspring, it would be to the night watch.

It was another ten miles to drive; but Maddox had to admit that his women had been right, it was a very nice house. A generous old-fashioned family house, on a big lot; it sat at the end of a dead-end street called Starview Terrace, northeast in the Verdugo Woodlands section of Glendale. Gleaming white with green trim outside, its little gabled windows on the second floor looked like friendly eyes, welcoming; and gleaming white with fresh paint inside, if the rooms looked a little empty, it was still going to be a warm family home. They wouldn't need to furnish the other two bedrooms until Sue started a family, and both his females were assiduously haunting the secondhand stores for more downstairs furniture.

He kissed Sue; he kissed Margaret Carstairs; he said, "Good day?"

"I suppose so," said Sue vaguely. "I haven't finished those damned curtains." Neither of them had wanted to attempt formal drapes for living and dining rooms; they'd got those on sale, but Sue was still struggling with the bedroom curtains.

"We'll get there," said her mother cheerfully. "Dinner in twenty minutes, Ivor, unless you want a drink first."

They were nice to come home to, his females. Sue neat and dark and slim, and Margaret—in about twenty years Sue was going to look a lot like Margaret Carstairs, which would be fine with Maddox. "Anything new down?" asked Sue.

"The ape man again. She wasn't knocked around quite so much, but it was him all right. And no new leads, of course."

"And NCIC a broken reed for once," said Sue. The National Crime Information Center had been a very good idea, a pool of information available to lawmen nationwide; but the men who devised it and set it up had a strong aversion to anything smacking of a permanent computerized file on the citizens, communist-style. NCIC dealt only with current crimes and currently wanted criminals. Whenever a crime was cleared, either by arrest or getting shoved in the unsolved file, all the information on it was removed from NCIC's computers. "Damn. I'd like to get that one. You know he'll end up killing one of them."

Maddox drifted out to the kitchen to build himself a Bourbon and water. "All too likely." There was a delectable smell of pot roast and gravy in the kitchen. "Did you go to see those dogs?"

"Oh yes," said Margaret. "The puppies are perfectly adorable."

"Utterly adorable," said Sue. "Of course they're only three weeks old, they won't be ready to leave home for a while."

"Um," said Maddox noncommittally. They'd only lost the well-loved little Welsh Corgi, Gor, six months ago. The new house had a very large fenced yard; but more to the point, it was a rather isolated house on this very quiet dead-end street, and Margaret would be alone here except on Sue's days off, and if Sue ever started a baby the two of them would be here alone—

(He had walked into the old house on Janiel Terrace, that day last January, to find Margaret bleeding and unconscious after the assault by the burglar, and it had been like that terrible time the high school principal had called him into his office and told him, fumbling and hunting for words, about Mother and Dad and the plane crash—)

The little Corgi. Another little Corgi. Nice little dogs, and plenty of guts and spunk. But a little dog.

He was supposed to be off on Thursday, but there were two witnesses coming in to make statements about the latest checks. He had been on that since it first erupted, so he'd go in this morning at least to type the statements. It was very nice these days, with no morning rush as the two of them got ready: Margaret had breakfast ready when he and Sue came down, and they got off separately by seven-thirty.

The witnesses straggled in at a quarter of nine: a clerk from a Lucky Market and another from Thrifty Drugs. Both stores were located in busy areas of Hollywood.

"I never gave it a thought," said Marcia Williams. "She had perfectly good I.D., and it looked like a perfectly good check, a salary check from Robinson's, for something over three hundred, and I do know they pay every two weeks because my sister used to work there, so it looked perfectly all right."

"Yes," said Maddox. It was all more of the same. The professionally printed checks looking so authentic, the amounts plausible: the big markets, the chain pharmacies, cashed a lot of salary checks automatically.

He made notes on what they could tell him, typed up the statements, and got them signed by ten o'clock. It was another handful of nothing. He was re-reading the statements, the witnesses gone, when Sue and Daisy came into the office in a hurry. Everybody but Rodriguez was out on something: the several heists they were still working, the daylight burglaries, the new body.

"You'd better hear about this, if there isn't much we can do," said Sue in a quiet voice. Maddox cocked his head at her; her mouth looked a little grim. Daisy was looking serious. "Mr. and Mrs. Rittenhouse."

"Yes?" Maddox got up and offered chairs.

They were probably in the early forties: an ordinary-looking couple except that they both looked ravaged and desperately worried. He was tall, dark, in crumpled sports clothes, losing his hair; she was middle-sized, a little plump, ash blond, wearing a navy pantsuit, her mouth taut, her eyes wild.

The man said, "I've got to try to make sense. Did she say Sergeant? I thought, telephone—but no way to get it across to you, we had to come. We drove all night—I never got home to see it till nine, I was showing a house—and we ran into that damn detour—we just got here—an hour ago, went to headquarters downtown and they sent us up here. Made the best time I could, but it's an eight, nine hour drive—Stockton." He sagged in the chair. Sue had gone down the hall, practically, for coffee. She set the paper cups before them on Maddox's desk silently.

"Yes, sir, what's it about?"

Sue laid something on the desk before him. "In the mail yesterday," said Rittenhouse. "That. We've been wild—just wild. Never had a minute's worry with Sally—always a good girl—and it was a silly little argument, her staying out past eleven with Ken, he's a good boy—and Marjorie going with her—God, we couldn't reach the Burnses, they were out somewhere—and we had to come—you've got to find them, you've got to start looking—"

Maddox picked up the thing on his desk. It was a crudely manufactured envelope, made of thick white paper Scotch-taped into folds, and addressed in a scrawl to Robert Rittenhouse, a Stockton address. It bore a fifteen-cent stamp and a Hollywood postmark. Inside, there was a folded half sheet with a ragged edge of the same paper, and more hasty scrawling.

Dear Daddy, I hope I can get some man mail this I dont know please we only meant to scare you some, go overnight but we got Hollywood and a lady and man said help us get jobs a Mrs. Aggie and his name Joey they lock us up and we have do awful sex things or they dont give us anyth to eat I think it said Vermont avenue where we are please please come get us we want go home please Daddy.

CHAPTER 2

Maddox managed to calm him into more coherence with a few sharp questions, and more background emerged. The two girls were good girls, never any trouble with disciplining them, they'd never done such a thing or threatened to before. There'd just been that little argument over Sally Rittenhouse's tardiness, and she'd flared up the way teen-agers would—they thought, just a little spat. The other girl, Marjorie Burns, hadn't had any trouble with her parents, but the two girls had been best friends all their lives and it was likely that Marjorie had gone with Sally for company—the kind of silly damn thing the teen-agers would do—Rittenhouse was half raging, half weeping.

"Yes," said Maddox, looking at the letter, "they didn't mean to run away for good."

"Three weeks yesterday!" said Rittenhouse. "Three weeks! We've been wild, and the Burnses—Marjorie's an only child, as if that makes it worse—I don't know if the police really tried, they kept saying how many kids run away these days—but not kids like ours! We—they didn't seem to—"

The two girls had just turned sixteen, only begun being allowed to date. "They're both young for their age," said Sally's mother sadly, drearily.

They might have had twenty or thirty dollars each; both had been saving from their allowances for summer clothes. They just hadn't come home from school that day; none of their friends knew anything— "And they're all good kids, they'd have told us if they knew." The police had checked the bus station, the railroad station, but both were fairly busy and nobody remembered selling them tickets; they could, of course, have asked somebody to do that for them. In the next four or five hours buses and trains had left for every major city in California, and points east, north, and south.

"—Nightmares about these crazy rapists killing girls, but now this—"

Rittenhouse was pacing agitatedly. "You've got to find them—knock on every door along this Vermont Avenue—"

Maddox said, "I'm sorry, sir, that's just not feasible. Vermont runs for twenty miles right down to the harbor." In Los Angeles all the way, of course; it was, in fact, in the mile-wide strip retained by the city so the harbor could be called Los Angeles Harbor instead of San Pedro. "The postmark on this says Hollywood, which is why the Central office sent you up here, but that just says it was mailed here." He picked up the letter again, and Sue took it from him.

"You know what it is, Ivor," she said suddenly. "It's shelf-liner." The thick coarse paper was old and grimy; their eyes met, and they shared a mutual vision of a bare-furnished room in a ramshackle old house somewhere, the aged torn paper lining in a cheap chest of drawers—they had had the Scotch tape, or filched it somehow? Maddox shrugged, and Sue gave him a brisk sharp nod. The two girls could be confined on any beat—Hollywood, Central, Harbor—but the Vice office downtown was always busy these days.

"The FBI—kidnapping—"

"It doesn't work that way, Mr. Rittenhouse," said Maddox. "The technical charge is contributing to the delinquency of minors. This isn't the first time we've run into this sort of thing, you know. For a lot of runaway girls, Hollywood is still a sort of mecca, and we've had too much of this—the older girls and pimps hanging around the bus stations, offering help and jobs to the kids landing here. Occasionally they're held against their will, more often just inducted into prostitution."

"But, my God, you've got to look—you've got to find—"

"There are things we can do, but you can't expect results tomorrow. Though, when your daughter got this smuggled out, maybe the luck's running— It is her writing?"

"She writes better than that," said Mrs. Rittenhouse on a hiccuping sob. "She's always had good, neat writing—but I suppose—"

"Yes, she was in a desperate hurry," said Maddox. "And talk about luck—it's a miracle that any man going to a place like that could be persuaded to buy a stamp and mail this."

"But what are you going to *do*? How can you— You are going to look? Now we know they're here, somewhere—"

"Believe me, we'll be looking. But it may take time. And there's nothing you can do to help, sir. If you'll take our advice, you'd better just go home and wait. I know it's not an easy thing to do."

"Wait!" said Rittenhouse in agony. He bit his knuckles. "God, have to tell Bill and Elly Burns—"

His wife looked at Sue and Daisy. "The other children—our older daughter looking after the boys, but— Bob, we've got to believe they know what they're doing. These police are supposed to be good, here."

"We'll be looking, Mrs. Rittenhouse," said Sue gently. "We'll be in touch with you. It's the only thing you can do, leave it to us. You'd better check into a motel, have a good rest, and just go home."

It wouldn't, of course, be easy for them. Daisy shepherded them out, and Rodriguez, who had been a silent spectator, said, "Now that's a bastard. The backpacking drifter's one thing, usually fairly tough, but these two poor innocents— Aggie and Joey. ¡Vaya! How many in the files?"

"Well, it's a place to start looking," said Sue. "And put the word out that we want them."

It was, in fact, about the only place to look. With the word out on the street, sooner or later one of their regular snitches would pass on the required information, possibly even the address. In the city jungle community of drugs, prostitutes, pornography, and pimping, a lot of people knew a lot of things, and there was a price on everything.

There might be a short cut to be found in records. Sue was already on her way out, car keys in hand. "Many hands make light work, they say."

"It's supposed to be my day off," said Maddox. Daisy had gone back to the office across the hall to answer an insistent phone. "You're looking concerned for the poor waifs, César—you can tag along."

"Well, we can look," said Rodriguez pessimistically. He went after Sue. Maddox looked at Sally's pathetic little letter again: the biggest miracle of the year the thing had ever got mailed, all right. The poor kids, more than they deserved for the flighty little impulse to scare the parents momentarily. It was very unlikely that Questioned Documents could tell them anything more about the letter, but they were supposed to be thorough: he supposed he ought to send it down there.

He was rummaging for a manila envelope when Feinman came in looking pleased, with a sullen-looking girl in tow. "You'll do for a witness," he said. "I didn't expect the idea to pay off so soon, but it did. This is Marion Potter. I had a little hunt for her, she made bail this morning, but of course she had to give an address at the jail and I dropped on her just as she was walking out with a suitcase."

"Damn fuzz interfering alla time," she said, dividing a resentful glance between them. "I'm getting out till the heat goes off."

"You can go as soon as you answer some questions," said Feinman. "You identified a body at the morgue last night, just after you were picked up." He offered her a chair.

She collapsed onto it suddenly. "Jesus, that place. Take me a place like that, make me look at a dead body! I nearly passed out— Cops!" She was too thin, scrawny as a plucked bird, shabbily dressed in dirty jeans and a tight T-shirt, and her sharp-featured face bore the residue of several days' make-up, unwashed. She had crooked front teeth, gray with tartar. If as cops they had always known that the myth of the glamorous golden-hearted prostitute was just that, a myth, still these last few years they could marvel at just how much dirtier and uglier each new crop seemed to get. Not much to choose between them, maybe, the hookers and the johns, but how anybody could figure Marion Potter was worth ten or twenty bucks a throw was a mystery.

"You identified the body," said Feinman, "as Sheila Harris. What do you know about her?"

"Harris, Harrison, Harrington, something like that, I don't remember exactly. I only heard it once, at a party. I don't know nothing about her, just ran across her a few times."

"Where?"

"Around. On the street, in a bar, like that."

"Do you know where she lived?"

She shook her head. "Girl she seemed to know pretty good was Mary something, she's got a pad somewhere on Delongpre with a couple other girls, could be this Sheila was one, I don't know. It's an apartment house, I don't know the address."

"All right, do you know who was running her?" asked Feinman.

She gave them a swift half-scared look from downcast eyes. "Was it him—took her off?"

"The odds are on it, aren't they?" said Feinman. "Do you know?"

She took a quick breath. "Plenty of people could tell you that, but I don't know his last name. It's Randy something, he's a little guy with sort of red hair, he's got four-five girls, I heard. I don't know him. And that's all I could tell you, honest."

"All right," said Feinman with a sigh.

"Can I go?"

"Go, go. Thanks very much."

"Cops," she said. It was merely a comment on a fact of life. She went in a hurry, and Feinman wrinkled his nose.

"At least in ancient Rome they took baths occasionally," he said sadly. "When I think of all the legwork, just to find who took off that cheap hooker—small loss. So now we go look in records for Randy."

"You look," said Maddox. "It's my day off."

Feinman sighed and went out, and D'Arcy passed him on his way in. "We might as well throw all these latest heists in Pending right off, you know. We haven't even got any decent descriptions. Grope around in the dark questioning men with the right records. And we're going to have an early summer, it's up to eighty outside now. In May. Little smog too." He slumped at his desk and lit a cigarette. "Let's go have lunch early."

"It's my day off," said Maddox, and the phone shrilled on his desk. Resignedly he picked it up. "Maddox."

"You've got a new homicide," said Sergeant Whitwell on the desk. "Woman just called straight in to report it."

"Oh, hell and damnation," said Maddox. Nobody else was in. "All right. We've got a new body, D'Arcy. What's the address? Who called in?"

"All very businesslike," said Whitwell. "Nichols Canyon Road. A dame by the name of Gunther. She said her piece and hung up, and I didn't have a chance to ask for a repeat, but if I got it right we're going to have press swarming around and every TV anchor man in California. She said it's Jan Warden. The body."

Maddox said blankly, "Jan Warden. Somebody?" The name rang a faint bell.

"My God, Sergeant," said Whitwell. "Only the latest big superstar— didn't you ever see her? That 'Newcomers' Club' show—"

Maddox very rarely looked at TV. "Well, we're on it." He put the phone down. "You watch the tube much?"

"Now and then," said D'Arcy. "Did he say Jan Warden? The body? I'll be damned." He put out his cigarette and stood up. "We'll have the press around."

"So let's go and look at it," said Maddox. It was now after eleven o'clock and he was getting hungry.

It was a big sprawling house on about half an acre up in Nichols Canyon above Hollywood, a house half-brick, half-stucco, with a broad curving walk leading up from a broad curving driveway. It sat cater-cornered on the lot. To the right of the drive, which curved away behind the house, stood a neat little guest house designed to match the big place. It had its own short drive, and in it was a middle-aged Dodge sedan. Maddox braked the Maserati just outside the front door of the big house; the door was open and a woman was standing there waiting for them.

Maddox showed her the badge. "Mrs. Gunther?"

"Well, you were quick enough," she said. "Miss. Eleanor. Trouble enough to look after myself and I never fancied any of the fellows did come around. And God knows I've seen plenty, mixed up with these people, but it's the first time I ever ran into murder."

"Did you say it's Jan Warden?" asked D'Arcy. He sounded doubtful; the show biz people got up to some antics, but chiefly brawls in bars and shouting matches with the press.

"That's who." Eleanor Gunther didn't seem especially upset. She might be fifty or more, a big woman nearly as tall as Maddox and a good deal broader, but not an ounce of her looked flabby: a solid strong down-to-earth female, with her graying brown hair in a short no-nonsense cut, no make-up on her square sensible face. Her squarish glasses were tortoise-shell-rimmed; she was wearing a plain cotton dress, cotton stockings, and brown oxfords.

She stood back and they went in to a good-sized entry hall, tile-floored, with a double door at the left leading to a vast living room, a door to the right to a smaller dining room.

"I never found her till just now. Took it for granted she was gone, same as usual—she had to be on the set at six A.M. when she was working, and I don't get up till around seven. The garage being behind, I never saw it was still closed. I puttered around dusting and so on down here—"

"Excuse me," said Maddox, "you live on the premises?"

"Sure, in the guest house. I'd been meaning to wash the kitchen windows, I did that, and then I thought I'd start her room before lunch, so up I went, and—boo!—there she was. All the blood—well, I don't get shook very easy, but believe me, I was shook."

The mobile lab unit pulled up behind the Maserati. Maddox said,

"We'll want to talk to you some more, Miss Gunther, but right now—if you'll just tell us which room—"

"First on your right upstairs. I'd just as soon not look at it again, and how it'll all get cleaned up—" She shivered. "I'll be in the kitchen making some more coffee."

Franks and Baker came in lugging the Speed Graphic, the lab bag, and they climbed curving stairs. The carpet felt a foot deep. There was a wide hall upstairs with three doors to the right, four to the left; the first one on the right, at the front of the house, was open.

"God," said Baker. "What a mess." He looked suddenly shook himself, and like all cops he had seen a lot of messes. He put the lab bag down. "My wife used to watch that show regular. She was a damn good-looking girl—not that you'd know it now."

"Somebody going berserk?" said D'Arcy.

"She didn't do any struggling," said Maddox. "I don't think so, D'Arcy."

Jan Warden, superstar, was lying quiet and straight in the double bed. The only indication that she had resisted an attacker was in one upflung arm, the right, over the pillow. The bed, the floor beside it, the bedding, and the body were all but covered with blood, and blood not long dry; it seemed incredible that so much blood could have come from one body, and not a very large body. You could just see that she'd had a lot of dark brown hair; the blood obscured everything else. One small square of nightgown had escaped the red tide; it was pale lavender nylon. Parts of the blanket showed as light green.

Franks was starting to aim the camera. "The autopsy'll say," he said, fiddling with the strobe light, "but I've seen a few bodies, Maddox. She just lay here and died—and a lot of that was arterial blood, you can still see a little difference in color. Looks to me—"

"Um." Maddox didn't like looking at messes any more than the next man, but he forced himself to look closer at this one. "Could be. Seeing she didn't struggle at all—the first or second lucky hit right through the carotid artery, and if she'd got banged over the head first she'd just lie and bleed to death."

"That's what," agreed Franks. The camera clicked, and he moved away for another view. Baker was getting out the dusting equipment.

"Last night sometime," said Maddox, "at a guess."

"Well, have fun," said D'Arcy. He and Maddox came out and Maddox wandered up the hall, looking into all the rooms. Three more bedrooms, a full bath in green tile; the front bedroom had its own private bath. The rooms on the other side of the hall overlooked an outsize sparkling kidney-shaped pool surrounded by a broad stone coping.

"Today's prices, four hundred grand," said Maddox.

"Well, she'd have been raking it in," said D'Arcy.

"Know anything about her?"

"Not much. She'd made it big in that TV show—it's been on about four seasons, just went off and she was supposed to be doing a new series starting in the fall. I've got no idea what she'd be making, but you know TV—two or three hundred grand a year?" D'Arcy hunched his shoulders.

"And a cutthroat business," said Maddox. "Anybody getting to the top has maybe stepped on a few toes getting there."

"Or been damned lucky."

"And a lot of show biz people not exactly burdened by an excess of morality. Know anything about her background?"

"I don't read TV Guide cover to cover. I think she was on Broadway awhile before she tried TV."

"Um." It had been thirty-five years since the entertainment business had dominated the Hollywood scene. By the end of the Second War, big industry had been established in and around L.A., and it had grown and diversified. There were still the big studios, many moved out of Hollywood now but still around, and vast sums were expended on the films and TV shows. But with bigger money elsewhere, and with the more legendary greats of earlier days faded away, the glamour had long since died, and if the gossip columns still flourished in a few tabloids, it was for a much smaller audience than formerly. Los Angeles, no longer dependent on The Business, was also no longer an overgrown small town but impersonal big city, no longer awed by ephemeral fame and money.

They went downstairs and found the kitchen, which was large and long with a lot of gleaming green tile and a big table by a back window. Miss Eleanor Gunther was sitting there over a cup of coffee, and without asking got up and brought two more cups.

"Not so pretty now, is she?"

"Not at all," said Maddox. "Have you worked here long, Miss Gunther? You're the housekeeper?"

"Good a name as any. Just over two years. I was with Rhetta Preston, that was a good job, I was sorry to leave, but when she married the new one they went back East to live, and I don't fancy wading through snow." The name was vaguely familiar to Maddox: an older actress, much married. "But this hasn't been bad—I wouldn't have stayed if I hadn't liked it all right. It's a damn good living," said Miss Gunther frankly, "because these people pay through the nose for what they get. Your ordinary housekeeper, maid, houseboy, whatever, wouldn't put up with it for the going rate. They want to get catered to, they've got to pay—and it's all gravy because you get your living too."

"Show business people," said Maddox.

"That's right. They have to pay, to get the service. If you can put up with it, it's a gold mine," said Miss Gunther. She accepted a cigarette and bent to Maddox's lighter. "Of course some of 'em are worse than others, but even the quiet ones with a few manners, they keep funny hours. I don't say they're all a bunch of crazies with the morals of alley cats, but enough of 'em. Especially the new crop, say the last fifteen years. I don't know whether either of you go to movies much or watch TV, probably not, probably as cops you got better things to do with your time, but it's—dismal. I mean, there used to be some real talent around—the stuff they were turning out in the forties, and a lot of the first TV shows, but now—God. Most of these so-called stars, not much more talent than I've got—it's all smart publicity and gall and if they add in enough cussing and sex it's a smash hit. The people who know real talent from amateur night don't watch the tube much, or movies either." She reached for the pot and warmed up their coffee.

"Quite a lot of people would agree with you," said Maddox, amused. "The new crop are hard to work for, are they?"

"Most of 'em I know anything about," she agreed cheerfully. "The thing is, the ones anywhere under forty, they grew up without any manners or morals mostly because that's when it started to get smart to be that way. And practically all of 'em came up from nothing, all of a sudden having all the money to throw around, and they think they can get away with anything on account of the money—and mostly they do. I was with Johnny Camp until he smashed himself up in that race car, and you wouldn't believe those bashes he threw—the mess—coke floating around like it was sugar, and four-five people out cold. Him calling at five o'clock, saying twenty people for dinner. I had six girls under me there, and plenty of work for all of us."

"Was Miss Warden as difficult to work for?"

"Well, no, I can't say that. At least she was halfway serious about her job. Not that she had any more real talent than most of the young ones—pretty face, gorgeous figure, and that was it. And when the shows were shot for the season, she'd live it up all right. Parties, I'd have extra people in to help, and off on shopping sprees, she'd be out till all hours. But I will say when she was working she didn't go goofing off. She had to be on the set at six A.M. and she wouldn't go out much."

"So she didn't go out last night? When did you see her last?"

"She did go out. Just to dinner with the latest boy friend. It was her birthday. She said her twenty-seventh, but I'd add on about five years to that."

"The boy friend," said D'Arcy.

"Fellow called Toby Kelsey, he's in TV too, not very big—had a couple of good parts in one of those cop shows. She'd taken up with him just the last couple of months, she split up with Scott Dukard last January."

Both Maddox and D'Arcy recognized the name; Dukard had just been starred in one of the perennial cop shows last year. "He was the steady boy friend up to then?"

"Live-in," said Miss Gunther succinctly. "For about a year. But when he made it big, of course that she couldn't take. She had to be top bitch. She used to be married to that producer, George Maximilian —I guess it was him who really put her up on top, and I'd say it was the same story there, she couldn't stand having anybody more important than her around. I think she'd been married to somebody else before, back East."

"Last night. When did they leave?"

"About six-thirty, he came for her. They were going to that Supper Club Theater in Beverly Hills. There's some kind of revue on there, supposed to be good."

"Did you hear her come in?"

"I did not. I locked up the house and went home—you know, to the guest house—and I read awhile and went to bed about ten-thirty. Sometimes they'd be noisy, coming in—he might stay over—and my bedroom's right on the drive, so I just put some cotton in my ears and I never heard a thing. I couldn't say when she came home."

"Well, this morning. Was the door locked when you came in here?"

"Yes, it was. She was careful about locking up. Well, she had a lot of stuff here—clothes and jewelry. There wasn't anything disturbed, just like it was last night." A sudden new idea galvanized her. "For the

Lord's sake, you don't mean you think it was the Kelsey fellow did that? He never struck me as being anything much, one way or the other—sort of a mild guy, I'd say. But when the door was locked—"

"It's early to make guesses," said Maddox. "Did the other one—Dukard—ever have a key to the house?"

"Well, yes, he lived here about a year." The phone on the wall suddenly went off and she jumped, got up to answer it. Automatically she said, "Miss Warden's residence. Oh, Mr. Wells. Mr. Wells, I—what?—no, I know she didn't—listen, Mr. Wells—" She looked around at them. "It's her agent. The studio's after him to know why she never showed up."

"They didn't call here?"

"Naturally, or I'd have known before something was wrong. She never gave out her number, they always had to get her through him, and I suppose he just got to his office." The phone was making squeaking noises.

Maddox got up and took it away from her. Interrupting a high fretful voice he said, "Mr. Wells? This is Sergeant Maddox, LAPD. I'm sorry to tell you that Miss Warden is dead. It looks as if she was murdered sometime last night. Her housekeeper only found the body an hour ago. We'd like to talk to you, ask some questions." He listened to a breathless stream of astonished obscenities. "No, it's not a joke, sir. She's dead. We'd like to talk to you soon." Probably the agent would have a good deal of background information on the woman; at least he'd be able to tell them where to locate the other TV people she had known, about her immediate associates.

There was a little silence at the other end of the line, and then Wells said, "Jan's *dead*? On the level?" Suddenly he bellowed one violent four-letter word. "Thirty grand a year right down the drain!" and apparently he threw the telephone across the room; the line went suddenly dead.

Fortunately the R. and I. office was equipped with computers to check the voluminous files. Even just looking at the sex records, it would take an army to paw through them by hand. As it was, the computer turned up exactly what Rodriguez had said it would: thirty-six possible Aggies and forty-eight possible Joeys.

"And the relevant pair might not be in our records at all."

"Don't be negative, César," said Sue. "Let's look at some details."

They asked for all those files to be pulled, and started to look through them. An hour later Sue, who had taken the female stack, said, "Well, there we are. A place to start. Two Aggies who have the suggestive pedigrees—contributing to delinquency, enticing to immoral acts. One mixed up with the porn trade. Agatha Sutton, Agnes Tiller. Both off probation now."

"*Así*," said Rodriguez. "So far, I can give you fourteen Joes with a record of pimping, and I'll bet there are a few more in here."

"If we find her, we'll find him," said Sue tersely.

"And if I wasn't feeling sentimental about those two poor kids—oh, well, it's a change from chasing down heist suspects." Rodriguez abandoned his stack of records and got up. As they carried all the manila folders back to the central desk, Feinman came in looking preoccupied. "What are you after?" asked Rodriguez.

"A pimp by the name of Randy. All the damn legwork on this worthless hooker," said Feinman. They wished him good luck.

The last address on file for Agatha Sutton was Houston Street in Boyle Heights. It turned out to be a crumbling apartment building. No Sutton was known on the premises; after search and questioning a few tenants they located the apartment manager at a local bar, having a beer and watching an old game show on TV. He had to do some thinking.

"Sutton," he said ruminatively. He was a big fat man with a nakedly bald head. "Oh yeah. Dame about thirty-five, sort of a tough cookie. She got arrested while she was livin' in my place. That's right. They say every dog allowed one bite, hey, and if it hadn't 'a' been that kind of charge I wouldn't 'a' done it. But it was a vice thing, sex thing, you know, somethin' to do with ropin' in young girls, and that I don't hold with. Not atall. She kept the place on, fella came to pay the rent, but time she come back—she got ninety days, whatever—I told her to get out."

"When was that?"

He cogitated. "Best part of two years back. No, she didn't leave no forwarding address. I got no idea where she moved to."

Well, it was the way the dice fell. The last address for Agnes Tiller was in Culver City, and that was more recent, six months back. It was one side of an old frame duplex, and after rather a long time the door was opened in response to the bell and a dowdy-looking middle-aged woman faced them.

"We're looking for Agnes Tiller," said Rodriguez, producing the badge.

She looked at it noncommittally. "She hasn't done anything else."

"We just want to ask her some questions," said Sue. "Does she live here?"

"Not now. She used to. My husband Harry, he'd never have her in the house, and I don't say I excuse anything Aggie ever did—real wrong things, and I always been an honest woman myself. But she's my sister when all's said and done, and blood's thicker than water. I lost Harry two years back, and when Aggie turned up like that, way down and out, seems I had to take her in for Mother's sake. But then she got in trouble again—she needed money, I couldn't give her any—wouldn't even if I had it, for the drink—"

"Can you tell us where she is?" asked Rodriguez patiently. "After that, you wouldn't take her back?"

"Like it says, charity suffereth and is kind," she said stolidly. "No, when she got out of jail I let her come back, but it got too much and I couldn't keep her. The drink. She got real bad, and they said it was delirium something and took her to the hospital."

"When was that?" asked Sue.

"Last month. Just last month."

"Is she still in the hospital?"

"No," said the woman, shaking her head. "No. She died the week after. So you see she couldn't have been doing anything lately."

Rodriguez waited until they got back to the car to start laughing. "Really, it's not that funny," said Sue crossly.

"Not funny at all, come to think about the poor kids. Wait for the street people, Sue." The word would be going out via the Traffic detail, the front office wanted this info. But you couldn't hurry it.

They had stopped for lunch after leaving Parker Center, and it was nearly four o'clock when they got back to Hollywood. Astonishingly, there was a great jam of people on the front steps, all around the front of the precinct, and among the crowd TV cameras waved here and there. "What the hell?" said Rodriguez.

Inside, they found Maddox and D'Arcy besieged with the hall door to the front desk bolted. "That goddamned agent!" D'Arcy was raging. "Why the hell he had to call the press—"

"Automatic bid for publicity," said Maddox. "We'll have them on our necks from now on, damn it." He explained the press to Sue and

Rodriguez tersely. "Look, I'll try to fob them off with the bare announcement—for God's sake, we won't see a lab report for a couple of days—" They all went with him to hold the door while he slid through: the front office was jammed with the press. They listened to his deep voice raised over the hubbub, finally quieting it down.

"No questions—we don't know enough to answer any at this point, that's all I can tell you. Miss Warden is dead and we are calling it homicide. That's all for now, and I do mean all. No, you can't take any pictures—" But the whir of cameras had already sounded.

The press grumbled and milled around, but recognizing authority when they heard it started to drift off. Maddox came back to his desk and lit a cigarette, leaning back and shutting his eyes. Outside, the Traffic shift was changing, squads pulling in, men going off duty as the four-to-midnight shift came on.

Ellis came in and asked, "What's the press doing around, for God's sake?" He had a man in tow, probably one of the possibles on a heist.

"TV stars!" said Maddox tiredly, and the phone on the desk shrilled. He picked it up. "What now?"

Whitwell's voice came through distinctly, audible to the nearest men. "We've got a jumper, on the roof of the Broadway. Everard and Rinehart and Gonzales have been trying to talk him in, and now he's holding Everard and saying they'll both go."

"Sweet Christ," said Maddox, and shot to his feet. He went out at a run, Rodriguez and D'Arcy on his heels.

Sue sat down in his desk chair rather suddenly and said, "He might have given me a chance to say, be careful."

"Now, Sue," said George Ellis. "Don't fuss. It'll be O.K."

"Thank you, Pollyanna. It's just, I never did like heights."

Maddox didn't like heights either, and the Broadway Department Store was seven stories high. Not exactly a skyscraper, but that much of a drop would squash anybody as dead on the cement below as a drop off the Empire State Building.

There was, of course, a gaping crowd collected in the street below, all around the corner of Hollywood and Vine. The three patrolmen up on the roof, the other three who met the detectives—Stoner, Gardner, Cassidy—would normally have gone off tour at four o'clock, but they'd been stuck here for an hour. Cassidy gave them a quick run-down as they rode up in the elevator.

"His name's Siegel—Dave Siegel. About twenty-five—no record—lives with his parents but we haven't been able to locate them. His former girl friend works here, clerk in handbags downstairs—gave him the brush-off a couple of days ago. He hung around from about noon, trying to argue her into making up—no go—so he's bluffing suicide—bulled his way up to the top floor where all the offices are—"

Up on the seventh floor, the damn fool people were hanging out windows, craning up. There was a pull-down ladder to a trap door, the trap open. "Access to the elevator housing," said Gardner. Maddox climbed the ladder, Rodriguez and D'Arcy behind him, and stepped off onto the roof. Down below it was warm, a pleasant still day; up here there was a stiff little breeze blowing, but it was a lovely golden afternoon, the sky a deep blue without clouds.

Cassidy was saying, "He grabbed hold of Perce about twenty minutes ago, and we haven't dared make a move at him—he outweighs Perce by twenty pounds, he got a hammerlock on him and got his gun—"

"Bluffing?" said Maddox. Everard was a rookie, just over a year on the job; a year from now he'd have known better than to get too close to one like Siegel, for you never knew what one like that would do. But Everard was a good man. Lately, they'd been getting the good men in younger and younger, wanting to make a career of the job; Maddox didn't think Everard was more than twenty-three.

The little tableau was frozen there at the very edge of the roof overlooking Hollywood Boulevard. There was a stone parapet about two and a half feet high. The uniformed men—big dark Gonzales, shorter blond Rinehart—stood tense and motionless about six feet back from the parapet, eyes alert. Right against the parapet, his back to the drop, Siegel had one arm clamped around Percy Everard, holding him tight against his body. Siegel was at least six-two, bulky and broad-shouldered, and he was waving Everard's Police Positive .38 in the other hand.

"Don't you come any closer! I will! I'll do it! I told Marge I will! She'll see—you'll all see!" His voice was high and wild and his eyes moved whitely.

Hair trigger, thought Maddox. It might have started out as bluff, it usually did when it happened in public—the craving for notice and attention, I'll show you, I'll show everybody—egotist acting like a kid in a tantrum—but inevitably the very notice he wanted had driven him nearer the real act, anticlimax if he backed down now—

Hair trigger. One way or the other in a second.

Everard was standing still as a rock; he looked a little white, but he was in control. His eyes focused steadily on the new men on the scene.

"David! David, my boy, I beg you to listen to me!" The firm sonorous voice rose in a confident boom. "You must listen to me, David! What you are threatening is contrary to God's laws—you must—"

He was an impressive-looking man, standing between Gonzales and Rinehart, a big round man black-clad, with a crest of silver hair.

"Waste of time," muttered Cassidy. "Rabbi from the synagogue down on Third. He isn't getting anywhere."

"You don't think I buy all that crap, do you? *Don't you come any closer!* I'll do it—I'll shoot the cop first—so Marge can see if I'm a—a—a *stupid mama's boy!* What are you going to do?" The gun wavered on Maddox, swung to Rodriguez beside him.

"Nothing right now," said Maddox. He stopped where he was, six feet in from the parapet a little to the left of Siegel and Everard. "Suppose you go on talking. Is that what Marge called you? She hadn't any right to say that, had she?"

Rodriguez turned and walked about ten feet away to Siegel's right, close up to the parapet. Well away from him, he peered casually down to the street. D'Arcy drifted in the other direction. The gun wobbled nervously; Siegel turned to look at Rodriguez. "What are you doing?"

"Nothing," said Rodriguez. "I'm not bothering you, Dave. Just giving you time to make up your mind. You've really got that crowd down there interested."

"Nobody believes I'll do it but I will! I'm going to!" He had Everard in a bear hug, tight. Maddox held his eyes and began to talk, easy and patient.

"I guess you will, if you decide to. Nobody can stop you, can they, but you know, it seems a little damn silly, Dave, because you wouldn't be able to appreciate all the excitement, would you? It'd all be for nothing really. You'd be out of it, you wouldn't see how that crowd of people down there would react, or the big headlines, or see the TV news stories. There wouldn't be much point to it, would there?"

He was listening, the gun loose in his hand. "I—don't—know," he said draggingly. Maddox held his eyes by sheer will power; he mustn't look away.

"After all that's the whole point, Dave, to get all the people thinking and talking about you, interested in you, in what you're going to do and how you're going to do it—and if you're not here to see it all— Now let's talk about that, Dave. You just said you don't believe in God's laws and all that—do you think there's any kind of life after death or do we just go up in smoke and that's all there is? Because if that's so, there wouldn't be much sense in killing yourself just over a silly girl, would there?"

Rodriguez, edging step by step, was three feet to Siegel's right. D'Arcy was about the same distance to his left. "What do you think, Dave?" asked Maddox, staring him firmly in the eyes.

"I'm—going to do it—I said I would—"

"Finally decided, have you?" said Maddox. "One, two, three." Rodriguez and D'Arcy both leaped on the count, and Maddox took one long step forward and fastened both hands on the front of Everard's uniform jacket at waist level below Siegel's arm. Rodriguez had tackled low and had Siegel's right leg like a vise; D'Arcy had his other arm, but it was the wrong arm, the gun arm.

Siegel screamed hoarsely and pulled violently backward, away from the restraining grips; the gun went off and he bent back over the parapet at an impossible angle, he went in slow motion, and he was going to take them all with him, the arm around Everard holding tight, Maddox fastened like grim death to the thick navy-blue wool, Rodriguez and D'Arcy—

Men fell on them from behind, and the sheer weight of the three big men—Gonzales, Rinehart, Cassidy—pinned them down to the gritty floor of the roof. Gravity tore Siegel's arm loose from Everard, and he went over backward, screaming all the way, and Maddox lay prone on the roof with Everard under him and the other five on top of him.

The crowd below made one concerted, excited long moan of appreciation.

CHAPTER 3

That kind of thing didn't happen every day, or every ten years, on the job; it only had to happen once, if it went the wrong way. With the action over, Maddox was just damned annoyed about the probably irreparable tear down the front of his suit jacket, a suit not new but with plenty of wear left in it. And now there'd be a certain amount of paperwork on this for the coroner's office, and an inquest to cover.

Adding insult to injury, they had just got back to the office, leaving the morgue wagon to clean up the mess, and the end of shift was coming up, when the senior Siegels descended on them, finally located by Whitwell, and Mama proceeded to have screaming hysterics all over the office. In the end they called an ambulance for her.

Maddox and Sue got away together, and he followed her old Chrysler up the Glendale freeway, got off at Verdugo Road, and turned up La Cañada Boulevard to the little narrow side street leading up to Starview Terrace. They came in the back door together—the house had an old-fashioned large service porch—and Margaret Carstairs looked up from something on the stove and said brightly, "Good day, darlings?"

"Well, it was a *day*," said Sue. "Oh, that you can say. And we're lucky still to have a man around. And why I ever got involved with cops—"

"I think we both deserve a leisurely drink before dinner," said Maddox, shedding his ruined jacket.

"In that case," said Margaret, "I'll have a sherry to keep you company. What's been happening?"

They sat in the still rather bare big living room—but at least he had got that antique curio cabinet of Mrs. Eady's for Sue—and told her about their day.

"And now he'll be talking to all the gorgeous TV girls," said Sue. "That is rather a funny thing, though—those people drink and dope and play around, but they don't get involved in homicide very often. I wonder if there could be a dope angle to it, Ivor."

"It looked more to me like personal hatred," said Maddox. "See if the lab gives us anything. But also"—he rattled ice cubes in his glass and laughed—"what that Gunther woman said. Think they can get away with anything on account of the money. That could enter in too. Just another homicide, except for the damned press horning in."

"I wish to God," said Sue moodily, "there was more we could do about Sally and Marjorie."

"Now that," said Margaret, "is an awful thing. There isn't? I see you couldn't get a search warrant for every building on Vermont, but—"

"We don't know that it is Vermont, Sally just thought so. They could be anywhere—moved around. The word's out, love, we ought to hear something from the snitches sometime."

"And meanwhile those poor kids—"

"I'm still wondering," said Maddox, "how in hell that letter ever got mailed."

On Friday morning, with Rodriguez off, Siegel's girl friend and a few people from the personnel office of the Broadway were coming in to make statements. Paperwork the curse of the twentieth century, but the thing had to be all tidied away in records for the coroner's office.

There would probably be an inquest on Siegel set up for Tuesday; there was an inquest scheduled on the hooker, Sheila Harris, on Monday. Yesterday, just before the press had come down, Maddox had managed to get hold of that agent, Wells, and set up a meeting for this morning. See what he could tell them, anyway. But just as D'Arcy came in nearly half an hour late, a messenger arrived with a manila envelope. A lab report. And all it said was that they'd found nothing but useless smudges, no liftable latents at all, on the door of that laundromat last Tuesday night where the ape man had raped Linda Thorpe. "Well, we didn't expect anything else," said Maddox, handing over the report to D'Arcy. "Hell's fire, if we had just one little lead—"

But the way he'd been operating, spotting the women alone, in fast with the attack and knocking them right out, naturally he wouldn't be leaving any evidence, the nice latents on the washers or dryers, or in this dry weather footprints, anything else useful. Like most of the heisters, he left them nowhere to go on it; at least on the heists they had the legwork to do.

"This agent," said Maddox.

As they went out to the parking lot, D'Arcy was yawning his head off. "I'm not running on all cylinders. I didn't get in till after midnight. I could have used another cup of coffee before we got going."

"You ought to get married so you can stay home nights." Maddox grinned at him, wondering a little: not a bad-looking fellow, D'Arcy, with his lanky height, long thin dark face. Rodriguez had a theory that he shied off anything permanent because what would a wife call him? He was ultra-sensitive about his very funny first name, had everybody trained not to use it. At the same time he was given to falling rather suddenly for the girls, but he never seemed to stick to one long. Maybe they got tired of calling him Hey-you. The last Maddox knew, he'd been dating quite a nice girl who worked at the phone company, Joan Berry; but he might have found another by now.

The agent's office was out on the Sunset Strip, high up in one of the newer high-rise office buildings there. The gold-leaf legend on the door said merely Ringo Wells Theatrical Representative, and Maddox raised his eyebrows at it. "Real name?"

"Who cares?" asked D'Arcy, yawning.

In the anteroom, all limed oak and thick green carpet, a sleek blonde challenged them and gave way before the badges. She opened an inner door and murmured, and the next minute it was swung wider and the representative advanced with outstretched hand, beaming on them.

"Say, I'm sorry about putting you off yesterday, officers, it's just that I had to do some figuring on all the angles on this thing. God, what a thing—Jan dead! Right in the middle of shooting the season's episodes— Si's jumping up and down yelling blue murder, stands to drop a quarter million on it. Hell of a thing. I thought a hell of a lot of Jan—and a very hot property she was, believe me. But that's not your business, and I don't suppose I can help you find out about it, I wouldn't know a thing, but anything I can do, count me in."

He was a plump, shortish blond fellow, very dapper in handsomely tailored sports clothes, all in shades of brown and beige, toning beautifully with his smooth yellow hair fashionably touching his ear lobes. The voice was hearty and full of bonhomie; the hand was soft and plump like a baby's, with a big diamond in yellow gold on the ring finger. And the eyes were very shrewd, very cold, as hard as stones and the color of agates under running water.

"Now, anything I can tell you. Come in and sit down. I've talked to that housekeeper, heard how she found Jan. God!" He sat back in an enormous padded desk chair behind a desk about eight feet long; there was a panoramic view over Hollywood out the floor-to-ceiling window behind him. Maddox and D'Arcy took the two upholstered Danish chairs in front of the desk.

"Some background," said Maddox. "I suppose as her agent you know a good deal about her. We've heard about a few boy friends past and present. And a divorced husband."

"Maxim, sure."

"Let's hear what you know about her, since you've been her agent. Who she played with, who might have hated her, held a grudge, whatever."

"Oh, God," said Wells. He passed a hand over his shining hair. "You don't want to think of these people as ordinary, officer—"

"Sergeant."

"Sergeant, excuse me. They're all—high strung." Wells gestured extravagantly. "Up and down. Hate you one minute, love you the next— they don't mean a damn thing by it. You've got to make allowances, see? Hell, hell, hell, when I think—she was raking in three hundred grand a year, and she'd have lasted at least another five on top—maybe seven. God. What can I tell you?" He flipped open a leather box on the desk, took out a cigarette, lit it with a quick flick of a lighter. "She was a nothing back East—few parts off Broadway. Just another good-looking chick. But it's all in the publicity, the build-up, you can take nearly anybody and build them—Maxim spotted her, he was back there some reason, thought there was some potential—" At their questioning looks, he said impatiently, as to a couple of children, "George Maximilian, he's the producer. He handed her over to me—hell, he's always picking up new girls, but he only married a couple of them before, but then she was an eyeful. And very much on the make."

"Had she been married before, do you know?"

"I think she got rid of another one back East, yeah. She got shut of Maxim fast enough, when she got right to the top in that first series— funny, nobody thought that'd go, but it went right to the top ratings and lasted. She—"

"Did Maximilian resent her leaving him?"

"What? Oh, that—I think he already had another chick on the string, or did not long after. Nobody got hurt on that one. Then she played around with Greg Ryan just a little while, but hell, who hasn't?

That Dukard dude—he was just using her for contacts and all the free publicity, she finally woke up to see that and kicked him out. One thing about Jan," said Wells with a sigh, "she was all business. Reliable as hell on the set, no tantrums or temper—as long as everybody was nice and polite—she had the sense not to fight with directors. Unlike a lot I could name. My God, when I think—"

"This series," said D'Arcy. "I seem to remember seeing a little of it, flipping around." Wells looked at him incredulously: the smash hit, a hundred per cent of the people should naturally be glued to the tube. "There were a couple of other girls featured in it. How did they all get along?"

"Well, now there," said Wells, "we get into a little thing. Not much —I was leading up to telling you about it. Listen, nobody in his right mind expects these chicks to get along all lovey-dovey. They're in the business because they like the spotlights, they like the name on the marquee and in *TV Guide*, and do I need to tell you the females are always the worst? But the other two made most of the trouble—Sheri Wynn and Pam Roylston. All three of 'em starred in that 'Newcomers' thing, but Jan had just a little fatter script, more limelight. The other two didn't like it. Then when it folded— Sometimes I wonder what the hell I'm doing in this business." And that sounded plaintive, but the agate eyes were hard as stones. "They're not hurting. I got them both new spots, which would do till something better shows. Sheri's got a good supporting bit in Maxim's new picture, if she'll straighten up and fly right on it, and I landed Pam a decent part in that other new series, that sitcom Perry dreamed up—but I think that's going to bomb by mid-season, at that. Hell, I wonder if I could sell her to Si to pick up the thing Jan was doing—no, probably not. Damn. The fact is, there was a little fuss and argument about pulling Newcomers off, and I think myself it'd have gone another season, but this spin-off was in the works, Jan'd have it all to herself, the whole spotlight."

"And the other girls didn't like it, when the series folded?"

"Naturally not, Sergeant, no, they didn't. Look, this is all just ridiculous, if you're trying to tie it up to somebody, for God's sake, murdering Jan. Sure the girls were mad—thought Jan could have argued the producer into another season. So she could, but she wasn't about to with her own show in the works. The girls aren't hurting, they got jobs," he repeated. He gave them a friendly wide grin. "That's background for what happened Wednesday night. If I didn't tell you about it, somebody else would. It doesn't mean anything anyway. These people, especially the chicks, high strung. Impulsive."

"So you said. What happened Wednesday night?"

"Well, I took Sheri to the Supper Club Theater. I wanted to catch the revue, supposed to be a couple of good new acts. And Jan was there with that fugitive from the Pasadena Playhouse. That Kelsey. I told her he was using her the same way Dukard had, she hadn't listened yet. Well, Sheri got mad all over again when she spotted Jan. Nothing much," said Wells. "A little yelling and hair-pulling. Kelsey and I broke 'em up—well, Jan didn't do anything, I mean we pulled Sheri off her, and I took her home to cool down."

"A little public scene, in fact. Was the place crowded?"

"Oh, middling. As a matter of fact I noticed Scott Dukard there, I think he got a kick out of it, way he looked. Had a blonde with him, new face to me. Other people around, sure. Listen, it was over in a minute. Sheri calmed down, I got her outside. Sheri's a good little girl, just temperamental."

"So you took her home. Where?"

"West Hollywood. She wanted to talk, and I went in with her and as a matter of fact—well, she was upset—I stayed. She needed company."

"You spent the night with her. Do that very often?"

"Oh, Sheri and I had a little thing going a year or so—just on a friendly basis," said Wells easily.

"Miss Warden," said Maddox. "All business when she was working, but she relaxed off the set, we've heard. Did she dope at all?"

"No, no—she thought too much of her complexion. I've seen her get halfway stoned on booze, but she never touched even grass. That's gospel, anybody could tell you."

"You mentioned a Greg Ryan," said D'Arcy. "That'd be the English actor?" The name carried a little more serious reputation behind it than those of the ephemeral TV people. He had played modern Shakespeare on Broadway, starred in a film based on updated Shaw.

"Irish, Irish, and he wouldn't let you forget it—he got his start at the Abbey Theater, you know. Ah, that was nothing serious—it never is with him. Of course that wife of his—now there's a woman I could see doing a murder. But so far as I know she's three thousand miles away, and naturally she'll have a dozen later girls to worry about since Ryan canoodled a little bit with Jan. He picks them up like flies, but he'd never leave that woman—she's too good a buffer for him. Excuse, to get out from under if anybody takes him serious. No, the only thing Jan got out of that was the house."

"The house in Nichols Canyon?"

"That's right. It belongs to Ryan. He went back to Ireland to make that film for Paramount, and now he's in some legit thing in London, the last year. Jan leased the house from him when he left L.A."

"Do you happen to know if she'd made a will? Did she have a regular attorney?"

"I don't know. She'd know the name of mine Addy Shapiro, Wilshire Boulevard."

"And could you tell us how to contact Mr. Kelsey?"

"No idea where he lives, but he's handled by Ralph Goldstein, next floor down." Wells looked relieved as they stood up.

Waiting for the elevator, D'Arcy said, "My God, Ivor. The way these people seem to carry on, their feelings don't go deep enough to make a motive for murder. What a crew."

Maddox laughed. "The sudden passions—it doesn't always take much of a motive."

About eleven o'clock that morning, Patrolman Gonzales was cruising down Fairfax keeping an idle eye on the traffic. The radio had been quiet for some time. For once there was only one A.P.B. out, and he'd memorized the plate number. Since coming on shift he hadn't had much business, a minor accident over on Western, a couple of traffic tickets for an illegal left turn, overparking.

The radio was still mute, and he was thinking lazily what a nice day it was—sunny but not too warm; all too soon they'd be getting some real heat—when movement caught his eye, and he swung the squad hurriedly over to the red zone at the corner where a wildly gesticulating figure was waving him down. There was a pharmacy on that corner, and it looked like one of the pharmacists—at least, a middle-aged man in a white uniform—calling agitatedly, "Officer, Officer!"

Heist, thought Gonzales, automatically reaching for the mike. "X-212, investigating unknown, Fairfax and Burton." Broad daylight, but the punks were out in force any time nowadays. He got out of the squad, loosening his gun in the holster, and the man rushed up and grabbed him. "What's the trouble, sir?"

"I don't know, but they look terrible, they want police, I was just at the phone when I saw you out here—" He urged Gonzales into the pharmacy.

It was a little independent place, and there was a young woman clerk in a white smock, another woman, probably a customer, standing in front of a pair of straight chairs at the back, where the pharmacy counter was. Gonzales went up there and over the women's heads saw the forlorn couple crouched in the chairs.

"Oh, thank God!" said the girl to the uniform. "Please—I want to call my mother—"

The boy stood up very shakily, hanging onto the chair. "I'm Peter Byron and this is Francie Keach. I guess our folks—maybe reported us missing." He sagged into the chair again. "Man kidnapped us—held us some place—raped Francie, and I couldn't do a thing—" He looked about eighteen; there was the bare shadow of a beginning beard on his jaw, but it could be taken for dirt. He was filthy, in the torn remnants of gray slacks and blue shirt, his feet bare. The girl, half-crying, bent over double, was probably younger, and she was wearing a dirty nylon slip and incongruous high-heeled white sandals.

"Good God!" said Gonzales.

"Tuesday night—I don't know—what day this is," said the boy. "Nothing to eat since—and I couldn't stop him—hurting Francie—" He started to sob too.

Gonzales ran back to the squad and put in a call for an ambulance. Then he talked to the desk. And that A.P.B., he thought suddenly, it was on that car—registered to a William Byron, at a Santa Monica address.

All the men were out somewhere, and it seemed the sort of thing Sue and Daisy might be more welcome on, anyway. When they got to Hollywood Receiving, the two victims were being examined. Daisy had talked to a desk sergeant in Santa Monica, who said they'd get hold of the parents. The parents arrived before anybody was let in to see the teen-agers. The two mothers were tearful, clinging together, the fathers grim. Introduced to police, they asked questions, and Daisy had to explain that nobody knew anything yet.

Of course the hospital let the parents in first, and it was two o'clock before Sue and Daisy talked to a doctor.

"You can question the girl," he said. He was a spare middle-aged man; he smiled a little wryly. "Female of the species. They were both badly dehydrated, and no food for nearly three days—they've had some rough treatment. They've been bound and gagged—there are some bad rope burns on the boy—a few minor bruises. The girl's been repeatedly raped. But she'll be fine—give it time. The boy's lost some blood from a bad cut on one leg, we've got him sedated—you can talk to him later." He fiddled with the stethoscope around his neck. "In the middle of town," he said. "My God. I hope you catch up with this one, all I can say."

Francie Keach was propped up in the hospital bed sipping orange juice through a straw. There was an I.V. tube attached to one arm. Clean, with her hair combed, she was a pretty girl, round-faced with a fine milky complexion, bright blue eyes, brown hair. She acknowledged introductions politely. "I'm glad it's policewomen," she said. "And I guess it's just as well Mother's gone to get some clothes for me—not that I won't tell her, but she'll be so—so upset, you know. Is Peter going to be all right?"

"Yes, they think so."

"Then that's all right."

"We'd like you to tell us what happened"—Daisy smiled at her—"if it won't upset you too much."

"I guess," said Francie, "I've got a long way past being what you'd call upset, Mrs. Hoffman." She sighed. "It was all so terrible, but—it's funny—it won't take long to tell you about it. We went to the movies on Tuesday night. Just to the main feature, because we both had to be home by eleven, so I guess it was about a quarter of ten when we came out. It was the Miramar Theater on Beverly Boulevard. There wasn't anybody in the parking lot at all—we were going to stop for malts on the way home—and when we got to the car, there was this man with a gun. Peter couldn't do anything. He made him—Peter I mean—get in the trunk, and locked it. That's when Peter hurt his leg, he was trying to find a wrench or something to bang on the trunk or pry it open, and he cut himself on some wire his dad had in there. The man held the gun on me all the time, in the front seat, and we drove—well, I don't know how long." She took a breath. "Then we got to this house."

"Do you have any idea where it was?"

"I'm sorry. I was so scared—he turned right on Beverly out of the lot, but I lost track, I had my eyes shut most of the time. But wherever it was, it was—you know—an awful slummy part of town. All awfully old houses. And that one didn't have anything in it at all—nobody was living there, it was all empty. There weren't any lights or a refrigerator or anything. That was when he—he raped me the first time. Peter was still in the trunk. Then he tied me up with rope and put something around my mouth—ugh, like an old rag right in my mouth and tied tight—and he went away. I don't know if I fainted or went to sleep. When he came back it was daylight, and he untied me and—and did it again—I kept begging him to let Peter out of the trunk, I was afraid he'd suffocate—but he didn't until that night. He—he—he made Peter watch while he did it again, and then he tied us both up and went away."

"Just as we go along," said Sue, "can you give us a description of him?"

"I certainly can," said Francie. She shut her eyes. "I'll never forget him. He wasn't old, but he wasn't young either—maybe about Daddy's age, forty or around there. He hadn't shaved in a while, I don't mean he had a beard but just sort of stubble, and it was mostly gray—all rough. He's bigger than Peter, maybe about six feet, and sort of broad. Not fat exactly. He had on dirty old clothes—he was all dirty too—I think he'd been sort of camping in that place, and it was all filthy, the floor all dusty."

"Do you think you'd recognize a picture of him?"

"Oh yes! In your—your mug books? I'd like to look. I'd recognize him."

"Good. Go on—how did you get away?"

"I don't think we ever would have, if he hadn't let us go. Did I tell you that he never said a word all that while? It was—it was"—she shook her head—"weird. He'd untie me every so often—to do it again—but Peter was tied up most of the time. Once he got the gag loose and started to yell for help, and the man knocked him around some before he tied him up again. Then this morning—he'd gone somewhere and when he came back he told us he'd let us go if we did just what he said. He'd torn up most of my clothes, you know—I only had my slip. When he untied Peter, Peter could hardly stand up, he was all stiff and shaky, but the man got him out to the car—Mr. Byron's car, you know—and he tied blindfolds over our eyes—we were in the back. And after we drove around awhile, he said all of a sudden we could take the blindfolds off and get out. So we did—I had to help Peter—and we were right in front of that drugstore—"

Sue and Daisy looked at each other. That was an offbeat tale if there ever was one. And Francie said suddenly, "I'm sorry—I think I'm going to sleep. Such a beautiful bed—" And did just that.

In the corridor, Daisy said, "First thought, a real crazy. On the other hand, he could have killed them both."

"Anyway, a wild man." They talked to the doctor again, asked him when the two might be released.

"I'd like to keep them in at least another day. They've been through quite an ordeal. I suppose you people run into these things all the time, but—"

"Well, not quite so often," said Daisy. It would probably be Sunday or Monday, then, before Francie could start looking at pictures, to see if she could spot the wild man in their records. But he'd kept the Pontiac, and if he was driving it around much it ought to be spotted sooner or later.

"One thing I'll take a bet on," said Sue. "If he's not in our records, he's in somebody's."

"No takers," said Daisy. "He didn't get that way overnight."

"I don't know anything about it, but I'll be glad to answer any questions," said Toby Kelsey coolly.

"That's right." Ralph Goldstein's tone was hearty. "Always cooperate with the police. How the hell would you know anything about it? You'd just dated her now and then. No involvement." He was the physical opposite of Wells, a big florid man in shapeless clothes, but there was a certain spiritual resemblance. "You didn't mind, gentlemen, I asked you to see Mr. Kelsey here in my office where I can get filled in on how you're thinking. I'm his representative, after all. He's my responsibility."

"Your ten per cent," said Kelsey a little shortly. He might be almost handicapped in show business by his unusual good looks; pretty boys were out of fashion. He wasn't overly tall, but he had a Grecian purity of regular features, a mobile wide mouth, wavy black hair molded to a well-shaped head, liquid dark eyes. "I suppose they know I took her out on Wednesday night."

"To the Supper Club Theater," said Maddox. "And there was a little scene with Sheri Wynn."

The wide mouth made a little grimace of distaste. "There was indeed. Some of these little sluts, no self-control—spoiled kids."

"What exactly happened and when?"

"Oh, they came in after Jan and I—we'd had dinner, there'd been a couple of revue acts, and it was in the intermission Wells showed up with the Wynn girl. They got a table just one separated from us, and it wasn't until about ten minutes later the Wynn girl noticed Jan and had the tantrum. It was—pathetic," said Kelsey. "Stupid. She stamped over to our table and started yelling at Jan, how she'd done her out of that part deliberately, couldn't stand any real competition, she was just jealous, a selfish bitch—and on and on. Wells tried to hush her up, but she was screaming her head off by then and the maître d' came up— A scene." Kelsey shrugged.

"How did Miss Warden react?"

"Oh, of course she was damned annoyed. I asked her if she wanted to leave, but she said no, it was all right. Wells had bundled the Wynn girl out then." Kelsey suddenly grinned and lost about ten years off his apparent age. "I had the idea that Scott Dukard got a little kick out of it."

"Out of seeing her humiliated?"

"Somebody trying to get back at her anyway."

"Was he sitting near you?"

"No—across the room." But Kelsey was looking annoyed again. "As a matter of fact, Mr. Frank Ballard and his wife were sitting at the next table, which didn't make me too happy about being part of that stupid little scene."

"Friend of yours?" asked D'Arcy. Anybody knew that name: a long-time fixture in the business, a very solid actor, who must be in the sixties now but had passed gracefully from romantic leads to character parts.

"My God, no. Just, he's a man I've always admired, I felt like a fool to have him see all that—not that he'd know who I am."

"You take yourself too serious, Toby," said Goldstein.

"All right," said Maddox. "What time did you leave?"

"After the first revue—ten o'clock. She had to be on the set early. We came out to the parking lot and the damned car was dead. I'd been having a little trouble with the starter, that's what it turned out to be, but right then— It was a nuisance, but I had to leave it and call a cab. I took her home in it and went home myself."

"Like a good boy," said Goldstein benevolently.

"What company was it?" asked Maddox.

"Yellow. It was probably around eleven-ten when I dropped her off.

I waited until she got in and shut the door, and that's the last I saw of her."

"Home being? Do you live alone?"

"West Hollywood. I don't suppose the Siamese cats would back me up." Kelsey regarded them with amusement. "You really don't suppose I was interested enough in that overrated clothes-horse to commit murder? Just good publicity to be seen with her."

"Yes, I gathered that. So thanks very much." Maddox was annoyed at wasting time, but that always happened on any case. This contributed nothing whatever, but it had to be rounded out and cleared away. He and D'Arcy would have split up, but they only had Maddox's car. They went back to Hollywood to the headquarters dispatching office of the Yellow Cab Company and spent an hour chasing down the log. The cab in question had been driven by Michael Gilroy, who was presently cruising somewhere around town; the dispatcher called him in and he took his time about showing up.

He was a stolid beefy fellow unimpressed either with cops or TV stars. "Yeah, that's right," he said. "About ten-thirty on Wednesday night, the Supper Club Theater to an address up Nichols Canyon and then back to West Hollywood. Yeah, I reckanized the dame. Big TV star. So what?"

"You're not a TV fan."

"I can take it or leave it alone. The sports are fine."

They had the name of the garage which had towed in Kelsey's car, and wasted the rest of the afternoon finding out that the car had indeed been out of action up until this morning.

"Listen," said D'Arcy, "anybody could have killed her. So the place was locked. The boy friends she collected, she could have had a spare who turned up and she let him in."

"All too possible, but why kill her?"

"I'm beginning to think," said D'Arcy, "that people like this don't work by reason. Temperament!"

They got back to the station at end of shift and heard about Francie Keach and Peter Byron. "Jungle getting wilder all the while," said Maddox wearily. And where that had begun, at least, was a decent enough section of town, not a place you would automatically walk warily in fear of muggers or heist men. But the wilder denizens of the jungle were apt to show up anywhere now.

Driving toward home—which was going to be such a gracious warm new home once they got some more furniture in it, and some kind of carpeting upstairs—behind Sue's old Chrysler, he thought some more about where that home was. The crime rate up even in quiet, bedroom-suburb Glendale. That was a secluded, very quiet area of town. The lot had an eighty-foot frontage, with only one house as a neighbor and that more than a hundred feet away. They hadn't met the neighbors yet; all Maddox knew was that they were a middle-aged couple who both worked, were away all day.

Anywhere, these days, the jungle could rise up. And neither of his girls was a fool; he trusted Margaret had learned her lesson about walking straight in when she saw a door kicked loose. And Sue was a pretty good shot.

But the little worry stayed at the back of his mind.

On Saturday, with Feinman off, a new heist overnight, the day started off with a couple of citizens coming in to report another burglary. They'd come home late last night to discover it; but they hadn't been home all day, and Maddox, kicking it around with George Ellis, placed it with the rash of daylight burglaries occurring over the last three months, roughly concentrated in central Hollywood. All of those had occurred at single houses, places of an age to be vulnerable, with old-fashioned back-door locks, loose windows. All of the entries had been effected like that, and it was all very anonymous and amateur. The lab had picked up some unknown latents. The little loot would be long gone; all too few householders kept the serial numbers of tape recorders, radios, small appliances, cameras—stuff easily pawned. The jewelry missing was all small stuff worth very little. They could go through the motions here, see if the lab could lift any more latents possibly to match those they had; but that was about all they could do.

The press was still pestering the desk for information; there wasn't any even if they'd wanted to hand it out. With luck, the lab would have come up with some significant evidence; wait for it. There were always the heist suspects to chase down.

But then of course he had Rittenhouse calling from Stockton. Hadn't they found out anything? Were they looking? Why weren't they looking, why hadn't they found out anything? When they knew the girls were somewhere here— Maddox was soothing and patient; but when he put the phone down he swore at it. There just wasn't any other way to look, in this sprawled city jungle. Not every wild one was on file in their records, as witness the ape man. In jungles, you had to depend on jungle grapevines. But those two kids—

Rodriguez had been on the phone; now he put it down and said, "A little progress, *amigo*. The lab picked up some latents on the cash register on that latest pharmacy heist. The stupid lout's still on P.A. Let's go and pick him up."

Maddox started to get up, and a voice from the door said, "Hey, Sergeant. Mind giving me ten minutes?"

"I think George is somewhere around," said Maddox to Rodriguez. "Hello, Barney."

The man who wandered in to take the chair beside the desk was in the sixties: a little stoop-shouldered, with a comfortable small paunch below his belt. He hadn't much hair left, and from long habit he had cultivated a rather stupid expression. But he'd been a smart cop for quite a while, and when he'd retired ten years ago from Central division, he'd missed the job; he was still a smart cop, Barney McCaffrey.

"I've got something funny I thought you ought to hear about," he said.

Maddox sat back and lit a cigarette. "So?"

"Funny in a couple of ways to start," said Barney, "though there isn't anything really funny about the flashers—too many times the prelude to something a lot worse. But just between you and me, all those prissy clubwomen types— Well!" He coughed and brought out an old briar pipe.

"A flasher at the hotel," said Maddox. Barney had been the house dick at the old Roosevelt Hotel on Hollywood Boulevard for the last ten years. In its heyday the Roosevelt had been the classiest hotel in town, drawing the big conventions, the celebrities, the merely wealthy; that was a long time ago. It was still a very good hotel, solid and quiet and ultra-respectable, but the connotations of class had moved on to the Beverly Hilton, Beverly Wilshire, the Century Plaza.

"For the last couple of months," said Barney. "All very cute—like a practical joke. Anybody can come in off the street, and we still get a full house as a rule, there's usually a little crowd coming and going in the lobby. And you know we always have a few single ladies, women traveling alone or with some other woman, who want a quiet place. It's been that kind he picks. Nineteen times so far, and probably more times it hasn't got reported. The women come in from somewhere, shopping or sight-seeing, and just after they get in their rooms there's a knock, and sometimes they ask and he says telegram, sometimes they just open the door, and there he is—er—showing all he's got, and a newspaper over his face with a hole in it so he can see the reaction."

Maddox choked on a mouthful of smoke, trying to laugh. "Yeah," said Barney, "but all the same—"

"I know, I know," said Maddox, with a composite vision of all those respectable matrons. "The warning symptom. The nut. You haven't got any lead?"

"It's not that that bothers me," said Barney. "Just the last week there've been other things. Somebody's been getting into linen closets and cutting up a lot of sheets and blankets. That means a key. Not the master key, but the same one fits all the linen closets. And now some of the guests—same kind, middle-aged women—have been finding obscene letters left in their rooms, and by God that does mean a master key."

Maddox sat up. "You don't say. What brand of obscene letters?"

"Threatening rape," said Barney unhappily. "Just the kind of thing flashers sometimes go on to. It looks like it's got to be one of the staff, and I can't buy it. I know 'em all. Nobody new in three years, and they've all got solid records."

"How many males altogether?"

"You count everybody, the manager, assistant manager, two room clerks, five bellhops, maître d' in the restaurant, five waiters, two cooks. Except the bellhops they're all forty plus and have pasts like new-driven snow. I just thought," said Barney, "you ought to know about it, because it might escalate, so to speak."

"How right you are, that kind."

"I've got the manager to hire a couple of security guards on a tempo-rary basis. I just wish I knew how the hell anybody got hold of a master key. Well, if you have any bright ideas about it you know where to find me." Barney knocked out his pipe in the ashtray and got up.

It was a funny little problem: not so funny for the dignified Roose-velt Hotel.

And Maddox seemed destined to be tied to the desk today; as soon as Barney had wandered out the phone rang again. It was Captain Lyons down in Fraud. "Just catching you all up to date. We've got seven new checks." To be expected: it was just after the fifteenth of the month, and all those accounting departments, aware of the bogus checks, would be looking for them. "Four made out to Standish, three to

Simms. Total just over a thousand dollars. Cashed as usual at markets, all on the Central beat. Four of them May Company refund checks, the other three Safeway salary checks. The damn things look so good, Maddox. A real pro printing job. We've also got a little something from New York. Rebecca Simms moved out of that apartment in 1972 —it was on Seventy-second Street—and nobody remembers anything about her. No forwarding address."

"Yes, anonymous," said Maddox. "I'll pass on a thought you've already had, probably, about that VISA card. I only carry one myself to get checks cashed—I don't believe in charge accounts. You don't have the money, you don't buy it."

"Yes, you've got a Welsh name," said Lyons. "Worse than any Scot. So?"

"The lunatics," said Maddox irritably, "are running the asylum. You don't owe a dime to anybody, your credit's no good. Prove you owe money all over town, fine, come borrow some more. When that card isn't being used to buy anything, just as I.D., no busy clerk is going to check the expiration date or write down the address. All they put down is the account number. The damn thing could be years old."

"Well, I suppose so. When was it Bankamericard switched to VISA? Yes. We've still got their headquarters checking, probably get fuller information on that soon. I'll keep you posted."

Maddox put down the phone, wondering absently where everybody had got to—even Sue and Daisy were out somewhere—and Dr. Bergner came in.

"I thought you'd probably be in a hurry over your TV superstar. I watched that series a little—silly sort of plot. But such gorgeous lovelies, maybe the sponsor figures that's all they have to offer." He plumped himself down in the chair beside the desk, paunchy and bald and comfortable. "Don't know what sort of female she was, but it's a damn shame, see that luscious body cold."

"I don't think she was a very nice female, Doctor," said Maddox. "You've done the autopsy?"

"You'll be getting a report. Nothing very abstruse," said Bergner, bringing out the inevitable cigar. "Somebody set about her with a short, sharp knife—blade only about two and a half inches long—something like a paring knife. There are eleven superficial cuts on her face and shoulders, but the operative one I'd say was a fluke—it severed the carotid clean across, and of course that was it. There was a very slight bruise on the occiput—may have been enough to stun her for a few minutes—"

"Just long enough for the rapid arterial blood loss to—um—immobilize her. Yes, I see."

Bergner sighed. "Whatever kind of female she was, a beautiful girl. Pity. That's the gist of it—I'll send up a report. Healthy female specimen, approximately early thirties, no evidence of drug abuse—she'd had a couple of mild drinks about three hours before death—she'd borne at least one child. Still had her appendix, by the way."

Maddox sat up. "She'd had a child?"

"At least one," said Bergner. "Could be more."

CHAPTER 4

Rodriguez and Ellis came back with a hot suspect for one of last week's heists and Maddox sat in on questioning him; he came apart when he heard that two witnesses had picked his mug shot out of the books, and Ellis took him over to book into jail while Rodriguez applied for the warrant. They went out for a belated lunch together, to a coffee shop down on Vine; that formerly favorite spot, the Grotto, had closed in March. A couple of gay bars had moved into that block, the straight citizens had shied off, and the business had died.

Up to three o'clock Maddox tried to get hold of Ringo Wells; his office wasn't answering, not even a recording service, and surprisingly he was listed in the book at a private address in Brentwood, but that number wasn't answering either. And Wells, of course, might not know one thing about that possible child: Jan Warden had only been out here how long, five years or so. Also, thought Maddox, so what about the possibility—people like these seemed to shed the past as snakes shed skins, no muss, no fuss, what might it matter? Probably more to the point was what the lab might have come across, and they always took their time making up reports.

He ought to talk to that lawyer, find out if she had made a will: about her money. If it hadn't been the lawyer Wells had mentioned, the Gunther woman might know, or the lab have picked up an address book. The lab boys would have gone right through the house, picked up anything that looked relevant. Lawyers, of course, didn't keep office hours on weekends: only a comparative few second-class citizens did, such as cops and firemen.

D'Arcy and Rodriguez had just come in empty-handed at three-thirty when a commotion erupted in the corridor and two of the Metro men —Conyers and Dietrich—came in towing a couple yelling imprecations at each other. There was a burly red-faced man about forty, in grimy tan shirt and slacks, and a spitfire of a skinny little female a few years younger, frizzy black hair figuratively on end and eyes shooting sparks. The air turned slightly blue, and Conyers kept bellowing, "Knock it off! Simmer down! Simmer down for God's sake, it's all over— Quiet!" without much effect at first. He and Dietrich planted them in two chairs flanking Ellis's empty desk and Dietrich stood guard.

"For God's sake, the citizens!" said Conyers to Maddox. "It's all yours, Sergeant, you can take the statements and book her in, nothing to do with our little operation. Of all the damn things."

"Lousy big bastard—after all I did for you—out of a job half the time and me work my fingers to the bone—knew you was runnin' after other women, but if I ever thought—"

"You're crazy, you're just crazy, try to kill people—"

Conyers laid a gun on Maddox's desk. It was a Smith and Wesson .32 automatic. "Mr. and Mrs. Ferryman. Fred and Myra. She thought he was chasing other women, so when he said he was going out for a beer she hid in the back of the car. What really teed her off was finding he was picking up a common hooker. When he made the deal and they started to make out in the front seat—Bob and I were just waiting to move in—she stood up waving the gun, and they exploded out of that car in about half a second flat. Yeah, funny. She fired off the whole clip, got the girl in the body but she'll live, the ambulance boys said. Assault with intent."

"—Go with the goddamned cheap whores, insult your own wife—I never had such a shock—"

"At least they don't nag alla time, crap about baths and sayin' I stink—"

"You do, you big bastard, you stink stink stink and I never want to lay eyes on you again—"

"Just crazy, shoot the poor kid—"

"I was aiming at you, you big bastard!"

There wasn't anything to hold him on, and once he was out of sight she calmed down a little. The two girls were back by then and Daisy got a statement of sorts from her, and set up the machinery on the warrant; Maddox booked her into jail.

Daisy and Sue had been out on a reported child molestation; not much to it, said Sue. The girl was more scared than hurt, and the mother had only got a glimpse of the man getting over a back fence.

But it was very, very nice, these last few weeks, that Maddox and

Sue didn't have to scurry around getting dinner after the day's work. They came home to the table all set and waiting, savory smells in the kitchen; Margaret was a good cook. It was nice to be part of a family again. Now if Sue could ever get started producing a family of their own—

"Oh, Mrs. Boardman called," said Margaret, busily dishing out tossed salad. "She's had dozens of calls about those puppies, and she said if we want one we'd better make it definite. They are darling pups, Sue."

"Absolutely," said Sue.

"I thought, maybe we'd have a girl this time. For a change. We could call her Bronwen."

"Well—" said Sue.

"Or—or Genevieve. What's another Welsh name? I'll have to look in the dictionary of names—"

"Isolda," said Sue. "Jenny?" She looked doubtful.

"Well, we'll think of something," said Margaret comfortably. "Just as well to get the housebreaking job over before we think about new carpets."

And of course any dog would bark at the prowler, let you know when strangers were around, thought Maddox. Little dogs quicker to bark and bite.

They were still working on those curtains, and departed upstairs to do some more measuring after dinner was cleared away. Maddox wandered into the big study, where all his books had finally got put in order on the built-in shelves last week, and at random took down *A Night to Remember* to re-read.

He was just stepping out of the shower at ten-forty and reaching for pajamas when Sue put her head in the door. "Brougham," she said.

"Oh?" Maddox flung on his robe and ran down to the phone. "What's up, Dick?"

"The ape man again," said Brougham. "But we may get more on him this time, Ivor. Very helpful victim—she's not much hurt—and keep your fingers crossed, we may get some prints. I thought you'd like to know."

"God, yes. Where are you?"

"Leaving the scene for the hospital. You want to come and listen to her?"

"I'll be there." He put some clothes on hastily. There wasn't much traffic at this time of night, and he got over to Hollywood Receiving in twenty minutes. Dick Brougham, solid and fair in a rather loud plaid jacket and slacks, was sitting smoking on one of the benches along the corridor in the emergency wing.

"This was a little switch, but it's got to be him," he told Maddox, "by the description she gave us right off. She's not much hurt. It wasn't a laundromat this time—service station over on Third. She'd stopped at the self-service tanks, the station's closed of course, and he drove in and jumped her. That's all I've heard except the description—at least six-three, hairy, acted hopped up."

"Women!" said Maddox. "Stopping at a place like that, at that hour —I know, the middle of town, but—"

"This one wouldn't scare easy," said Brougham with a grin.

When she came out under her own power, Maddox could believe that. "I can go home to take aspirin, about all I need," she was saying testily to a young nurse. "Lot of fuss over nothing. I was head surgical nurse in this place when that interne wasn't housebroken yet. And if you think I'm going to leave my car sitting there to be hot-wired before morning—"

"We'll take you back to it," said Brougham. "This is Sergeant Maddox. Mrs. Katharine Gorman. Right now we'd like to hear a few details, and then you can come in and make a statement tomorrow, if you will."

"Surely," she said. "Anything I can do to help. Men like that are dangerous." She was a tall thin woman with a halo of curly white hair; she was probably in her sixties. The plain white uniform she wore had been torn down the front, was fastened neatly together with safety pins. She sat down on the bench beside Maddox and asked, "What have you done with my handbag?"

"You can have it back tomorrow," said Brougham. "You said he grabbed it away from you."

"Oh. Fingerprints." She nodded. "Well, I'll borrow a cigarette from one of you." Maddox supplied her. "I suppose you want all the details," and she inhaled thoughtfully.

Listening to her, Maddox thought she was telling them a little more about the rapist both wittingly and unwittingly.

She was an old warhorse of an R.N., expectably efficient and practical. She was a widow, lived alone in a single house on Loma Linda Drive, and she was assistant manager of a private convalescent home on

Crescent Heights Boulevard. She'd stayed overtime tonight to finish up some paperwork, and thought it would save time in the morning to fill the tank on her way home. Third was a main drag; the station was closed but she hadn't been the least nervous about stopping. No pedestrians along then, but cars passing. She'd been opening her handbag to get out money for the slot in the self-service tank when the other car had pulled up right behind hers, and he got out and ran at her. She realized then that they were far enough back from the street that no one in a passing car would notice what was happening. He'd grabbed her handbag and tossed it away, and dragged her farther up from the street, behind the regular full-serve tanks, and knocked her down on the cement.

"There wasn't any sense fighting him," she said. "He was a great big strong fellow, he might have killed me. I just pretended to faint. He didn't waste any time, I can tell you—he tore my uniform right down the front, and yanked off my underwear. Lord, as if a rape would be any great big matter, woman my age and I hope some common sense—" She laughed sharply. "I just hoped he'd stop at that. And he did. He got up and ran back to his car and drove off."

"You gave me a rough description."

"He was at least six-three, about two hundred pounds. Young. In his twenties. Hairy—a lot of thick curly hair, I'd say dark brown. You understand, there wasn't as much light as if all the station lights had been on, but there was some. Enough. He was clean-shaven, and he had on a dark brown jumpsuit. And I think he was high on marijuana."

"Professional guess?" said Maddox.

"Well, I do know something about the effects of drugs," she said dryly. "The habitual heroin addict usually loses most of his sexual urge, and you get the same thing with LSD or cocaine. Marijuana causes brain damage, but it's a little slower in effect in that area. You could smell the stuff on him, his breath reeked of it—of course that doesn't say he'd just been smoking, but I think he had. There's a look in the eyes—"

"The car," said Maddox.

"It was an old Chevy Nova, white. Couldn't tell you the year, but an old one, and filthy dirty. I'm sorry I can't give you the plate number, there wasn't quite enough light for that and it all went too fast, but I can tell you it's one of the old plates, orange on black." California was still using two different kinds of license plates, the newer ones gold on blue.

"Um, yes," said Maddox. That wasn't much practical help. But maybe she told them something else about him, now he thought about the other victims. This was the fifth woman he'd raped in about a month, a little less. The others had all been young, and now Maddox thought back, they'd all been blond—at least more fair than dark. The ape man had got a good look at the others, spotted alone in the glaring bright lights inside the laundromats, before he rushed in at them. This time, he wouldn't have had such a good view: the partially darkened station, Mrs. Gorman twenty feet up from the sidewalk, thirty feet from a car on the street. A tall thin woman whose halo of white hair might have looked blond in that light.

Rapists were unstable to start with, and most of them—not all—had quirks. They specialized in redheads, or stole the victims' shoes or underwear—other queerer things. This made it look as if possibly the ape man went strictly for blondes, which was interesting if it didn't point anywhere to look for him.

But possible prints on the handbag, that would be a long step on. Maddox looked at it on the bench beside them. Brougham had slid it neatly into a plastic evidence bag. It was a generous-sized bone-colored bag made of shiny plastic vinyl, and it ought to hold latent prints just fine.

And something else, too. Those other women had been young and scared, had tried to struggle with him, so he'd used more force and knocked them around. They had said they might be able to recognize a picture, but could they be certain? In fact none of them had. But Mrs. Gorman, steady and sensible, had played 'possum, and in spite of the bad light she might be more likely to recognize a mug shot, if they had him on file.

She said she'd be glad to look, she'd know him all right. Brougham told her he'd drive her home, bring her car back—she'd left the keys in her uniform pocket.

Maddox got home at twelve-thirty, and the big house was so solidly built that he got in and upstairs and into the front bedroom before Sue stirred slightly. A burglar—

He went to sleep still thinking about burglars.

Sunday was just another day to cops, unless the routine fell so they got it off. Daisy and Ellis were off, but everybody else was in.

Maddox glanced at the night-watch report—Saturday nights were usually busy. There'd been another heist for the detectives, that was all. The Traffic detail would have taken the brunt of Saturday night, the drunks, the brawls, the family fights, the accidents. He filled Rodriguez and D'Arcy in on Katharine Gorman, and they went over to the other side of the building where there was a small and efficient lab. Any of the more erudite lab work would be sent down to the big one at Parker Center, a lab world-known for its near miracles. The run-of-the-mill things could be handled here.

"Are you," said Maddox, "going over every inch of the superstar's house?"

Baker looked up from his tiled counter and grinned. "We do like to be thorough. You'll get a report tomorrow."

"And about time. What we'd like to know right now—Brougham left something last night. That."

"I saw it when I came in. You just want it printed? Hang on a second." Baker maneuvered the handbag out of the evidence bag, looked at it and got out equipment. Delicately he puffed an insufflator full of gray powder. "Beautiful surface, you could bring up prints on this with chalk." In a minute he added, "There you are. Lovely. Nearly see the type with the naked eye. You've got at least eight liftable ones here."

"Well, I suppose most of them—let's hope not all—will be Mrs. Gorman's. She's coming in this morning to make a statement and look at some mug shots. We'll get her prints then and you can sort them out."

They'd just got back to the detective office when the desk called: a new homicide down. "Things to come," said Rodriguez. "Summer's coming in, and the rate always goes up." Rowan, Dabney, and Feinman had already gone out on legwork; they left D'Arcy to take care of Katharine Gorman, and went to see what they had to work on now.

It was Finley Street, a rather short side street off Vermont just below Los Feliz. This was old central Hollywood, and it wouldn't have changed much in thirty years. The houses along most of the streets here were old single frame or stucco houses dating back to the thirties, but neatly maintained, with patches of green front lawns: solid middle-class urban houses, on quieter streets than further down in town.

The squad was parked at a corner a short half-block down from Vermont, with Stoner waiting for them. It was, he said, another body in a car. This wasn't a neighborhood where people would flock out to make crowds, and it was Sunday morning; but already a couple of faces were peering out the front window of the nearest house.

The car was a nine-year-old gray Ford sedan, and the body was in the driver's seat: a young man in nondescript sports clothes, slumped over the wheel.

"You've got an ident, anyway," said Stoner. "He was spotted by a neighbor who knows the car. A James Rogers, lives up in the next block. He was walking up to Vermont to get a Sunday paper, and went to break the news before we got called."

"So what do we have so far?" asked Maddox.

"He's Bill Wagner, a college kid, lives with his mother—Mrs. Louise Wagner—in the next block." Stoner added the address. "She didn't know he hadn't come home, thought he was still in bed. He was out on a date last night. I think he's been shot."

"Well, there's a lab unit on the way." They got back in the Maserati and drove up to the next block. The house was unpretentious, a comfortable frame bungalow with a straight walk up to a wide porch, lawn and roses in front, neatly manicured.

And it was just one of the difficulties of the job that they had to deal with the bereaved families, the shock of sudden death; it made delays in getting answers. But in her neat and rather shabby living room, Louise Wagner just sat upright on the couch and looked bewildered, looked confused.

"But how can Bill be dead?" she asked them numbly. "I don't—I can't take it in. You—they're sure it is Bill?" She looked at the man sitting stiffly in the chair beside the couch: a tall gray-haired man in an old-fashioned formal dark suit. "Mr. Rogers—"

"Yes, they're sure," he said gently. "Mrs. Wagner, the police officers have to talk to you. Would you prefer I went away? I'll be glad to stay if you want me to, but—"

"Oh," she said. "No, you stay, please. It's good—to have someone— But I don't understand. I didn't hear him come in, but I took it for granted—he was in his room. How—" She was probably in her late forties, a pleasant-faced woman with rather bright brown hair, crystal-rimmed glasses; she was wearing a long pink quilted housecoat.

Rogers cleared his throat. "Ah, did you say Sergeant Maddox? I should perhaps tell you that I saw Bill come home last night. I can't understand this either, it's a terrible thing. Terrible. I knew Bill ever since he was a baby. Most of the people on this block have been neighbors for a long time, I live just across the street—my wife and I."

"You saw him come home?"

"Well, I saw him drive in—"

"He was out with Marylou," said Mrs. Wagner. "Marylou Searcy. I think they were going to a movie."

"What time did you see him, sir?"

"I had just been listening to the eleven o'clock news. When it finished, I went to bolt the front door before going to bed. There's a street light in front of this house, and I saw Bill's car turn in the drive."

"The Ford. You're sure?"

He nodded. "Of course he must have gone out again for some reason. But I can't understand what could have happened—Bill as nice a young fellow as you could want. Good son to his mother. Ambitious young fellow."

"Could you see if he was alone in the car?"

Rogers shook his head. "Took it for granted he was. That hour."

Mrs. Wagner seemed to wake up and catch echoes. "A good son," she said. "Of course he was. Of course. I never had a minute's worry with Bill—he never got into any trouble—some boys now, the drugs and girls—but Bill was always steady, I could always count on Bill to be— reliable. Never any worry to me. A good boy." She looked at them blankly. "How could he be dead?"

She was divorced, she told them, had a job in the office at Capitol Records. He had been an only child; he was twenty, going to L.A.C.C. on a government loan. They got the names of a few of his closest friends, the girl he'd been out with last night. They all went to L.A.C.C., and addresses could be got there for the friends; she knew the girl's.

Maddox and Rodriguez split up to talk to a few neighbors; Maddox tried the house next to the Rogers' first. That was a funny little detail, the car driving in and then being found a block away. He wondered if anybody else had noticed it in the drive.

The woman who answered the door was young and would have been pretty with make-up, smart clothes; on Sunday morning she was wearing a loose shapeless green muu-muu, and her light brown hair was tangled. She had a tilted nose with a scattering of freckles on it.

"I didn't know—there was anything wrong," she said, staring at the badge. "I've been busy with the children—" Two children, about seven and five, a boy and a girl, nice-looking children. He asked her about the car, and she said, "Oh, I wasn't home then. I couldn't tell you anything. That's awful about Bill Wagner. His poor mother—I didn't know him very well, but she's nice. You might ask Mrs. Keeler, she lives two houses down. You see, I work nights, I'm a hostess at a restaurant, well, it has floor shows and people come in late, so I'm out all hours, and Mrs. Keeler always stays with Bobby and Rita. She doesn't mind it being so late, she says she has insomnia anyway."

Rodriguez had drawn a blank at the house next to the Wagners'; on the way back to the Ford they tried Mrs. Keeler. She was a thin, bright-eyed old lady, pleasurably shocked at the news, and voluble. "A mugger," she said. "It must have been—what a terrible tragedy— because Bill wouldn't be mixed up in anything wrong, such a good boy, the real steady kind. Some boys his age, you don't know what they'll be up to, but Bill was such a nice boy. He wouldn't have had much money, but these criminals around now, they'd kill you for a dollar." Maddox asked if she'd seen his car drive in next door. "No, why would I when he didn't come home? I thought you said it was up the street. Well, I'm sorry you bothered Amy Dorn, she's always fussed in the morning, poor girl, having to be up with the children after getting in so late. I wish she could get a daylight job, but that one pays good money, acourse. Poor thing left a widow so young—her husband, he took sick and died just after they moved here—be nice if she'd meet some nice young man— Well, I usually settle down with a magazine or the radio in the den at the back, so of course I wouldn't have seen anything."

Back at the Ford, the other lab unit was still there; the morgue wagon was just pulling up. Carew and Douglas had evidently done all they would here, were standing at the curb talking. "Well, what's it look like?" asked Maddox.

"He was shot. The slug'll still be in his head. There was a shell casing." Carew was holding an evidence bag. "Looks as if somebody in the front seat with him just put a gun to his head." An automatic, by the casing. "We'll tow the car in and go over it. There was a wallet on him with I.D. and twenty-six dollars."

Maddox sighed. Another anonymous one. Of course, mothers didn't always know everything about sons. It could be when they talked to other people who'd known Bill Wagner, his friends, his girl, they might find out that he'd had a run-in with a dope dealer, or annexed somebody's best girl, or in some way invited the bullet in the head. It always came back to the solid legwork, getting around and asking questions.

Mrs. Gorman came in at eleven o'clock, and Sue took her over to be printed, and typed up her statement. Feinman had just come back from somewhere and was talking with D'Arcy, when there was a call from the desk. D'Arcy took it, reached for a memo pad, and said to Feinman, "Well, what do you know about that? Out of the blue." He lounged over to Sue's desk and smiled at Mrs. Gorman, who smiled back. "You won't mind if Mrs. Maddox takes you down to look at the pictures instead of me?"

"I could say I'd rather have a personable young man," said Mrs. Gorman smartly, "but of course I don't. I like to see young women *doing* things. Being useful. This must be an interesting job."

"Too interesting sometimes," said Sue, thinking of Sally and Marjorie. "At the moment I'm hoping to start producing a family so I can stay home for a while."

"Oh, yes, that's important too," said Mrs. Gorman. "But you want to keep your mind occupied. You can just stagnate, at home all the time."

Sue thought, but didn't say, that that sounded very restful. For a change.

The anonymous caller had told Sergeant Whitwell he had it on the wire the fuzz was interested in Randy Janovich. He was just passing on where they could find him, a pad on Thirty-first.

"Randy Janovich," said Feinman. "Are we? It's more than I knew. I came across five Randys in records who might fit the general description, but Janovich wasn't one of them." Feinman was always inclined to be pessimistic. D'Arcy, looking up at him lazily, wondered just what was going to happen in August. It would be damned nice to have a lieutenant who pulled his weight around the office, but a new man might shake things up some. The best thing that could happen, and they were all holding the good thoughts on it, was that George Ellis as the senior sergeant should get promotion and the lieutenant's desk; if that happened, Joe Feinman would be in line for promotion to sergeant, next senior to Maddox. Then if they got, say, three new detectives, even green ones— They could use double the number, but that would be a help.

"I suppose we'd better go and take a look at him," said Feinman. "Somebody who doesn't like Randy, maybe just trying to make trouble."

"Or somebody who liked the hooker," said D'Arcy.

"Even hookers have friends." They took D'Arcy's Dodge.

Thirty-first was down on the edge of a black area. The address was an old apartment building, the left front. The bare old wooden floor of the narrow lobby was thick with dust, and except for a handful of black children playing in the street outside, there wasn't a sound. Feinman pushed the bell. There was a name slot above it, but it was empty.

The door was opened by a good-looking sharp-featured Negro girl. She looked at the badges and stood very still. "Randy Janovich," said Feinman. "Is he here?"

After a moment she shrugged and stepped back. "We don't want no trouble. Randy, it's the man. Don't you go busting up the place, now."

"Damn you, Lila—" But he didn't look the type to do much busting up. He was a weedy little man with yellow-red thin hair and buck teeth. He didn't move from the battered old couch he was lying on, just looked up at the two tall detectives, a grimace frozen on his mouth. D'Arcy spotted the gun lying on the coffee table, and scooped it up in a hurry.

"Scared I turn into a cop killer?" said Janovich with a feeble sneer.

"Let's put temptation out of your way," said D'Arcy gently.

But he was, of course, very small-time; not the kind to make trouble. They didn't bother to cuff him; Feinman rode in back with him up to the station, and they brought him in and sat him down on a chair.

"Let's take things in order," said Feinman. He got Baker in the lab. "Did the morgue send over a slug from that Harris girl? What was it?"

"I thought I sent up a report. It was out of an old .22 Colt revolver. Oh yeah, distinct marks—it's an old gun, used a lot and not cleaned very often. We can make it."

"Thank you so much," said Feinman. He picked up the gun D'Arcy had laid on his desk. It was an old Colt .22 revolver with part of the grip broken off. "Now I don't know about you, Randy, but we're pretty busy here and we don't like to waste time. So suppose you just tell us why and how you shot Sheila Harris with this little equalizer—that's all we want to know."

"I never shot nobody," said Janovich. "You can't prove I did."

"That's just what we can," said Feinman patiently. "Even you can add two and two, Randy. The lab will match the slug out of her to this gun, you know that. Open and shut. You had the gun."

Janovich sat head down for a long minute. But if he wasn't exactly a great brain, he understood a few facts of life as a judge would see them; and he said sullenly, "Oh, for God's sake, I never meant to kill the damn little bitch—I just wanted to scare her. That's all I went to do, show her the gun. Scare her good. Little bitch holding out on me—she just needed a little lesson how to act. I never meant to kill her, the damn thing went off. The heap wasn't running anyway, I just junked the plates and left it."

"That's a good boy, not wasting time," said D'Arcy. But he felt tired, tired of all the little punks dirtying up the place with their mindless squabbles and violence. This was the kind of crime police saw mostly, and there was nothing at all exciting or even very evil about it: it was just dirty and random.

Janovich would get charged with Murder Two and probably get a three-to-ten. He might stay in for two years and then get out on P.A., likely to slither off to some other city jungle and start up his dirty trade again.

"And my mother wanted me to be a rabbi yet," said Feinman sadly. "Sitting in a nice clean temple studying Mosaic law. Come on, Randy. We'll get you booked in."

D'Arcy called the desk and started the machinery on the warrant.

Maddox and Rodriguez finally talked to Marylou Searcy when she got home from a wedding shower at four o'clock. She was shocked to hear about Bill Wagner but not devastated; they hadn't even been going steady, he was just a fellow she dated occasionally. "We both had plans, you know? I want to finish college before I even get engaged, and he was all out to make his first million fast—he wanted to go into a brokerage, and I'll bet he'd have been good at it. I'll bet he'd have made that million. When you want something very much, like that— They'd always just got by, he used to say, and he wanted to make it easier for his mother, give her things. I ought to go and see her—" She was just an ordinary-looking girl, dark and slender.

They'd gone to a movie last night, she said, but it was terrible and they came out in the middle and went and had a drink at the Brown Derby and Bill had brought her home about eleven o'clock. He hadn't said anything about a later date; she thought he'd be going right home.

"I might think it was muggers at that," said Rodriguez, "if it wasn't that he hadn't been robbed. And why did he go home and then out again?"

"We don't know that he did," said Maddox. "Street light be damned, it was dark and Rogers wears glasses. That could have been another car similar to the Ford getting onto a wrong street, turning around. Well, poke around some more and see what shows."

Mrs. Gorman spent three intensive hours looking at mug shots and regretfully didn't find a picture she recognized. "And I would have," she said.

Of the prints lifted from her handbag, three didn't belong to her. At a guess, said Baker, a man's prints. Those had been isolated this morning and sent downtown, and of course they had a computerized filing system down there. Just before the end of shift the downtown lab called. They didn't have those prints on file; they'd been wired to the FBI and NCIC.

Those outfits had computerized systems too, but also a backlog of requests from all over the country; it might be a little while before they got a kickback from them.

They now had two new heists to work, pulled on Sunday night at a bar and a pharmacy.

The inquest on Sheila Harris was scheduled for ten o'clock on Monday morning, and now they had Randy Janovich for that; Feinman would have to offer the whole packet of evidence, not to waste the court's time with an adjournment. He hauled Baker out of the lab for the ballistics testimony.

Francie Keach came in with her mother, and Sue took them down to Records and Identification at Parker Center. "Peter wants to try too but he's still in the hospital, did you know, Mrs. Maddox? He has to have therapy on his leg, something to do with the circulation getting cut off so long. I just begged and begged the man to let him loose—"

"Don't think about it, darling," said Mrs. Keach.

"But we've got to think about it," said Francie resolutely. "You've got to know about the awful things that happen, or you can't stop them happening. Like I've got to look at all the pictures to help the police catch him."

Francie, thought Sue, had the root of the matter in her.

But she didn't pick out any mug shots, and at one o'clock her mother took her home.

Maddox and Rodriguez spent a wasted morning on the L.A.C.C. campus talking to students who'd known Bill Wagner. The first thing they heard was that his closest pal, Ron Kreuger, wasn't around. His grandmother had died back East and the whole family had gone back for the funeral. Aside from that, all they heard was more of the same: Bill a very straight guy, and ambitious, hard-working, never looked at drugs, dated moderately but all nice girls. Oh, he could tell a blue story, he wasn't a square, just a nice guy.

In the afternoon, they went to see Adam Shapiro at his law offices on Wilshire Boulevard.

"I don't know how I can help you," said Shapiro. "Maybe you do." It sounded abrupt; it was only blunt. This was a very classy office, but not as fancy as Wells's: good solid furniture in leather, not vinyl; a plain big desk, comfortable chairs. The view out the window wasn't spectacular; this was only the second floor.

"We don't know one damned thing about this yet," Maddox told him frankly, "and it looks like—well, shall we say an emotional motive —but we don't know. Money is always a dandy motive. Do you know anything about Jan Warden's money, Mr. Shapiro? Mr. Wells seemed to think she'd have gone to you if she needed a lawyer."

"Oh," said Shapiro. He was a middle-sized dark man with thinning black hair, a quiet voice, a sensitive mouth. He pinched his nose between thumb and forefinger. "Yes, she did. Wells asked me to arrange the funeral. I turned it over to Forest Lawn, and he was annoyed. Funny little man. I suppose he's really laid it on, for tomorrow—all the fanfare, every two-bit show biz name he can get contributing eulogies. And the press out in force."

"I would bet," said Maddox. "She was raking in the money. Do you know what she did with it?"

"Show biz people," repeated Shapiro. He lit a cigarette and looked at it. "I've known a few. All shapes and sizes like most people. Quite a few of them have had the sense to hire business managers, set up investments. Some just blow it. A lot of them, you know"—he pinched his nose gently—"never had any money to speak of before, and they tend to go hog-wild. Well. I couldn't tell you what Miss Warden did with her money. All I did was advise her. She came to me to have her contracts looked over—redundant, after Wells had practically dictated them. I gave her the name of an investment counselor—Richard Parish, he knows what he's doing. I mentioned the advisability of an annuity. I had to explain that to her."

"She didn't know much about handling money?"

"She knew how to spend it," said Shapiro dryly. "No, you could say that. I don't know whether she went to Parish or anybody else for advice."

"What about the house in Nichols Canyon?" asked Rodriguez. "She was leasing it, we heard."

"Yes—I put that through for her, with Mr. Ryan's attorney. Actually the Gold Carpet Realty people handled the details. She was paying two thousand a month for that."

"My God," said Maddox mildly. "Look, she was raking in about three hundred grand a year, the last four or five years? She couldn't have got rid of all of it on clothes and jewelry and so on."

Shapiro shrugged. "She could have—but if you ask me, there was a streak of caution there. I think she realized that the ride on the merry-go-round couldn't go on forever—her type, it's all looks and youth, and when that's gone they've got nothing to offer. I think she'd have stashed some of it away. You can ask Dick Parish. He's close as an oyster, but if she did anything through him he'll probably get on to me when he hears about the murder."

"It's four and a half days," said Rodriguez.

Shapiro looked amused. "He's been in Hawaii since last week. He doesn't read newspapers or follow the news on TV when he's on vacation."

"Well, all right," said Maddox. "Did she make a will?"

"She didn't want to," said Shapiro. "Like some—er—immature people, she was superstitious about it, make a will and you're going to die. I tried to explain to her, it's only sense to see it goes where you want it to go, just in case. She only laughed and said it didn't matter if she couldn't have it. Then one day—it was last March—she walked in without an appointment and wanted to talk about it. She said somebody had told her that if you died without a will and had any relatives, they'd get everything. I told her that was so, broadly speaking, and she said in that case she'd have to make a will. She did." Shapiro sighed.

"And how does it read?"

"I had the hell of a time with her," said Shapiro, "about the relatives. She wouldn't tell me anything. She had a quick mind in some ways, but she was extraordinarily obtuse in others. I told her seven different ways, and finally got it across, that if she had living blood relatives when she died, and hadn't left them a dime, it'd be grounds for them to contest the will. It's legal precedent, comes under a statute of Unnatural Provisions. She finally gave me a name. A sister. She said"— Shapiro carefully lit another cigarette—"that she'd hate like hell for any of that bunch of snotty snobs to get a dime of it. On my advice, she left the sister a hundred dollars. That would get round the statute. The rest of it—and she wouldn't spell out what, just the residue of estate and all personal property—is divided between Wells and George Maximilian."

"Hell!" said Maddox.

"She said it was a joke. When she was through with it, she owed it to them anyway."

Maddox sat forward and stabbed out his cigarette in the ashtray on the desk. "We've had an autopsy report, Mr. Shapiro. Did she say anything about any other relatives? Just the sister?"

"That's all. Mrs. Esther Price. Tarrytown, New York. I suppose she'll have seen the papers, but I sent her a telegram on Saturday. Why?"

"According to the autopsy," said Maddox, "she'd borne at least one child. We don't know anything about it, if the child's alive or dead, but—"

"Now isn't that interesting," said Shapiro. "If there's a living child, with proof of parentage, that will isn't worth the match to burn it."

"Exactly," said Maddox. "Mr. Shapiro, what was your honest opinion of Jan Warden?"

"Why, I thought she was an egotistic, mercenary little bitch," said Shapiro. "But there are plenty of those floating around in show biz. And I apologize for the word, I've got a little Dachsie girl at home with more integrity than that girl knew existed."

"Yes, I rather gathered that's what you thought," said Maddox.

CHAPTER 5

The press had not given up trying for any scrap of information: all the local papers, TV stations, the wire-service agents, had been hanging around every day, and fobbed off, had fallen back on old clips of Jan Warden's early and late career, repetitions of the bare facts handed out about the murder. But on Tuesday, they were going to have a full and eminently satisfying day, and they turned out in droves to make the most of it. There'd be the inquest in the morning, the funeral in the afternoon.

They wouldn't get much copy out of the inquest, Maddox reflected. There wasn't any evidence to hand the court except the fact of murder; the police would put in the autopsy report, the coroner's instructed jury would hand out the open verdict, homicide by person or persons unknown, and that would be that.

In fact there was just slightly more to it. Maddox was covering it for the police, and the coroner's office had brought in Kelsey to testify to the time she returned home that night. Wells was in the court with Sheri Wynn, probably eager to take the stand if he was called, but he wasn't. Before proceedings opened, the press flocked around those three —"Pictures, Mr. Kelsey?"—"Pictures, Miss Wynn?"—which was how Maddox had spotted her. She was a small curvaceous blonde with the figure shown to advantage in what Sue would probably say was unsuitably elaborate for the occasion, stark black with ruffles. She had a vapid little heart-shaped face with a petulant mouth. Maddox thought Wells would have brought her along for the nice free publicity.

It didn't take forty minutes once it got started, and the jury docilely handed out the open verdict before eleven o'clock. Maddox managed to escape while the press was busy with Kelsey, the girl, to a lesser extent with Wells—"Any comment on the verdict, Mr. Wells? As her long-time agent"—the cameras steadily whirring—"I can only say, and friend, gentlemen, I feel I've lost a dear friend, as I'm sure all of her loyal fans feel too—"

Maddox got back to the office before noon, and Baker came in with the completed lab report ten minutes later. "I thought you'd like to kick it around." It was D'Arcy's day off and Dabney and Rowan were out chasing heisters, but everybody else came up to take a look at the sheaf of glossy 8×10 prints the lab man spread on Maddox's desk. "We give you this and that interesting. First of all, we don't give you a weapon. Nothing more lethal than a nail file anywhere. Yes, we looked at the knives in the kitchen—there's nothing to say that X was anywhere but the front hall, stairs, and bedroom. But, as you can see by most of these shots, there was the hell of a lot of blood. By what we can deduce from the autopsy, the strike that severed the carotid artery was probably one of the first struck, or she'd have put up a lot more resistance. When that artery got cut, it'd have spurted blood like a jet stream—you can see some of the pattern on the blanket—and X would have been right in the path. Must have been in a little mess. Look at this." Baker plunked down another 8×10. "Nice. In just a couple of minutes, blood on the floor, and X still there."

"*Que bello*," said Rodriguez softly. "And possibly very helpful." The glossy print was a many-times enlarged view of a section of carpet, and showed the fairly clear print of two shoe soles in the blood lying wet there.

"As X stepped back to get away," said Baker. "You can see the pattern of the crepe sole. A flat moccasin, and by the measurements it might be a woman's size seven."

"And those shoes will now be in some Goodwill bin or buried in the back yard," said Maddox.

"That's your business. But X had realized by then that she was a bloody mess, so—" Baker substituted another photograph. "The light switch in the bathroom. Unfortunately only smudges, no liftable print —she went in there to clean up as well as she could, and she used every towel there—one of those big bath sheets as well as regular size." Another print: the heavily stained wadded-up towels left on the floor. "She probably took off the shoes and carried them, got off the worst of the wet blood—only left a few more traces, a couple of smears on the stair carpet, a bigger spot on the tile in the entry hall."

"Going out the front door," said Ellis, nodding. "You didn't pick up any prints at all?"

"A lot of hers, naturally, and the Gunther woman's. Two unknowns from the left bedside table. They're not in records, and nobody else knows them. But I don't suppose this got pulled by a pro."

Maddox thought of that quiet curving road—dark up there at night, if there had been a moon. The car left in the road, and Gunther dead to the world in the guest house. "All right, the locks. Any blood on the front door?"

"Nope. There are good dead-bolt locks on both back and front doors. No sign of any blood except these places. You can read it that she came, got in and did the killing, cleaned up and left. By the front door. Back locked up tight."

"Yes," said Maddox. "A little snib on the doorknob inside you push to activate the lock—I noticed it. Above the knob, the bolt to turn. And a key used on the outside would release both bolt and lock. But Gunther wouldn't have known whether both were in place, or only the lock."

They looked at him. "Well, that's so," said Baker. "You mean, X could have shoved in the snib and left the door locked behind her—but what's the point? There's all this clear evidence to show she was there—"

"The point is," said Maddox, "that X might have pushed in that snib automatically—it's a common kind of lock. That door might not have been locked before that. The autopsy report says she died between eleven and two. Well, we know she got home about eleven. Kelsey maybe was anxious to get rid of her—he didn't play the little gent and escort her to the door, just waited in the cab until she got in. He can't say whether she locked the door. Could be she was tired and out of sorts—she hadn't had a very nice birthday, what with the Wynn girl making the scene and her escort just out to be seen with her, which she must have suspected—she could have walked in and banged the door shut and gone upstairs to bed, forgetting both lock and bolt."

"I don't know," said Feinman slowly. "The Gunther woman said she was careful. And since Manson, people up there tend to be nervous, take the precautions."

"It's a long time since Manson," said Maddox.

"Listen," said Rodriguez cynically, "what we've heard so far about boy friends, and this Ryan who owns the house, there could be keys to that place all over. Were the locks changed when she moved in? Have a bet?"

"Which is also a thought," agreed Maddox. "And I'll tell you something else." He picked up the print showing the footprints. "You're so confident of pronouns, Baker—these could just as well be men's shoes. Crepe-soled moccasins are unisex like they say. They're blurred a little by the wet blood, you can't be sure of exact measurements. Wells could take this small a size in men's shoes—and also Kelsey, if that's far-fetched. That Scott Dukard—I wonder if he'd have had any sort of grudge on her."

"I've seen him a couple of times on the tube," said Feinman. "He looks fairly big, I think he'd take a bigger size. What the hell kind of motive could Wells have, Ivor? She was paying him a hefty part of his yearly income."

"And if he knew about that will, she was worth more to him dead," said Maddox. "She wasn't going to stay on top forever, hauling in the six figures. And then there's this Maximilian." He looked at the other objects Baker had laid on top of the prints. A leather address book, a checkbook, a folder of keys. He picked those up. It was a miniature leather envelope with a snap; on the front of it in gold leaf was an evident replica of a sprawling careless signature—*Jan Warden*. He unsnapped it and looked at four keys only.

"It was on the top of a dresser, with the bag she probably carried that night," said Baker. "Cosmetics, handkerchief, cigarette case to match that in the bag, nothing else." Maddox nodded. "The address book was by the downstairs phone. The keys are for the Mercedes in the garage, the house."

"And," said Maddox, "a safety-deposit box somewhere." He prodded the fourth key with a long forefinger: a long narrow steel key.

"Looks like it."

Maddox leafed through the address book. There wasn't much in it of significance: hairdresser, make-up specialist, a Mercedes agency, Kelsey, a crossed-out number for Dukard, listing for Wells, office and home, Maximilian. She hadn't much sense of organization; he supposed she wouldn't have been a letter-writer. But at the back he came on a terse three lines—*Esther 167 Orchard Tarrytown NY*. "Well," he said, "she hadn't quite cast off the relatives after all, maybe? I'd better talk to Shapiro about that key."

"He'll be out to lunch," said Feinman.

But the secretary put him on without argument. "Yes," said Shapiro. "I thought I'd better talk to Dick, I got hold of him last night at the Honolulu Hilton. She'd gone to him all right, he says she was into real estate—he'd bought her a new office building on Wilshire, that's clear, and investment property in Arizona, Palm Springs. About a million, roughly speaking."

"Now do tell," said Maddox. "Isn't that nice. Her checkbook's on the Bank of America, Hollywood branch. Probably where the safety-deposit is, with those deeds."

"I'm getting on it," said Shapiro. "I've got an appointment with Wells for after the funeral—apparently Maximilian isn't here. You'll also be interested to know that I've heard from the sister. Mrs. Price. She's flying out at the end of the week."

"And she may tell us more about the possible offspring. I'll want to talk to her."

"I'll be in touch," said Shapiro.

"Look, we can exchange more inspirations over lunch," said Feinman as Maddox put down the phone.

Maddox got up and pulled his tie straight. "You go on. I'll pick up a malt. I want to catch Wells before he leaves for the funeral."

"What are you after Maxim for?" asked Wells. "Jan had hardly seen him in three years or so. Anyway, he's up the coast shooting the background and process shots for the new film. It's a very funny thing, but all those marvelous sand dunes up around Pismo Beach look exactly like the Sahara, it's very handy when you need such a thing. He's so fussy, has to superintend everything personally. I wouldn't know, but Sheri's off the chain until he gets back to go on shooting the main scenes. I saw him before he left last week." Wells was looking a little haggard, his smooth gold hair disarranged as if he'd been running fingers through it. He was wearing the same sober navy suit, white shirt, and dark tie he'd had on at the inquest. He hadn't asked Maddox to sit down; he wandered over to the window and stared out at the view over the city.

"I also want—"

"Oh, didn't I see him." Wells hadn't heard that. "Bitch, bitch, bitch. And do I blame him? I'm the one sold her to him, Sheri. Can't get along with the rest of the cast, never on time, keeps blowing her lines. The damn little fool ought to realize she's no Monroe or Minnelli, get away with that. And hitting the sauce some— Goddamn it, she could be on the skids faster than she got her name in lights, and so I told her."

"Mr. Wells. Can you tell me what George Maximilian looks like?"

"What he looks like?" Wells was momentarily diverted. "What the hell? He's about five-ten, getting a little too fat nowadays—black hair—"

"All right," said Maddox. "How do I contact Pam Roylston?"

"What do you want with Pam? She hadn't seen Jan since the break-up last December."

"Can you give me her address, please?"

"Look—" Wells glanced at his watch. "I've got to get going. If you want to see Pam, we can set up a meeting here, I can fix it."

"No, Mr. Wells. Address, please."

"Oh hell," said Wells unhappily. "All right. But you're wasting your time. The more I think, It must have been some nut— God knows there are plenty around—got in and killed Jan. Nobody had any reason—" He turned to the desk and scrawled an address on a memo sheet. "There you are. They're shooting this new series like I told you, but she ought to be home by six unless they got hung up some way. Look, I'm in a hurry—"

Francie Keach came in again on Tuesday afternoon to look at mug shots, but again she didn't make any, and at three-thirty Mrs. Keach firmly called a halt, "I'm sorry," she said to Sue, "but you can see it's no use, and it's just too much for her—keeping it all in her mind. She's co-operated, so let's not drag it out."

It was queer, thought Sue on the way back to Hollywood, that in a full week that A.P.B. hadn't turned up the Byron car. But it could be undercover somewhere.

As she turned into the lot behind the station, the Traffic shift was changing, the squads coming and going, getting gassed up in the underground garage. She went in the back door and found her husband on the phone, Rodriguez and Feinman looking over that lab report again.

"Damn it"—he slammed the phone down—"I want some information about that house, and the damned realty company says this Von Bazen's the one who'll know, and he's off somewhere in the boondocks inspecting property, won't be back until Thursday."

"Well, it was just an idea, about those keys," said Rodriguez. And just then Sergeant Moore, on the switchboard on Whitwell's day off, buzzed Sue and told her he was sending another burglary victim in, so Sue went to meet the woman.

She was a fat elderly woman in dowdy clothes, Mrs. Dora Chase, and she admitted to Sue at once that it was their own fault. "My husband's always said we should get a better lock on that back door, it just opens with a straight key." It was another of the ongoing daylight burglaries by the amateurs, and they hadn't got much loot: an old radio, some costume jewelry. Mrs. Chase had been out to the market, only gone a couple of hours. "But the funniest thing"—she opened her bag, rummaged around in it—"they dropped something. I never saw it before, and it was on the floor of the service porch just inside the back door. This."

Sue took it. It was a Hollywood High School class ring. And if it had been loot from some other job, why would they be carrying it around?

"Funny," said Mrs. Chase. "Well, this'll stir Harry up to do something about the locks, anyway." She signed the report form obediently before she went out.

Sue was still looking at the ring when Carew came in. "We haven't done you much good on the Wagner car," he told Maddox. "The morgue sent the slug over—it's out of a .32 Smith and Wesson automatic. The only blessed thing we got in the car was a cigarette stub in the ashtray. It's an unusual brand, pure Turkish—I didn't know they were still made—a Murad. No lipstick on it. Should we run a saliva test?"

"Leave it, leave it," said Maddox. "We'll see." Carew shrugged and went out.

Sue took the ring over to show. They agreed that it had probably been dropped inadvertently. "So the amateur burglars are from Hollywood High," said Rodriguez, turning the ring in his fingers. "There was a time that would have caused a little tut-tutting, respectable old school. Nothing surprises us nowadays. I think most of the juniors and seniors might have one of these—what, maybe a thousand kids? No way to find out who this belonged to. It's not worth much—ten-karat gold, a fake stone, it'd retail for about forty bucks."

Maddox slid down in his chair, lit a new cigarette and grinned at Sue. "And now I've got to go out and see this TV star tonight. You want to come along and hold my hand in case she tries to seduce me?"

"Oh, I'll trust you to remember," said Sue sedately, "what you promised the minister."

It was, by the size of the living room, a big apartment, high up in one of the newer buildings in West Hollywood, on the edge of

Trousdale Estates. He could guess, around six hundred a month, more with full maid service. The living room was violently modernistic in purple and white, with a carpet six inches thick and a contorted brass sculpture on one wall.

And she was a gorgeous girl all right, a dark Latin type, and probably a good deal smarter than Sheri Wynn. He wondered if Pam Roylston was her real name. She was almost insolently tailored in a royal blue velvet house-robe high to the throat, long to the wrists; the dramatic effect was spoiled a little by the yappy little white poodle.

"Don't bark at the man, Frou-Frou, he's not a burglar."

At least, thought Maddox, Sue and Margaret hadn't set their hearts on a poodle.

Pam Roylston looked at him with her head on one side. "You're sort of cute, Sergeant. Ringo said you wouldn't eat me, but why you wanted to talk to me—I hadn't set eyes on Jan since last December. You wouldn't be thinking I'm the one murdered her, would you?" She laughed trillingly. "That's just stupid. Jan wasn't so bad. She just took what she wanted, and most of us do that."

"I understand you had quite a fight with her over that TV series that folded," said Maddox. "You and Miss Wynn."

"Oh, that. Are you sure I can't give you a drink, Sergeant? Well, after all, it's every girl for herself. 'Newcomers' would have lasted another season without slipping too much, but Jimmy had to have that bright idea for a spin-off series. At first it looked as if they'd write in all three of us, and then it turned out there'd be just the one big part, and it was pretty damn obvious the deal was all cut and dried between Jimmy and Ringo. Ringo's a pet but he can be tricksy-tricksy. Frou-Frou, darling, quiet while Mother's talking."

"You were annoyed about it."

"Naturally we were annoyed, as annoyed as all hell, Sergeant, but that's the way things go in this business. At least I'm working, if the thing is a bit stinko, I don't see any future in it but you never know what might show up." She was drinking rum and pineapple juice, and now stuck her finger in the glass and let the poodle lick it. "Next year I might be right on top. I'm sorry for Jan now, she didn't get to enjoy it long, did she?"

"About last Wednesday night," said Maddox.

She widened her eyes on him over her glass. "Are you asking for an alibi? My God. I'm afraid I can't oblige you. Quiet, darling. Do you re-

alize how hard we have to work in this business? I'm on the set at six
A.M., and four days out of five some damned thing goes wrong and we
have to do retakes up to the middle of the evening. You were lucky to
find me home tonight. I didn't get home until after nine on Wednesday, and I was beat. I had a drink and went to bed."

"You live here alone."

"I'm between boy friends," she said with a laugh.

"You have your own car?"

"I do. In the garage downstairs, and there's no attendant, so I could
have gone out and murdered Jan, but really, you know, I didn't. I
hardly ever thought about her anymore—I've been too busy."

"But you knew where she lived."

"Oh, everybody knows that. That she had Greg Ryan's house. Sure,
I'd been to parties there, in the old days when we were all chums and
'Newcomers' was running top in the ratings. If you ask me," said Pam
Roylston thoughtfully, "that's a jinx house, I wouldn't want it. I
wouldn't live up in one of those canyons if you paid me, I'd be terrified
of fire. But besides that—it's a jinx. I don't know Ryan, but what Jan
used to tell us about his wife—she laughed, but I didn't think it was
funny. Like a Gorgon or something, suspicious of anything female he
got in ten feet of—and with the hell of a lot of good reason too—and
then going back to Ireland every year to have another baby. And before
Ryan bought it, it belonged to Doreen Guardeau." He knew the name:
another actress from way back, another one much married. "I didn't
know her either but I remember somebody talking about it when Ryan
bought the house. She was married to that last husband right in the
house, and then they were both killed in a head-on collision on the way
to Palm Springs for a honeymoon. It's a wonder that house isn't
haunted. Maybe it will be now."

"Well, thanks very much," said Maddox.

"Have I convinced you I'm not your murderer? I wouldn't mind if
you stayed awhile, Sergeant." But it was automatic coquetry. Whatever
it was about Ivor Maddox that attracted the females, this kind was im-
mune; most of them with a larger than normal amount of egotism.

And actually he wasn't convinced of anything, either way. The thing
was all up in the air. She'd been in that house, to parties. So had Sheri
Wynn. And Wells. And a lot of other people, who would know which
was Jan Warden's bedroom. Those unknown prints. He hadn't any
evidential reason at all to ask for Pam Roylston's prints.

And queerly enough, going by the lab evidence, that murder had been done in the dark. Well, the light from the window at the front of the room. The bed on the side wall, and X coming in to stand at the left of the bed, between bed and bathroom door—he could see X touching that bedside table there, inadvertently, getting oriented in dim light. But Jan Warden quite visible enough in the light from the window. And afterward, the hasty makeshift cleanup in the bathroom—

The door unlocked, or a key used?

He came home to find Sue and Margaret admiring the finished curtains, now hung in place. He agreed absently that they looked fine. "Well, they'll *do*," said Sue. "Neither of us ever set up to be a seamstress. At least it's my day off tomorrow, I want to find that secondhand furniture place in the valley. If we could possibly find one of those old round oak tables—"

"They're asking a fortune for them now," said Margaret. "Everybody wants to cut them down for coffee tables."

"Now, Mother, don't be a pessimist. You never know until you look."

Maddox had just got to his desk on Wednesday morning when Captain Lyons called. "We've got the word from VISA headquarters," he said. "They had to dig for it. You were right about that Simms card, Maddox. It's an oldie. It was never renewed at all. It was issued in 1970, and they're good for about eighteen months and then if your credit's paid up you get a new one with a new expiration date. The Simms card never had much on it, less than four hundred, and it was paid up in April of 1971. It's been dormant since, that is she never asked for a renewal and of course it's no good."

"Except as I.D. for cashing checks," said Maddox. Lyons laughed rather hollowly and said he had other calls to make.

Rodriguez passed over the night report. For once there wasn't anything new for them to work. Feinman and D'Arcy came in behind Ellis; Dabney was bent over his typewriter across the room. Maddox sat back and told the other three about the Roylston girl.

"There's nothing to get hold of, it's all up in the air," complained Rodriguez.

"I'm out of ideas on it," said Maddox, "if I ever had any. I just have a fond lingering feeling that Wells would be the ideal X."

"He was with—"

"Yes, and the glimpse I had of Miss Sheri Wynn in court yesterday morning, she's the last person I'd pick to share a dangerous secret with. Empty-headed little egotist. But there wasn't anything to stop him slipping a little something in a last drink with her, and next morning saying, why, of course I was here all the time, lover."

"Well, I can't say he'd be my idea of a bosom buddy," said Rodriguez caustically, "but we've got absolutely nothing to say—" The phone went off on his desk and he went to pick it up. Maddox's phone rang again.

"Maddox speaking." It was an outside line.

"Oh, Sergeant Maddox, this is Marylou Searcy. I don't want to bother you or waste your time—"

"Quite all right, Miss Searcy. What is it?"

"Well, you asked me if Bill had said or done anything at all unusual lately. I didn't think about this, and I don't suppose it means anything at all, but I thought maybe I ought to tell you." A conscientious girl.

"What was it?"

"Well, nothing much. It's just, the way I told you, money was usually sort of tight with him, he didn't have any to throw around. But the last couple of dates I had with him, up to Saturday night, we went to places that were a lot more expensive than usual. The Tail o' the Cock, and that dinner theater in Beverly Hills. I know I was surprised, and asked if he'd inherited a fortune or something, and he just laughed and said sometimes you had to enjoy yourself and forget the tab."

"Oh, really," said Maddox.

"I wondered about it, but it didn't seem to worry him, so I let it drop. Of course on Saturday we'd just gone to that movie. I don't suppose it's important, but I just thought I'd mention it."

Maddox thanked her, and sat back and thought about that. It was a very little thing; maybe Bill had just been feeling reckless. But after a while he got up, feeling for his car keys, and noticed that the office was empty except for D'Arcy, who was slouched at his desk reading a large book with a colorful jacket, *The Art of Photographing the Desert*. Photography was D'Arcy's only outside interest, unless you could put the girls first. "Goofing off?" asked Maddox.

"I'm waiting for a witness. That pharmacy heist last Saturday. This clerk got knocked down and had a concussion, couldn't come in until now. César and Joe went to look at another body."

"What the *hell?*" said Maddox. "We didn't used to get the homicides so fast and furious."

"Oh, it was called in as a suicide," said D'Arcy. "Just a little paperwork."

The Capitol Records building had been a source of wonder and tourist interest when it was built; only the tourists stared at it anymore, a completely round building some twelve stories high, in the middle of town on Vine Street.

Maddox asked for Mrs. Wagner at the desk, and finally found himself facing her in a small anteroom with a door marked *Manager* behind her. "Oh, have you found out anything?"

"No, I'm sorry. Just a couple of other questions I'd like to ask you. If you could take a break, maybe I could buy you a cup of coffee?" She was a nice-looking woman for her age, had kept her figure and dressed well; but today her skin looked gray, and her voice was apathetic.

"Oh, I don't think—well, we could go down to the employees' lounge. Mr. Finch won't mind—he's been kind, he said I needn't come in, but you have to go on somehow." She put her head into the inner door and murmured, after a moment shut the door; she led him down the hall to a big square room with wicker furniture, a coffee machine, a sandwich machine.

"You can't give way," she said, accepting the paper cup of black coffee with a nod. She clasped it in both hands as if they were cold. "Only it all seems just for nothing now, Bill gone and me all alone. It was just the two of us all those years—his father died after we were divorced—and he was always so good, Bill I mean, such big plans he had for making money—" She smiled faintly. "Maybe he would have. You read about the crime rate being so high, but you never really think anything like that could happen to you or your family. It just seems such a waste, that's all."

"This may sound like a peculiar question, Mrs. Wagner, but had you noticed whether he seemed to have a little more money than usual, just lately?"

She sipped coffee. "It's funny you should ask that. He never had much, the loan just covered tuition and so on, and I couldn't make him much of an allowance. I don't know where he could have got that hundred dollars. I just found it last night, under his handkerchieves. I was thinking—what I'd better pick out—for the funeral, you know. Somebody called me just this morning to say I could claim his body."

"He never mentioned the money to you? It was cash?"

"That's right. Five twenties. I can't imagine, unless he'd been saving up a long while for something. He did like to plan ahead. The neighbors have all been so good—Mrs. Keeler brought over a casserole, and Mrs. Rogers came with a cake, and even old Miss Robbins made me gingerbread. Old-fashioned, but it's nice. Neighbors aren't always so neighborly in a city, but we always have been somehow, up there. Of course most of us have lived there a long time. Even little Mrs. Dorn brought me some flowers and was sympathetic, she's the newest one on the block but of course she's a small-town girl and a little old-fashioned too. Those children of hers so well-mannered—" But all that was from the surface of her mind. She looked at Maddox and her eyes were full of puzzled pain. "He was all I had," she said. "I used to look forward and think, it'd be such a wonderful thing when he found a nice girl, was earning good money, could get married and they'd have a family—I'd have grandchildren. But it'll never happen. He's just—gone. Just for nothing, the robbers in the street happening to pick him. All the years I worked and planned—it's all for nothing."

Sometimes there wasn't anything to say to the ones left in the receding wave of violence. He left her there crouched over the cup of cooling black coffee, and knew she was looking down the long empty years ahead, with nothing left to plan and work for but herself.

"And just who's going to clean up all the mess, I'd like to know—people got no right to do things like this on somebody else's property—I never seen such an ugly mess—" The high bitter voice of Mrs. Stella Goodman ranted on breathlessly as she climbed the stairs, and Rodriguez and Feinman after her, thinking instantly of the mess in Jan Warden's bedroom revealed in those photographs, were wondering how that had got cleaned up. "He was overdue with the rent, I was goin' to get it or tell him to get out, three months he'd been here and never on time with it once, a quiet fella but I will say I always thought there was something funny about Mr. Orde—"

This was a ramshackle old house on Harold Way, long cut up into a rooming house. Makeshift particle-board partitions made two rooms of bigger ones; the place smelled of dust and stale food. "Such a shock when I opened the door—maybe this is the time I really do it, I'm always sayin' get rid of this place and go to live with my daughter in the country— It's in there."

They had left the uniformed man downstairs. The door indicated was at the back of the upstairs hall on the left. Rodriguez shoved the door open.

It would be a little mess for somebody to clean up. The man lying on the thin mattress on the old iron bedstead had neatly slashed his wrists with the old straight razor beside him on the bed, and there was quite a lot of blood all over. But it had happened, at a guess, at least twenty-four hours ago, and the blood was all dry, darkening to a dull brown.

"I'll go tell Stoner to call the morgue wagon," said Feinman.

"There's a note." There wasn't always. This was a neat envelope, cheap dime-store quality, propped against the table lamp on the one rickety chest of drawers. Written across it in ballpoint pen were the words *To the Police.*

Rodriguez picked it up. It wasn't sealed, and there was a single sheet inside. He unfolded it, and Feinman looked over his shoulder uninterestedly.

The large but legible writing covered both sides of the sheet.

To the Police, I come to see this is the way its got to be because I keep on doing things. Everybody always kept telling me I should not do such things and I know that but I think there is somebody else inside me that does the things one of the doctors told me it was something like that. It is a different somebody not me because when I am me I am very sorry about the things. I guess I should not ever take a drink because when I do that lets the other one out but I like to drink especially whiskey. I thought I would use a rope to hang myself or rather both of us but there is nothing in here to tie it to. This is a very cheap place but I have not much money. I would like to say I am sorry very much about Irma Elwood the others too but she was the first and if they had hung me after that he would not have done all the rest. Sincerely Yours Fenton L. Ordway.

"Well, of all the rigmaroles," said Feinman, and Rodriguez clapped a hand to his head and let out a smothered yell.

"¡Santa Maria y todos angeles! Ordway! Fenton Ordway—my God, Joe, he's been on the Ten Most Wanted list for the last five years! Those rape kills in Louisiana, and some people burned to death somewhere in Wisconsin—they send a new flyer on him every now and then—"

"My God, sure," said Feinman. "Morgue wagon be damned, we'd better leave Stoner on the door while we get the Feds—"

Mrs. Goodman gaped at them.

At least the Feds would have all the paperwork on it. By the time they got back to the office with the two FBI men, Deforest and Anders, everybody else was back, and interested in this; it made a little break in the monotony of routine.

"I'd have to look at the record, tell you how many murders," said Deforest. "Since he was about fourteen. The Elwood youngster was the first, her father was chief of police—some little town in Alabama—and Ordway was nearly lynched. Pity he wasn't, like he says. He left a trail of robberies, rapes, and murders from Alabama all across the Midwest, and he was arrested and charged four times."

"I could guess the rest," said Maddox.

"Oh yeah. Stashed away in the nut houses, violent schizophrenic personality, and the next thing you know some damn-fool head doctor lets him out. At least the last time he was supposed to be in for keeps, the criminal-insane institution in Illinois, but he broke loose with another nut named Quigley, who'd got committed for killing his grandmother. And he killed Quigley three days later. Well, good riddance—we've got him off the books, and at least he won't be killing anybody else."

"The ultimate solution," said Feinman, "talking about Mosaic law."

What was in all of their minds was, of course, that that unpredictable body, the California Supreme Court, had just ruled the death penalty back in. All lawmen were pleased about that, but it remained to be seen how many killers would still slide out from under it with the plea bargaining and reduced charges.

Into the little silence the phone on Maddox's desk went off, and he reached for it. "Maddox."

"Say," said Sergeant Whitwell, "I just had a snitch on the line. He hears the fuzz are interested in an Aggie with a house of girls. He wants a meet and a C-note. It seemed a little high, but I know you've been waiting on this one."

"Hell, yes! Did you set it up? Good. My God," said Maddox, starting to laugh, "Sue's going to be mad—it would break on her day off!"

Patrolman Percy Everard, riding X-214 down Cahuenga, at twelve-twenty, was just thinking of calling in a Code Seven and stopping somewhere for a hamburger, when he got a call. It was an interesting call: the first time since he'd been on the job that he'd had this kind of assignment. One of the street informants with some information the detectives wanted; he was to meet him and get it, and he was authorized to give him a police department chit for a hundred bucks, redeemable in cash downtown. Every police department relied on snitches for big or little information, but the snitches were usually shy birds.

He was to meet this one around at the back of the Pan-Pacific Auditorium. There wasn't anything on there now, it was closed, but the parking lot would be open. Everard accelerated the squad a bit down to turn right on Melrose, down to Gardner, and left there to Beverly.

It was funny, he thought, but ever since that thing had happened last Thursday—Siegel up there on the roof of the Broadway—he'd been feeling, somehow, more alive than he ever had before. He knew he'd never again come so close to death without actually dying, and maybe it had made him appreciate being alive more than he ever had. Appreciate being young and strong and happy and satisfied with where he was in life.

He hadn't told Rosemary all about that—there'd only been a little paragraph in the papers—because if she knew she'd be all upset and nervous. She was a sensible girl usually, but with the first baby due in August— Either John or Linda, they'd agreed. He didn't exactly mind carrying a name like Percy, but he wouldn't wish it on a son.

It was a nice sunny day, and it was good to be alive, and good to feel he was in a job that was important, on a team with a lot of good men all pulling together. And someday he'd make rank on the team, detective and sergeant, maybe even lieutenant.

Right now there was this interesting little assignment. He pulled the squad into the big empty parking lot of the Pan-Pacific Auditorium and looked around. He couldn't see anybody at first, and then he saw a skinny dark-colored figure slide out from the shelter of the building and lift an arm, and skulk back again. He slid the squad up there to the rear of the building and cut the engine.

Somebody ducked out and in one quick move got into the passenger seat. "You got the paper?" asked a squeaky voice.

Everard looked at the snitch curiously. He was a scrawny unhealthy-looking little man, about forty. He had a foxy face, thin and sharp, with bleared eyes, and he wore ancient dirty old pants, a raveled black sweater, sneakers. This wasn't the first time he'd sold information; he examined the official form narrowly, said, "That's good. You want a dame named Aggie, got some girls and a regular setup for johns. It's on Hoover." He recited the address parrot-like. "Aggie Moreno."

"O.K.," said Everard. The snitch was out of the car in another quick move, and the next second he had vanished round the side of the auditorium.

Everard picked up the mike and relayed the information. This would be interesting to tell Rosemary about.

Maddox said to the phone, "O.K., we're on it. That's the Central beat, below Santa Barbara. You'd better get Central to send a squad to meet us as backup." What he was thinking was, if Aggie (and presumably Joey) were holding two minors captive, there might be others. It wasn't unprecedented. Sue was going to be furious that it had broken when she wasn't there to help with the great rescue. But Sally and Marjorie had been at the back of Maddox's mind too, and he didn't waste any time getting out to the parking lot, D'Arcy and Rodriguez behind him. They took D'Arcy's Dodge.

The snitch had called in at twelve-ten. Sergeant Whitwell would be relieved for lunch by one of the policewomen in the Communications office at twelve-thirty, and his stomach was already growling. The switchboard was quiet until twelve-nineteen, and the policewoman was just coming up to the desk, when a call came in.

"Los Angeles Police Department, Sergeant Whitwell, may I help—"

"Listen, I've got that A.P.B.—the Byron car—but tell the front-office boys to get up here pronto—" It was the hurried, breathless voice of Patrolman Ramon Gonzales, and Whitwell was momentarily confused because Gonzales shouldn't be on an ordinary phone line, out of the squad—he should be talking to Communications from the squad— "What?" said Whitwell.

"The A.P.B., for God's sake—chase somebody up here, it's Stanley Avenue—" He added the address. "This one we'd better get on, he's held these people hostage—I've got an ambulance coming—"

Whitwell broke the connection and plugged in to the communal detective office. Feinman and Daisy Hoffman were the only ones in, probably just thinking about going out for lunch.

CHAPTER 6

Stanley Avenue ran straight as a die up through Hollywood, mostly residential all the way, but up here above Franklin where it began, it was exclusively residential and tailed off in a curve to a dead end with only three houses on a short half block, expensive houses if not over-large. The black-and-white squad was sitting double-parked in front of the last one, and Gonzales was standing on the little front porch. It was a neat Dutch Colonial house painted gray and white.

"Where the hell's the ambulance?" he said to Daisy and Feinman. "There you are, right out there—" He stabbed a forefinger. "I get this call, unknown trouble, and the first thing I spot when I land here is that Pontiac there's the A.P.B. on, right in front." They were in the house by then.

"Dan—please, you've got to help Dan—" A thin old lady was half-lying in a chair just inside the living room from the small entry hall. Her gray hair was wild; there was blood on her dress.

"The ambulance is coming, Mrs. Cobb. The guy had been here since Monday afternoon, holding them hostage. Shot them when he left just a while ago, in their car." Across the room, a man was lying on the floor, a stout bald old man in a white shirt and dark pants; there was a great patch of blood on the shirt, but he was still breathing.

"She just managed to get to the phone—" The ambulance siren came howling; the ambulance pulled up in the street.

Feinman squatted down beside the old lady as the ambulance men came in with a stretcher. "A minute, boys," he said. His voice was gentle. "Mrs. Cobb? Can you tell me quick, anything the man handled? Glasses, plates, furniture?"

Her faded blue eyes focused on him. "He sat—watching TV, drank all that beer— Want to tell you about, so awful—only I'm afraid for Dan, he's hurt—his heart not too good—" They were taking the old man out first. Her eyes moved to Daisy, and she said clearly, "Please, would you call our son—Rodney lives in Brentwood—"

"Yes, it's all right, we will," said Daisy. The attendants were coming back for the old lady.

There were a dozen empty beer glasses on the living room floor, around a big chair pulled up to the color TV.

Feinman said, "You'd better ride along. Gonzales, get on the mike and call up a lab unit."

Daisy rode down to the hospital in the ambulance, and waited forty minutes in the emergency wing before a doctor talked to her. "I don't know if the old man will make it—the bullet's lodged dangerously near the heart, I wouldn't attempt to go for it until he's more stable, but the outlook isn't good. She took a bullet in the shoulder, but she's patched up and we've given her something to settle her down. She's very anxious to talk to the police—just don't fuss her with too many questions. I gather she's been through quite an ordeal, and she's an old lady."

She looked a very frail old lady, lying flat in the hospital bed; a nurse was standing by. "I have to tell—the police. Want to tell—so they can find him— Are you police?" She stared fuzzily at the badge in Daisy's hand.

Daisy bent over her and said clearly, "I'm a police sergeant, Mrs. Cobb. Just take your time and tell me what you want to. We'll try to find him." She had her notebook ready.

"Oh, I'm so afraid Dan's hurt—badly. His heart's not good. He came —the man—on Monday afternoon. Rang the doorbell—and he had a gun. Walked right in. We couldn't—couldn't do a thing. Big strong man—such awful language—he was hungry, I had to fix dinner for him, and he took all the money we had in the house—about a hundred dollars. He locked us in the front bathroom, and it seemed—so silly, you'd think something we could do, but the window so high, and Dan's heart and my arthritis—"

"Yes, take it easy now."

"He got all that beer—sat watching TV, we could hear it on so loud. He let me out to fix him another meal— Oh, but it was awful, the things he said! All the time I was fixing something, and he made me wait on him—we'd told him and told him, just take anything he wanted and please just go, but he wouldn't, so I didn't say that again. He kept saying he should have killed those two kids, he was crazy to let them go, they'd seen him. He should have killed them. He said, you don't think I mean it, but I killed lots of people, what would two more be. I killed those cops, he said." She took a breath. "And he locked me in again—that bathroom's on the side without any neighbors, and we couldn't call loud enough to carry to the neighbors on the other side, and besides we were afraid if we tried, he'd do something worse—"

"Yes. He left this morning?"

"We were so tired—couldn't sleep, that little space—he made us go in the living room, he wanted the keys to the car, he said don't worry, he wouldn't be back, and he laughed, and he just—stood a minute looking at us and I saw him decide to kill us—like I'd swat a fly—he just aimed the gun and shot—so worried about Dan—"

The nurse nodded at Daisy as the voice trailed off, and she put her notebook away and went out to the corridor. "We've contacted the son," said the nurse at the nearby station. Daisy didn't see any point in wasting time until he arrived; she called the office, they sent a squad over to pick her up, and she had an initial report nearly typed up when Feinman came back.

"Franks is still poking around there, but Baker got a dozen latents off those bottles and came back to have a closer look."

"I have a hunch he's not listed with us, but he'll be on file somewhere, Joe. They don't think the old man's going to make it."

"Hell of a thing," said Feinman. "I don't suppose she could tell you about the car. Never mind, we'll get it from Sacramento." He went over to Communications, and shot an enquiry up to the D.M.V. office; in five minutes the information came back. Daniel Cobb's car was a two-year-old Mercury, plate number thus and such. An A.P.B. went out on it with the warning tacked on to approach the driver with caution.

As soon as Maddox spotted the address on Hoover he had a sharp stab of apprehension that they were going to be disappointed. It was an old block of store buildings; the store just below, in the middle of the block, was empty and for rent, but a narrow doorway beside it led to steep stairs, a sign with an arrow pointing up: *Massage Parlor.* The Central beat squad had been waiting for them, with two men in it.

"Hell, don't tell me," said Maddox. They pounded up the stairs with the uniformed men behind, and up there all they found was the expectable setup, repeated all over town, if this was a third-rate example and cruder than some. There were a couple of customers on the premises, five girls, and Aggie Moreno, who was a tough blonde about forty. The girls were all in the twenties, and there wasn't any evidence that anyone had been confined anywhere; the way makeshift rooms opened out, no locks on any doors, it wouldn't have been possible.

They came across the usual equipment stocked to cater to different tastes, and a little pile of cash money, and that was all except the human flotsam and jetsam.

One of the Central men, looking around, said, "One every six blocks, some areas. What was the big hustle and bustle, Sergeant?"

"We just thought there was," said Maddox disgustedly.

Rodriguez laughed sharply. "We'd better spell out the wanted info a little more specific from now on, *amigo*. This was a damned expensive way to flush out another cheap whore house."

Maddox swore along with him. But having landed on it, they called up another squad and took all the women over to the central jail.

"What the hell is it with you damn fuzz, anyway?" said Aggie. "You never take a roll in the hay like anybody else? It's a girl's own business, she wants to peddle it, we don't kidnap the johns off the street, do we?"

The girls in business for themselves, maybe it was their own business; but so few of them were. Most of them were exploited by the pimps, their female counterparts like Aggie; and anywhere above the street-level operation like this, it was all tied up with big organized crime.

At any rate, this had been the wrong Aggie, and they were no nearer to locating Sally and Marjorie. Rittenhouse had called again on Monday; he'd be calling some more; and there was nothing to tell him.

These women would make bail, and depending on their previous records might get probation, or thirty days in the county jail, and next day be back at the old stand.

The Hollywood men got back to their own precinct about four o'clock and heard about the Cobbs. "Baker wired the prints to NCIC," said Feinman, "just in case." They might hear something on that right off the bat, or not until tomorrow; NCIC was always quicker than the FBI, because they were always operating on very current files, and were set up to give service. In fact, a call came up from downtown at five-thirty; the prints weren't in L.A.'s files. But just at the end of shift, there was a teletype from Washington: NCIC had come through with an identification.

The man they wanted, who had abducted Francie and Peter, and held the Cobbs hostage, was Gary Anderson Lewis, and he had a long and bad record back to age seventeen. It read tersely, without details, theft, robbery, robbery with violence, assault, assault with intent, manslaughter, Murder Two. He had served time, mostly in federal prisons; he was currently supposed to be serving a twenty-year term in Leavenworth for bank robbery, but he had escaped three months ago with another prisoner. In the course of police pursuit, the other prisoner had been shot and recaptured, but Lewis had got clean away after killing a deputy sheriff and badly wounding a city cop. His official description read, male Caucasian, forty-one, six-two, a hundred and ninety, brown and blue. He had usually run with a gang, but as of right now all the rest were behind bars.

"Yes," said D'Arcy, rubbing his jaw, "he wouldn't care what he did, would he? When he's dropped on, they'll try him for that lawman." NCIC was sending on photos. They could do a rush job on it, get a lot of flyers made up for distribution to the patrols county-wide, and hope that that, or the A.P.B., would flush out Lewis soon.

He wasn't a man to be out wandering the streets.

And of course Maddox had to pass that on to Sue, about the abortive Aggie, and Sue said, "Damn! Stupid street snitches." They talked about other things over dinner, but he knew she was still brooding over Sally and Marjorie. When she came into the living room after dinner she said, "I wish there was some way to *look*, that's all. I know, I know, there just isn't. They could be anywhere. Sixteen. Just wanting to scare the parents a little. Damn." She bit her lip. Neither of them had to discuss what they both knew. On the face of it, it might seem that it would be unnecessary trouble for the Aggies and Joeys to hold onto prisoners, when there were enough girls available eager to oblige. But there were too many potential customers who got the big kick out of the unwilling ones, the scared ones, and the Aggies and Joeys would cater to the offbeat lusts. It wasn't nice to think what might be happening to Sally and Marjorie.

Maddox thought about the manager of the Egyptian Theater. Supposed to be more or less civilized. But there were a lot of dirty dark alleys still in a supposedly enlightened era, and nobody knew that better than cops.

Sue went and got a book from the study, but he didn't think she was really reading it. Margaret came in massaging cream into her hands and said brightly, cheerfully, "You know, I've been thinking about it, Sue, and there's no reason we have to be so purist and faddy, just because Corgis are Welsh. We could call her Taffy. Or Amber. Or—"

"Oh!" said Sue, and started to cry. "Oh, Mother! I'm sorry but I c-couldn't—I haven't said anything because you were so c-crazy to get another— But it wouldn't be *Gor!* I couldn't bear—"

Margaret looked startled, and then she started to cry a little too, and she was laughing at the same time. "Sue, darling! I just couldn't bear the thought either—but I wouldn't say so because I thought you wanted—" They were both laughing then, and hugged each other a little tearfully.

"Something who looked like Gor and wasn't. We can't," said Sue.

"Yes, that's it. Almost any other kind of dog at all," said Margaret.

Maddox put down the *Herald* and cleared his throat. "Well, you've settled that. As a matter of fact I've been thinking about dogs lately, and you know, the little ones are quick to bark and bite, but—well, they are little. Can't really do much damage to a determined burglar or rapist."

They looked at him. "Well, for heaven's sake," said Sue, "would you like to get an attack-trained Doberman, or something? Who'd likely murder the meter reader?"

"No, no," said Maddox hastily. "It was just a passing thought."

Sue and Margaret smiled at each other. "Let's just leave it and see," said Sue. "Maybe we'll feel different after a while, but I don't think so."

"I'll call Mrs. Boardman in the morning and tell her."

Thursday, and he was off, but he wanted to talk to that realtor about the house in Nichols Canyon. Nine o'clock found him in a comfortably shabby back office of the Hollywood branch of Gold Carpet Realty, talking with Eugene von Bazen.

"You know, that house has a kind of funny history," said Von Bazen thoughtfully. "When my secretary said the police had called, wanted to ask questions, I got to thinking about it. Got out the file on it." He was the senior partner here, a man in the sixties, still with a plentiful head of hair and a spare figure. He clutched a briar pipe without filling it. "As it happens, we've handled it every time it's changed hands. Well, we're about the biggest outfit here, of course. But—funny. To start with, the contractor who built it got stuck with it—the fellow he was building it for went bankrupt. We sold it for him to Mrs. Ferensky. That was in 1960." He had a thick manila envelope on the desk in front of him, but didn't open it. "She was a retired prima ballerina, with a New York company—came here for the climate. Woman about sixty, and she looked as fit and healthy as a woman twenty years younger. But she died of cancer just the next year. Well, it isn't always easy to move property like that, you know—property in that price range, that is. We sold it in late 1961 to Robert Medford—I expect you remember his name, well-known film director. He and his wife lived there until 1969, when she died and he killed himself. Then that actress, Doreen Guardeau, bought it. She lived there until 1973, when she and the latest husband were killed in an accident. Almost as if there was a jinx on the place."

"Mr. Greg Ryan owns it now?"

"Yes, he bought it after that, in 1973. But he's written us that he wants to get rid of it, he'll be in England indefinitely. Miss Warden's lease will be up in December, and then it'll go on the market again."

"I see. Well, all I'd like to know," said Maddox, "is about the locks. Have they ever been changed? Any new owner putting in different ones?"

Von Bazen looked a little surprised. "Now that I wouldn't know. But it doesn't seem too likely. That's a very well-built house, solid value. Everything in it first quality. Why would the locks get changed?"

"And damn it," said Maddox, "anybody who might know seems to be dead."

Von Bazen said slowly, "Well, I know how we can find out. I told you I got out the file on it. We've handled it every time, as I say, and things do pile up in any office. Shoved on shelves out of the way. When I went to look up the lease, when her lawyer called, I found a lot of old papers on that along with it, and something I'd forgotten about—well, it was twenty years ago." He opened the envelope at last, reached in and brought out a key. It had a tag tied to it with string. "Mrs. Ferensky's daughter came out from New York to settle the estate. We sold the house for her to Medford, but not until after she'd gone back East. I remembered when I saw this—she found an extra key among her mother's things and sent it to me. I probably meant to pass it on to Medford, and it got buried with the papers." He held it out. "You see the tag."

"Yes." It had the address of the house printed on it in block letters, and the date, 1960, and the name and address of the realty company. A key the realtors had used when they were showing the house. "So," said Maddox, "let's go see if it still works." Von Bazen got up with alacrity.

They drove up there in his car. "Miss Warden's lawyer said it would probably take until at least the end of the year to settle her estate, there's no question of breaking the lease. But I don't like the idea of leaving it untenanted until then. It's full of valuable furniture to be sold with the house. I don't know what we can do about that—have to think. And inflated values—unless we can find another millionaire, it won't be easy to move. Ryan paid three hundred and eighty-five thousand, and that's seven years ago. We'll ask at least five hundred thousand. It's a prestige area."

And it was indeed a handsome house, elegant with its combination of stucco and stone and brick, its white shutters and outsize blue pool, the neat little guest house, the manicured lawns. Eleanor Gunther's car was in the guest house drive.

As they got out at the front door, she opened it. "Oh, you," she said to Maddox. "I was afraid it was more reporters. They've been around like flies. I didn't know anything to tell them, but they took a lot of pictures. I didn't let them in, though. The other policemen put a seal on that door—after she was taken away. I didn't know if I should—"

"That's all right now," said Maddox absently. "We're finished with it."

"Oh, you are. And am I expected to clean up—all that?"

"Um," said Maddox. "No, I see. I'd ask the lawyer. I suppose there'll be money to hire somebody."

"Best just bundle everything up to take to the dump," she said with a shiver.

And Maddox, eying the serene sweep of green lawn to either side of the drive, thought that he wouldn't care for this house himself. It had a funny history, all right. He put his hand out and Von Bazen gave him the key. He tried it in the front door, and it slipped in easily, obediently moved the latch and dead bolt. "Bloody hell!" said Maddox. César's hunch.

There might be any number of keys to this house floating around, the last twenty years. Now he thought about it, the house had always belonged to show biz people, and there would have been servants—

funny hours, Miss Gunther had said; yes, servants who wouldn't ordinarily be given keys might have had them, here.

He asked Von Bazen about those various households, if he remembered anything, had ever known anything. Von Bazen scratched his nose and said, "Well, I see what you mean. I don't know how we'd ever find out. I can tell you this and that. The Medfords hadn't any family, it was left to a nephew and he sold it through us after probate was ended. I believe they did a lot of entertaining, they had a couple who lived in the guest house—we had them stay on as caretakers until it was sold. Mrs. Ferensky—there was an old friend who lived with her as companion, and she had a personal maid, and a housekeeper. Miss Guardeau—she left it to her only daughter in a new will, and the daughter lived in Virginia, didn't come out to see it. At that time there were three servants living in. I remember the lawyer had some trouble with them, they claimed she'd owed them more money or something. I couldn't tell you anything about the Ryans."

"My God," said Maddox. He looked at Miss Gunther, who was listening interestedly. "Do you remember, when Miss Warden gave you a key to the house—did she have several, or what?"

"Sure," said Miss Gunther. "Just after she hired me. She took me upstairs to her bedroom, and she rummaged around in the bottom of an old jewel box and there was a handful of keys. I couldn't say if they were all the same—"

"She took the place after the Ryans left," said Von Bazen, "but he didn't decide to rent it until they were in England—his lawyers turned the keys over to us, and I seem to remember there were three or four."

"But the same key fits the guest house, you know," said Miss Gunther. "It makes it handy, not having to carry a bunch. It fits the front and back doors and the guest house."

"Oh, now that is really too much," said Maddox. This put the thing, not merely in the air, but in the stratosphere.

"I remember Mr. Wells had one once, I don't know if he just borrowed it. He came to borrow some records when she was away working. I told you Mr. Dukard had one when he lived here." You could see the avid speculation in her eyes.

My good God, thought Maddox. Anybody who had ever lived here, to twenty years back—servants, friends, whoever. Show biz people tended to be careless. And something else—nobody needed to know who lived here, to know it was somebody with money, loot to be had. It could be—wait for it, the idea sliding into his mind— "Tell me," he asked Miss Gunther, "was she neat about her clothes? Hung them up as she undressed?"

"Oh, goodness, anything but. They'd be all over in the morning, where she took them off. She kept her nightgown and robe in the bathroom, but she'd just drop everything else—"

So there we are, thought Maddox, and the picture slid into his mind complete. That could be the answer. Somebody—once a servant here, down on his luck—somebody, in any case, knowing what door a key fitted, a key however come by, and taking a chance on it. Casing the place? And another thing, if he saw her leave, he might reasonably have thought she'd be out much later. Giving Miss Gunther a chance to settle down after her light went off—he might just about have got up to that bedroom when Jan Warden walked in at eleven o'clock. And caught flat-footed, he took refuge in the closet. The closet in front of the bathroom. And when he tried to get out quietly, after she was in bed, she sat up or called out, and he hit out in fright with a pocket knife or whatever, and then found he was in worse trouble.

Keys. How many keys casually handed out among how many people? And come to think, who did change locks, coming into a new house? Take it for granted that all the former owners' keys had been handed over.

He also thought that right now he was going to see that realtor, Parrott, who had sold them the house, and find out for certain who might have old keys to the house on Starview Terrace. It had belonged to an old lady, but you never knew. And if there was any doubt about it, damn the expense, he'd get that lock changed right away.

The autopsy report on Bill Wagner came in, nothing much in it. At three o'clock on Thursday afternoon the hospital called to tell them that Daniel Cobb had died. The photos from NCIC were in, and the lab downtown busy getting those flyers out.

Rodriguez was just saying to D'Arcy, looking at the autopsy report, "The only obvious thing about it, he knew whoever it was. Somebody sitting in the front seat with him just reached over and shot him. Slug was in the right temple."

"And the only little suggestive scrap Ivor turned up was that he had a little more money than he should have. A hundred bucks or so."

"Chicken feed," said Rodriguez. "What could that say? Somebody owed it to him, or he saved it up." The phone rang on D'Arcy's desk.

"Say, I just had a call from Cassidy," said Whitwell. "He says they're bringing in a whole crowd of people you'll have to sort out. Something about assault, assault with intent. A wedding party, he said, and the priest insisted on coming along."

D'Arcy held the phone away and looked at it. "Assault? On a wedding party?"

"Don't ask me," said Whitwell. "He just said I should warn you."

Fortunately Feinman and Ellis were in, questioning a heist suspect. When the wedding party started to arrive, in five squad cars, they were needed to help on the sorting out.

The wedding had been a fully formal one, at St. Mary's Church up on Vermont. The bride, though she was in floods of tears, looked lovely in a long creamy satin gown with lace and a train, a long lace veil. She was Maria Luisa Scarola, née Donato. Two of her bridesmaids were still with her, also in tears. There were also four ushers, the best man, and eight of the wedding guests, all male. The bride and the bridesmaids were the only ones unscathed. The rest of them were utterly disheveled, bruised and bloody, their wedding finery in shreds. It had, said Cassidy bitterly, been quite a donnybrook. He and Stoner had been called out first, and had to call up reinforcements. He had a long tear in his uniform jacket, the makings of a black eye; Stoner and Burke looked bruised and battered.

The groom, his father, and the bride's father, were down in Emergency with a lot of knife wounds. So were the other two ushers and assorted wedding guests.

The priest, a Father Angelo Dominari, still in his official robes, was trying to comfort the bride and chastise the rest of the party at once. Everybody was talking, and it was all a little confused until George Ellis lost patience with all of them and started bellowing for quiet. They simmered down and a few facts emerged.

It seemed that Roberto Donato, who was an electrician working for the city, had borrowed some money from Carlo Scarola, who owned a small restaurant on Western, some time last year. It hadn't been a formal arrangement, but as time went on Scarola began to feel that he'd like to see his money again; Donato said he didn't have it. Their working hours conflicting, their orbits didn't often cross, but of course they had today when Scarola's son Tony and Donato's daughter Maria were united in holy matrimony. The ceremony in the church was over, everybody had adjourned to the church hall for the reception, and that was when the donnybrook got under way.

"All Mr. Scarola said was," sobbed Maria, "it must be c-costing a fortune, there were four c-cases of champagne—and two cakes and a lot of f-favors— And Papa said nothing was too good for me, the money didn't matter—"

"And then," said the best man Hugo Volpi, nursing a bloody gash down one cheek, "Scarola said if he could spend all that on a wedding he could sure as hell pay up his debts, and Donato said he wasn't like some people who owned their own businesses, and then they started shouting at each other and Donato grabbed up a knife and naturally Tony jumped in to protect his father—"

It was just coincidence that the reception was to include a sit-down dinner with roasted duck, and that the tables were all set with sharp and serrated knives.

"My God, you should have seen it," said Cassidy. "The funny thing is, nobody was tight—nobody had a chance to take a drink before it got started—there were broken wine bottles all over the floor, and the tables all knocked over, and both the cakes squashed flat—"

Stoner was feeling his face. "Most of the groom's side took out after the bride's side, and God knows who stabbed the two papas—"

"They stabbed each other," said Volpi. "I saw that much. Then I got knocked down over a table and I got no idea who knifed Tony."

Nobody seemed to know. They talked to them separately, but fairly soon it was evident that nobody had been noticing much of anything, and probably they'd never know who had knifed Tony. A call to the hospital confirmed that the groom wasn't in any danger, but he'd be spending a few days of his honeymoon in the hospital. Donato and Scarola were both in more serious condition.

"Dear me," said the priest, "and who is to clean up the hall I don't know. This is all very distressing—very distressing indeed." He took the bride away still in tears, and they let the rest of them off with a charge of disturbing the peace. It was all a little waste of time, unless the two papas died or got charged with assault.

Dick Brougham and Ken Donaldson, sitting on night watch, were left undisturbed until nine-fifty, when they got a call from the dispatcher about a body. It was Melrose and Formosa. They both rode on it.

The body had been found fifteen minutes ago by a dog-walker, who had called in from a public phone up on the main drag. It was just a little way down the side street, in the parking strip by the curb: the body of a young woman. Brougham and Donaldson looked at it and instantly read the story. She was lying there with her head hanging over the curb, and her dress had been ripped open down the front; panties dangled from one leg, and there were bruises on her face; her long blond hair was tangled, trailing in the dirt in the street. The body was still warm.

They got the dog-walker's name and told him he could go. He went thankfully. "Any point in calling up a lab unit?" asked Donaldson.

"Pictures, anyway," said Brougham. The girl had on a gray cardigan with pockets; he felt in both, and came up with a key holder. It was a folding one, and inside the flap was a plastic slot that held an I.D. form, and it was neatly filled in. Wanda Bates, an address on Formosa, an apartment number. "That's just up the block," said Brougham. "What's that?" His flashlight caught something there in the grass in the parking strip; he reached for it. It was a big stiffened manila envelope addressed to Private William Tucker at an APO address, New York; it bore Wanda Bates's return address, and postage. There was a postal box ten feet away at the corner, down from the main drag. "Now I just wonder," said Brougham, "if he grabbed that when he reached for her. You can't be too careful." He went back to the car for an evidence bag, slid the envelope into it.

They called a night-crew lab man for the pictures, left the uniformed man waiting, and walked up the block to that apartment. It was a fairly new and small one, about sixteen units on two floors; the one they wanted was upstairs. When they rang the bell, a girl's voice said instantly, "Wanda? I thought you took your keys—" The door was pulled open and her eyes widened on them, on the badge in Brougham's hand.

Her name was Lyn Hofstetter, and they had to give her a little time. She told them that she and Wanda had just moved in last week, and then she began to cry; they waited for her. But she pulled herself together, shakily, to tell them a little more. "I'd just started to worry—she should have been back. She'd just got those new photographs, she wanted to mail them off—to her fiancé. She just went up to the corner —I was washing my hair so she took her keys—" They hadn't known each other long. They both worked at one of the gift shops in the

Farmers' Market, had decided to share an apartment to save expenses. Wanda had said she'd just go up to mail her parcel, and she might stop in the pharmacy on Melrose, it was open until nine-thirty. "She left about ten to nine, I expected her back any minute—just wondering where she was, the pharmacy would be closed—"

"Could you give us an address for her parents, any relative?"

She blew her nose again, wiping her eyes. "She didn't have any. Her parents were killed, her grandmother brought her up and she died last year. Oh, I shouldn't have let her go alone! But just half a block up to the corner, and lights there—it wasn't really late—"

They didn't like to ask her to come in, make the formal identification. They asked about the employer.

"Mr. Hope. The Old World Shop. Oh, why did it have to happen? She'd just got engaged last month, before he got sent to Germany— It doesn't seem fair."

Brougham and Donaldson walked back up the block, and around the corner onto Melrose. "You know, Ken, bells are ringing in my head," said Brougham.

"There's nothing to prove it," said Donaldson.

"Not yet. There may be prints on that envelope, and we've got the others off Mrs. Gorman's handbag." Brougham stood on the corner of the street and looked up the block: a block of business. On the corner was a big laundromat. The lights were still on inside, bright and white on the glistening lines of washers and dryers, the big tables for sorting laundry. Next to that was a dry cleaners', dark completely. Next to that was the pharmacy, one faint night light inside and the one neon sign left on outside. Up from there was a card shop, a fabric shop, a small independent liquor store, all dark.

"It's his beat, sort of," said Brougham. They had been in on the beginning of all of those, of course, on night watch. "The Unger girl was at a laundromat five blocks up from here. The Sawyer woman at a laundromat about four blocks down. The Ritter girl—I wonder if she's still in the hospital—at a laundromat just a couple of blocks down La Brea from Melrose. And the Thorpe woman at one a few blocks down on Highland. If he's cruising, looking, those are both main drags he'd naturally pick. And Mrs. Gorman on another main drag only a couple of blocks down."

He went over to the laundromat and peered in. The sign on the door said *Hours 6 A.M.–12 P.M.* "I suppose," he said, "there's an automatic time lock or something. There aren't any attendants at these places." The door was still unlocked but there wasn't anybody in there now. "She was still warm, Ken. It wouldn't have taken her five minutes to walk up here—not even right to the corner, the post box is on the side street. It could have happened a couple of different ways. He cruises past, spots a woman inside alone, and by the time he parked the car and came back, she was gone, or a couple of other people have gone in. And just then Wanda comes up to the post box, and it's only ten, fifteen feet down to the dark side street."

"Oh, I see it. We said he could end up killing one."

"How did he?" The night lab man, the squad car, were gone; the morgue wagon had come and gone. Brougham went down to where the body had been, squatted down and moved the flashlight. "Well, I trust our scientific expert got a shot of this." The curb there was jagged and broken, the edges rough; and there was just a little blood along the roughness. "Yes," said Brougham. "Put him there just foiled of his intended prey at the laundromat—a couple of minutes before nine—when the girl comes up. He goes for her instead—we know he's fast. He grabs the envelope—or, of course, she drops it to fight him, he gets her down and knocks her back onto that curb, finish. I'll bet the autopsy will say, skull fracture."

"And that's nice deduction," said Donaldson. "Sure, that's probably so. But if we ever catch up to him, this is one they won't charge him with. There's no solid evidence."

"Unless there are some prints on that envelope," said Brougham. "I think I'll call Maddox and pass it on, anyway."

Back at the office, he did, and Maddox agreed with him. "But we haven't had a kickback on those prints yet. They're only useful if they're in somebody's files, after all. NCIC is usually pretty quick, and we sent those in on Sunday. You know what that says."

"Yes, damn it," said Brougham.

NCIC might once have had those prints, but by their continued silence it didn't look as if they had them now.

But whether it could ever be proved or not, both Brougham and Maddox were morally convinced that the ape-man rapist had graduated to homicide.

The usual paperwork had to be done. And on top of everything else they had to think about— "We'll have to get statements from the two idiotic papas, and the groom," said D'Arcy, "and see if the D.A. wants to bring assault charges—" Maddox spent a couple of hours locating Wanda Bates's employer, getting him to make the formal identification, listening to his shocked comments.

By the time he got back, at least they had some concrete evidence. Baker had raised one clear print on the manila envelope, and it matched one of those from Mrs. Gorman's bag.

"Half a league onward," said Maddox irritably. "And if they aren't in any files, what the hell use are they? But forgetting the ape man for a minute, I've got some damned frustrating news on the superstar." Ellis and Feinman abandoned typing reports to hear it, and D'Arcy laid down the photography book. "That Nichols Canyon house—"

They heard about the keys, and cussed fervently. "César is going to love that one," said D'Arcy. It was Rodriguez' day off. "My good God, Ivor—every servant who ever worked there, and those casual, come-and-go people—even if they got keys back when they fired somebody, anybody can get a key copied for sixty cents. And my God, with so many deaths, confusing the thing all the more, no way of ever finding out—"

"Yes, that just complicates it. Usually, when a house changes hands, both parties are alive and present. All the keys accounted for and handed over. Here, we've got the prima ballerina with a companion, maid, God knows what—they all probably had keys—where did they go? Moved out before the daughter came to settle the estate? Who knows? Medford—the nephew lives in Oregon, let the lawyers here settle things. Nobody knows what servants the Medfords had, now. Who they might have lent keys to—house guests, whoever. The Guardeau woman—there seem to have been several people living with her. In the confusion after the accident, where did they go, what happened to their keys? And Ryan—" Maddox sat back and snapped his lighter with a vicious little click. "It's just adding insult to injury that the same key fits the guest house. Handy! All I can say is, the fellow who built that house had a damned trusting nature. It follows—he did go bankrupt. Of course the guest house may have been originally intended for a mother-in-law or something."

"Ryan," said Feinman thoughtfully. Suddenly he smiled his slow crooked smile. "I'll just contribute to the jeremiad, Ivor. Religion, now. I suppose every one there is has something to say about hypocrisy."

"I would take a bet on that. Elucidate," said Maddox.

"Something that Roylston girl said to you. About Ryan, and Ryan's wife. He's pretty notorious as a womanizer. I don't read the gossip columns, but you see the occasional headlines. And she mentioned—his wife probably a faithful Catholic—that they've got quite a family. Wife going back home to Ireland to have another baby every year. The Ryans lived in that house for about five years. Would the wife be gone maybe three, four months a year? And Ryan handing out keys to any of his current lovelies, I might be detained on the set, sweetie pie, but walk in and make yourself at home."

Maddox uttered one violent word and shut his eyes. "Thank you, Joe. I hadn't thought of that yet. On the other hand, not to sound snobbish, I'm rather inclined to like my vision of the former butler for Medford or houseboy for Miss Guardeau being down on his luck and planning the burglary. Surprised by Jan coming home early. You buy that possibility at all?"

Feinman rubbed his jaw and said it was possible. "I don't know, Ivor," said Ellis. "Would one like that have attacked her? Even in panic? Why would he have had a knife all ready? I think he'd just have run."

"If he was somebody she'd have recognized—a former servant of Ryan's—she'd have been to parties there when she and Ryan were, um, canoodling— It's just, I keep thinking about all those keys," said Maddox dreamily. "A flood tide of keys, twenty years' worth of keys. And the hell of it is, they might not enter in at all. It's possible that she didn't lock the door. That some random cat burglar got in, and she woke up, and he'd been prying at a locked jewel case with a knife and—"

"Almost anything looks possible," said Ellis. "And the goddamned press—if we never get him, whoever, it'll be the stupid incompetent police getting called names."

Into a gloomy silence, D'Arcy said, "Well, we'd better call the hospital and find out if the wedding party can be talked to. Did anybody tell you that Daniel Cobb died?"

"Yes, that's another wild one we'd like to get."

"You didn't see the autopsy report on Wagner—I left it on your desk. There's nothing in it," said D'Arcy. Maddox found it and glanced over it.

"Damn all. Healthy specimen, no drugs, one mild drink. The money," said Maddox. "He was interested in money—never had any—

wanted to make it. He had a little more than he should have. Where did it come from?"

"Chicken feed," said D'Arcy.

"Yes, but— Hell, I don't know." Maddox stabbed out his cigarette. "But I can see one thing all too clear—there's just nowhere to go on the superstar, and it'll turn into one of the great crime classics. Rehashed in the tabloids, and paperbacks, and classy hard-covers, every few years— *Who Murdered Jan Warden?*—and the armchair detectives going all cutesy-clever to finger Maximilian or Wells or Dukard or Kelsey—or somebody's houseboy from fifteen years back." He laughed. "Or Gunther. Now there's a thought. I suppose we could dream up a lovely Freudian motive—"

Baker came in fast, looking happy. "The system does work, if it takes time. Here we are, boys. The Feds finally came through." He plunked a teletype down in front of Ellis.

It was the kickback from the FBI on the prints from Mrs. Gorman's bag. Naturally NCIC hadn't known him; he wasn't currently wanted anywhere.

But the Feds had him on file, and he was Russell John Barlow, with a record stretching back a little way. Assault, rape, assault with intent, narco possession. He had been charged with all that in Merced, California—his home town—San José, and San Francisco. He had served a little time, four years in Susanville. The description said male Caucasian, twenty-nine, six-three, two hundred, brown and gray, no marks.

They sent a query up to Sacramento about a car, and drew blank; he wasn't listed. Either he was using another name or driving a stolen or borrowed car. According to Mrs. Gorman, a white Nova.

But this was a long step on. At least they knew who they were chasing.

CHAPTER 7

D'Arcy went back to typing a follow-up report on a heist, and Ellis and Feinman went out on the never-ending legwork. Maddox just sat there for a while thinking about Jan Warden. They couldn't just forget about it, of course. They'd never get anywhere on it, but they'd have to work the damned thing into the ground. Periodically the headlines would say POLICE STILL BAFFLED IN FAMOUS BEAUTY'S MURDER. Go out and talk to everybody she'd known: talk to the cast of the new show she'd been doing, her hairdresser, ask Gunther who had been to the house lately; get Wells down here in the official atmosphere and talk to him some more, that fellow was slippery as a snake and probably completely amoral. Forget the damned keys; if they could get a line on the ones who might have wanted her dead, either for passion or advantage, the *modus operandi* would probably emerge. Somewhat regretfully he pushed the potential burglar onto a back burner; it had looked more like a purely personal attack.

Suddenly he remembered the sister. He sat up, pushed the button for an outside line, and dialed Shapiro's office.

The secretary put him through at once and he asked about Mrs. Price. "She's getting in tonight," said Shapiro. "I've been informed by a firm here, Troutner and Schell, that they're acting for her to contest any will Miss Warden might have left."

"Without knowing the contents?" Maddox was surprised.

"Apparently."

"Well, I want to see her while she's here. She was listed in Miss Warden's address book, they may have been in recent touch."

"I'll let her know," said Shapiro. "She'll be staying at the Holiday Inn on Highland Avenue."

Presently Maddox went out to have lunch with D'Arcy, Sue, and Daisy. They had found a fairly good new coffee shop called the Top

Hat around on Vine. When they got back Sergeant Whitwell was calling before they had a chance to sit down.

"I gather it's some more of your phony checks, some hassle going on at the Security bank, and the manager says you'd better come and hear about it."

"That thing," said Maddox. It was just another annoying fact about the job, that they couldn't follow a thing through consecutively from start to finish, but were continually getting deflected off onto something else. He went out again with D'Arcy.

The Security Pacific Bank on Western Avenue was on the ground floor and basement of one of the newer tall buildings in the middle of town. This had been the bank that the real John Standish had used, and they had talked to all the personnel before. When they came in the big triple doors to the high-ceilinged, hushed huge temple, an excited-looking redheaded girl was waiting for them. "Sergeant Maddox? You're to come to Mr. Dewberry's office." She led them around the line of marble and bronze tellers' counters to a little hall, a door labeled *Manager*. On a built-in bench in the hall, a ruddy, tall black-haired fellow was talking too rapidly to a younger man, stocky and fair, who was nodding absently.

In the inner office, which was somber and handsomely appointed, the manager greeted them punctiliously. "This is our chief teller, Mr. Corbett, I don't think you have met before." A roundish nondescript man in a brown suit. "I think you met Mrs. Lederer over this unfortunate business when you were here recently." He sounded annoyed; he was a pontifical pear-shaped man about sixty. "I realize that this kind of case is difficult for the police to investigate, and of course you should have had this information some time ago, but it's not surprising that you didn't. That's Mr. James Tabor out there—we'll bring him in presently. He's got some more of these checks for you—that is, I've got them here—and they're the oldest you'll have seen yet, I think."

"Should we know the name?" asked Maddox.

The manager raised his eyes to the ceiling as if mutely consulting his Creator. "We've had trouble with Mr. Tabor before—"

"Not a businessman, Mr. Dewberry," said Corbett gently. "You have to make allowances."

"Good God in heaven, Charles, I can make allowances for incompetency but not sheer idiocy! Unbusinesslike be damned, it's the greatest wonder to me that the man has been able to hang onto his money this long. Inherited money, Sergeant Maddox, and I suppose he has a bro-ker to advise him, but when it comes to the ordinary—run-of-the-mill—simple little matters which any ordinarily intelligent human being should be able to manage—"

Mrs. Lederer ventured a laugh. "I've known him to realize he was out of checks after he wrote the last one, and expect a new batch printed overnight."

"Yes. We've had trouble before," said Dewberry, "with his not open-ing statements, forgetting to pay the monthly charges on VISA, and so on. Oh, he's always apologetic—it isn't that he hasn't got the money, he's got too damned much money— I don't think," said Dewberry, be-trayed into indiscretion by his exasperation, "the checking account has ever fallen below twenty thousand. He keeps horses," said the manager distastefully as if that was a secret vice, "and goes deep-sea fishing. A three-acre estate up near the Hollywood reservoir, and I believe he breeds dogs—terriers of some kind."

"He's never had to think about money," said Corbett, "so he's care-less, that's all."

"My God," said Dewberry. "About two years ago there was a com-puter error in his statement, around a thousand dollars in our favor, and I called him to apologize. He hadn't noticed it. He said he never bothers to reconcile his bank statements, usually doesn't look at them. My God. Well, it seems he's just got married, apparently to a woman with some sense, and she got him to hire an accountant to get every-thing straight, and the accountant came across these checks." He handed them across his desk: eleven checks.

Maddox looked them over and passed them on to D'Arcy. "Some-thing a little different." He waited for Dewberry to elucidate. The checks were dated a while back, the earliest nine months ago. They had all been cashed at this bank; and one was made out to John Standish. James Tabor's name was written in round, careful script, like a child's unformed writing. "I take it they're forgeries."

"They're duplicates," said Dewberry, "except for the Standish check." He produced ten more checks. "These are the real thing." The signature on the forgeries was a passable imitation, but it was simple script, nothing difficult to imitate. These checks were written for the same amounts on the first ten, the largest sum a hundred and fifty, the rest all for one hundred dollars; there were discrepancies of two or three days between the real and bogus checks. All the checks were simply made out to Cash.

"Suppose we hear what he has to say about it."

What Tabor had to say was that he felt like a damned fool. "Nelda's never going to let me forget it," he said ruefully. He was about thirty-five, an instantly likable, easygoing personality, as uncomplicated as his signature. "Even I could spot those were forgeries, when Mr. Wengel found them. You see, I never bother to look at canceled checks."

Wengel, who had frighteningly intelligent eyes, said, "I still don't understand how these could be accepted by the bank, Mr. Dewberry. I agree the signature would pass a casual glance, but checks made out to Cash—"

Corbett coughed. "So are the genuine ones, sir. I can see how they slipped through easily. Mr. Tabor has a long-standing habit of making out checks to Cash, and sending his employees to cash them for him. It happens at least once a week, sometimes twice. It's understandable, as frequently as it does happen, that almost any of the tellers being offered such a check would take it for granted that the person presenting it was one of Mr. Tabor's employees."

"Well, damn it, what do I pay people for but to save me trouble?" said Tabor simply. "I'm usually riding morning and evening, or I'm busy with the dogs, or just puttering around, and if I need some cash I send somebody down with a check. Nuisance standing in line."

"Do you employ many people, Mr. Tabor?" asked Maddox.

"Well, a man in the stable, usually two kennelmen. Housekeeper and maid. They've all been to the bank for me, couldn't say how many times." Tabor looked uneasy. "I wouldn't like to think Mrs. Crowley was dishonest, she was with my mother for years, nice woman."

"But, excuse me," said Corbett diffidently, "you do change employees, Mr. Tabor. Just over the last year, I can recall perhaps six or seven different men bringing your checks in."

"Well, damn it," said Tabor, "it's damned difficult to find reliable men willing to put in an honest day's work. Fellows claim to be handy around a stable, turn out not to know a curry-comb from a bucket. And those kennel-attendants so damned slipshod about hosing down runs, exercising the dogs— And that one maid quit, she was going to be married or something, so we had to get another, and Mrs. Crowley didn't like the first girl and so—"

"Just a minute," said Maddox, looking at the two sets of checks again. "The printing on these looks absolutely identical to me." They were personalized checks of the ornamental kind banks offered customers now: stubless checks—the stubs would be at the back of the book, and Maddox didn't need telling that Tabor wouldn't bother to fill out stubs. There was his name and address at the upper left, and a faint superimposed background design on the face of the checks. Both good and bad checks were exactly the same: *James L. Tabor, Hidden Acres Kennels,* a box number at a Hollywood post office: the design was identified in tiny printing at the lower left corner, *Rustic Americana,* and consisted of at least six subjects, a mill, a farmhouse, a railroad station, a lighthouse, a covered bridge, a steamboat, all in faint sepia on a beige background. "How did a forger come by regular bank checks identical to the real ones? The real checks are supplied to the bank, I take it. Yes. But the numbers are different. The forgeries are all numbered in the four hundreds, the real checks in the seven hundreds."

"Oh, excuse me, but you see," said Mrs. Lederer, "they've all got to be Mr. Tabor's own checks. He never remembers the numbers. You know you don't, Mr. Tabor. You come and tell me you need some new checks, and I ask what number to start with, and you don't know, half the time you say it doesn't matter, start with five hundred or something."

"Well, that clears up one mystery," said Wengel with a faint smile. "In checks written just last month, I came across some numbered in the three hundreds and some in the seven hundreds."

"I thought I was out, and then I found another book at the back of the drawer," said Tabor.

The man nearly deserved to be robbed, thought Maddox. "Where do you keep your checkbooks?"

"Oh, any place," said Tabor vaguely. "In a desk drawer, but I don't use the desk much, don't like paperwork, you know. I usually have one on me—" He groped in three pockets of the expensive sports jacket, found a checkbook in the fourth.

Which could easily have been noticed by anyone; and Maddox could see him, the simple outdoorsman, taking off the jacket to rub down a horse or play with a dog. Damn the man.

"Honestly, I can't feel we're to blame, Mr. Dewberry," said Corbett. "It isn't even as if these checks came in at any regular time, or of course to any one teller. We were all so used to some ordinary-looking workingman presenting Mr. Tabor's checks to Cash—of course there'd be an endorsement, but—"

The forged checks were all endorsed on the back, in a careless scarcely legible hand: the name could be Peter Boone, Bourne, Bohn. "Did you ever employ anyone with a name like that, Mr. Tabor?"

"Not that I remember," said Tabor unhappily. "Look here, I feel like an idiot. I suppose you all think I am an idiot. It's just, I don't think about money, much." That they could believe.

As a gesture, Dewberry sent for the other tellers. They were all back from lunch now and came in in relays of three: six girls, Karen Hansen, Mary Black, Nita Woodman, Marion Paul, Nora Cooke, Rhonda Leach. None of them could remember any of the checks, good or bad. "But all of us had cashed checks exactly like those before," said Rhonda Leach. "There wouldn't be anything to remember—any of us might have had these. I remember, the first one I got, I wasn't sure about it, just made out to Cash like that, and I asked Mr. Corbett. He looked over at the man and said it would be one of Mr. Tabor's employees, it was O.K."

None of them remembered the Standish check either, but admitted that by then—it was dated four months ago—they'd have been so familiar with Tabor's checks that any of them would have taken it without question.

"Which," said Corbett when the last of them had gone out, "isn't surprising, Sergeant Maddox. Of course Mr. Standish was known by sight to Mr. Dewberry, myself, and Mrs. Lederer, and the girls in the safety-deposit vault. But he always came to me for his actual banking, the other tellers wouldn't have known him personally."

"Well, Mr. Tabor," said Maddox, "we'd be obliged if you could make up a list of all the employees you've had over the last year, say. With addresses, if you have any. Can you do that?"

"Oh, Lord," said Tabor in dismay. He looked at Wengel, who said there ought to be records somewhere. Names on salary checks. "Well, I'll see what I can do. The maids too? Well, all right."

"But," said Maddox to D'Arcy in the Maserati, "I think Tabor must have set the ball rolling. That far back. It's not at all easy to get hold of a personal checkbook as a rule, but Tabor was a gift from heaven, of course. It could have been the fired maid—never underestimate females —but I'm inclined to think it's likelier it was one of those unsatisfactory grooms or kennelmen, sent to the bank to fetch back cash, who took the gamble. And Tabor never said a word—didn't notice. The man may have realized he was on borrowed time on the job, and went on passing the checks as often as he dared. You noticed that every time there was a genuine check cashed, a couple of days later there was a bogus one for the same amount. Then he got fired. And he knew Rebecca Simms."

"That's a jump in the dark," said D'Arcy.

"Work it out. He must have. And I think it was probably Simms who knew Standish. Or of him. As we said, a lot of people would have known Standish, known he had a VISA card. She could have been a real estate client, a clerk in his office, the woman who came in to clean for him, anything. We're all very democratic these days, it says nothing that the original forger was the groom or kennelman. Anybody can know anybody. One thing a lot of people have in common is a simple liking for money. Anyway, they knew each other. He tells her about the sweet deal he had—and he's got one check left. She suggests the Standish name, and the check gets accepted with no question. And then one or the other of them had the bright idea how to expand the business. They couldn't hope to find any more Tabors, so the first problem was, how to get the authentic-looking checks? Find a tame printer. And it went on from there."

"Yes, I like that," said D'Arcy, "and at least it gives us some leads to work on, for the first time. A hell of a job to locate those former employees, but at least we'll have manpower to call on, with three precincts and the sheriff's boys working the case."

"I think Lyons will like it too."

On Saturday morning Tabor, looking subdued, brought in a list of eleven names. There were only three addresses appended, and he apologized. "I'd hand 'em their salaries on the job. No reason to have their addresses, was there?" But a couple he had contacted through employment agencies.

"Haven't we always said, if we had about three times as many detectives, we'd likely be more efficient," said Maddox, "and that's just what you're going to get on this one, you lucky boys. D'Arcy, you and César can go downtown with this and get Lyons to rustle up some more hands." He gave the list to Sue to make a few carbons of.

Rodriguez had been enthralled by the saga of the keys, and Maddox said it just made the thing more complicated. "We're not forgetting the superstar, we're going to do some real legwork on that—I want to see the people on that TV show she was making, everybody she knew, had been in contact with lately—something may point the way. And I want to pin Wells down, I don't think he's told us everything he could. But there's never a time we've only got one thing to work. You make a start on that list—at least we've turned up the leads for Lyons, and he can't complain if we leave the legwork to him after a couple of days."

But before he could get away himself, the desk put through a call, and it was Louise Wagner. She sounded, oddly, a little frightened. "I thought I'd tell you," she said. "I don't know if it's anything to do with Bill getting killed, but it—there's something wrong about it, Sergeant. Awfully wrong. I—I found five hundred dollars hidden in the pocket of one of his old jackets. Yesterday. I—the funeral was yesterday, you know, and I was sort of restless when I got home, I was just—going through things—and I found that. He couldn't have saved up that much."

Maddox was interested and also what the headlines would call baffled. "There wasn't anything he might have sold? That he owned personally, I mean?"

"What could it have been, to be worth that much? I just can't imagine. I can't help worrying about it. I asked Ron Kreuger about it, and he didn't know either."

Maddox had nearly forgotten Ron Kreuger, said to be Bill Wagner's closest pal. "Oh, he's back?" He supposed he ought to see him.

"Yes, and of course he feels just terrible about Bill, he came to see me last night, he's a nice boy. But where could all that money have come from?"

"It's queer all right. Could you let me have Kreuger's address?"

She gave it to him absently: Martel Street. "I don't feel right about it," she said. "I don't feel I have any right to it, because I don't know where it came from. I just thought—you ought to hear about it."

He sat back with his hand on the phone for just a moment, wondering about that; and just as he got up, the phone went off again. One of those days. "Sergeant Maddox."

"This is Esther Price, Sergeant. Mr. Shapiro said you'd like to see me while I'm here." It was a very clear, incisive low voice, sure of itself.

"Oh yes, Mrs. Price. I think you're at the Holiday Inn in Hollywood?"

"That's right. I'm only going to be here until Tuesday or Wednesday, I'm afraid. Of course I can't be of any help to you over the murder. But I'll be free about three this afternoon, if that would be convenient for you."

"Quite all right," said Maddox. "I'll see you then, thanks very much."

That time he got away. He didn't call before trying Wells's Brentwood address; if he didn't catch him now he would another time, and he wanted to have a look at the place.

It was, expectably, a modern high-rise building, but housing condominiums, and Wells had one of those at the very top. For a change, he reflected, they were seeing how the other half lived, on this one.

He pushed the bell and waited, and in a minute the door swung back to reveal a stout red-faced middle-aged woman, in a white uniform dress. "Well, and who might you be?" she asked with large good humor. "Oh, my goodness, one of the police officers, are you? You found out yet who killed her? The papers say it's a big mystery, but I hope you find out."

"Is Mr. Wells here?"

"No, and he won't be until maybe Monday or Tuesday, whenever he takes it into his head to come back. He decided all of a sudden just after I came this morning. It's my day to clean, see, and I was just starting to vacuum the rug when he made me shut it off. Decided to go down to Acapulco for the weekend, he says, got a lot of things to think over, Angie, he says—that's my name, see—and I don't want the something police butting in while I'm thinking. I wouldn't say the word he used, personally I think you policemen do the best you can, I don't hold with calling names. Anyway, he called around and found he could get a plane at International at eleven o'clock, and he packed a bag and went off."

Maddox was annoyed; it was exactly eleven o'clock now, and too late to stop him. Let Wells go: they would have enough to do without him. And then it struck him that he hadn't the slightest idea what studio Jan Warden had been working for, what the name of the new series was, or who else was involved in it. That Goldstein might know; or Kelsey.

He headed back for Hollywood, and he thought, six hundred dollars. Jan Warden raking in three hundred grand a year. Wells not doing at all bad either. But money was relative. To Bill Wagner, six hundred dollars would have been a lot of money. Where had he got it?

Martel was just over the line into Hollywood from the piece of county territory which held the Sunset Strip; on impulse he turned up it and found the Kreugers' address.

It was a modest frame house behind a clipped privet hedge, and Ron Kreuger was home alone. He asked Maddox in to a long narrow living room. "I never was so shook in my life, to hear about Bill," he told Maddox. "I mean, people get killed in accidents, young people too, but murder— I know, the crime rate. It's just, it doesn't seem that I can take it in, he's gone. We were all through school together." He was a big sandy young fellow, with a slow voice and big square hands, steady blue eyes.

"And now in college. Were you going out for stockbroking too, to make a million?"

Kreuger smiled gravely. "He was always saying that. No, I'm going in for accounting. Can I ask if you've found out who killed him?"

"We haven't. It's got us stymied too. This money that Mrs. Wagner found—you really don't know where he might have got it?"

"Not one clue, Sergeant. That was a lot of money for Bill."

"Well. You probably saw more of him than most of his other friends, would you say? Can you think of anything that happened recently, any little thing at all, that struck you as unusual? Anything he said or did— anything he talked about, or—"

Kreuger sat looking at the floor, his hands between his knees. After a pause he said slowly, "It's such a funny little thing—I'd almost forgotten about it—and then when I was thinking about Bill, talking to Mrs. Wagner last night, I got to wondering about it again. It couldn't be anything to do with what happened, at least I don't see how."

"What was it?"

"Well, I suppose you meant, just now, anything he said or did that was—out of character. For Bill. And that sure was. Do you really want to hear about this? It's sort of involved and also sort of ridiculous."

"Tell on."

"Well, all right. It was about two months ago, a Saturday night. Bill and I had been bowling that afternoon, we did sometimes, and we decided to pick up a sandwich and go on to a movie we both wanted to see. And we ran into Andy Merton at the coffee shop. He's in my trig class and Bill's accounting class, we both knew him sort of casually. And he said he'd go with us. So we drove out there—we were in Bill's car—it was a theater on Sunset—and the bill had changed, it was some English picture none of us wanted to see. So we just went along the Strip, no choice, there's no good place to turn around right there, and all of a sudden Andy said, hey, boys, let's go see some strippers. There was this place we were just passing, the Can-Can, it was called. Well, now, Sergeant"—Kreuger was young enough to look embarrassed and mad at himself for it—"I don't mean that either Bill or I are sweet innocents, but neither of us had ever gone for that stuff, and besides there'd be a pretty stiff tab. Andy argued, and finally we parked and went back to the place. Neither Bill or I meant to go in, if Andy wanted to fork out it was his business. Well, the admission was six fifty, and that was enough for us, and we were standing there telling Andy so when all of a sudden Bill got a funny look on his face and stopped talking. I thought he was looking at something over my shoulder, but there wasn't anything, just a side door to the building. And the very next minute, just like it had been all settled, he said, Well, come on, if we're going in let's go, and he walked up and put down the six-fifty. I was so surprised—Bill, spending that much all at once on a strip show—"

"And you waited outside for them?" asked Maddox with a grin.

"Now, I don't aim to be a mama's boy, Sergeant. But it was pretty raw, all right. But the point is, I don't know that I ever saw Bill act so—out of character, you could say. And after we dropped Andy off, I asked him, I said what the hell got into you, anyway? And he just laughed and said he thought it had been a good investment, it was a very instructive evening. He sounded—queer."

"Well, that's a queer little story altogether," said Maddox.

"But I don't see that it means anything. To do with what happened."

"Neiter do I at the moment. But I'll bear it in mind."

"It just doesn't seem possible that he's dead," said Kreuger. "Here and then gone. Whoosh. It doesn't seem more than a couple of years ago we were kids playing football in the street." He shook his head. "It'd be nice to feel there was—Somebody doing all the arranging, and a good reason for everything that happens. I can't always believe that—when a thing like this could happen."

At one-thirty on Saturday afternoon, Patrolman Harold Cummings of the Beverly Hills Police Department had just come back to the squad after a Code Seven. He was parked on Beverly Drive; he announced into the mike that he was back, and started the engine, and proceeded along Beverly into the rather narrow streets of exclusive shops just below Santa Monica Boulevard. About halfway along the area was a small branch bank, and a public parking lot alongside it. Cummings was a conscientious officer, and one to go by the book; in his three years of riding a squad, not once had he ever been the one to spot a car with an A.P.B. on it, but there was always a first time; and he turned into the lot and went down the lines of angled cars looking at license plates.

He was more surprised than gratified when he spotted one of those posted on his dashboard. He stood on the brake and checked it. That was it, all right: a two-year-old Mercury; and three terse letters were appended to the A.P.B—AWC. Approach with caution.

He debated. He had, he decided, better call a backup. It was possible the front office would want to set up a stakeout.

But of course he didn't have time. He ran the squad up to the alley at the top of the lot, where he could keep an eye on the Mercury, and he had just picked up the mike when a man went up to the Mercury and got in.

Perhaps if Cummings had spent three years in the LAPD instead of riding a squad in Beverly Hills, where violent crime is rare and the squads cruise down clean and lovely streets instead of through dirty slums, he would have acted less hastily. As it was, instead of staying in the squad and getting ready to follow the Mercury, he scrambled out from behind the wheel, drawing his gun, and ran down to the car just backing out of its slot. "Stop where you are—police!" he barked. "Cut the engine and come out—"

The slug took him high in the chest, and he spun and dropped. The Mercury backed out fast, and ran over his legs as it was gunned up and around to the exit lane. It was five minutes later that a shopper came into the lot and found Cummings, and three minutes after that that the dispatcher, sitting in Communications at the police station, heard an unfamiliar voice on the squad frequency. "Hello, is this thing working? I don't know how the hell— Police? Is anybody hearing me? There's an officer been shot, you better send an ambulance—"

In the ambulance, Cummings opened his eyes and whispered to the attendant, "That A.P.B.—tell—somebody. The Mercury."

D'Arcy and Rodriguez had just come back to look in at the station before going hunting again; downtown Lyons had had more copies of that list made up and called in some of the men working the case from other precincts, and they had kicked the Tabor thing around. It looked very much, on account of that one Standish check, that this had been the beginning of the caper, and it gave them leads to follow. D'Arcy and Rodriguez were now bound for the Acme Employment Agency on Western, where Tabor had hired one of his unsatisfactory kennelmen; but they walked in on a new call, and were sent somewhere else—a movie theater on Fairfax.

It was a very confused thing, and the patrolmen first on the scene had remembered all the rules about preserving the scene, but it had been an unprecedented situation. When D'Arcy and Rodriguez got there at two-fifteen, there was a little crowd of angry people herded into one corner of the theater vestibule outside, with Burke and Cassidy keeping them bunched, and Gonzales and Day had a rope stretched up the other side of the vestibule so nobody could get too near the body.

"People," said Gonzales. "That bunch up there, they came to see the movie, and they're upset not because they just saw a murder, but because we won't let them in to see the movie. We weren't sure just how far back in the line to go, we took the first ten people, let the others go in. They just heard the commotion, didn't see anything."

"What line?" asked D'Arcy.

"Waiting to get tickets. The booth opened at one-thirty and there seems to have been quite a line already waiting."

The body was lying flat on its back just behind the ticket booth. It was the body of a man in a rather tawdry uniform, navy blue with tarnished gold epaulettes and gold buttons. The front of the uniform jacket was darkened and wet, and blood had trickled down to the cement. He lay there with wide-open eyes looking surprised at the domed ceiling far above.

"The ticket girl had hysterics, she's lying down in the manager's office. He came out when she screamed, and called us. He's closed the booth now, I guess they're running the film for about thirty people," said Gonzales. Rodriguez looked up at the marquee; the theater was showing two old Disney films, 101 *Dalmatians* and *The Lady and the Tramp*. "Short and sweet, and I doubt if you'll ever pick him up. About ten people had bought tickets and gone in—that's the ticket collector, by the way, Nick Martino, he'd worked here for twenty years. About ten, fifteen minutes after the booth opened, a couple came up for tickets, and the man started to argue about his change. Claimed the

girl shortchanged him. Martino came down from the door to try to settle it, the guy was getting loud and rough, and when he couldn't simmer him down he says he'll call the cops, so the guy pulled a knife and
went for him."

"For God's sake," said Rodriguez.

"I guess it was over in about two minutes, everything went fast. The
guy ran off, down the other way from where the line was, and the manager came out and called us."

"Beautiful," said Rodriguez. He looked at the people: ten very ordinary people, both sexes, old and young. "So we are now going to hear
that he was tall, short, medium, old, young, fat, skinny, had a beard
and was clean-shaven."

"He had a girl with him. She ran off too."

"Lovely," said Rodriguez.

"I haven't called a lab unit. I didn't know whether you'd want to
talk to them here or take them in."

"Call the lab," said D'Arcy. "Then we'll get a few more squads to
ferry them in to the office. I'd rather talk to them sitting down."

The little crowd of people was trooping into the office just as Maddox was leaving; he stopped to hear what it was all about. "That'll take
you to end of shift," he said.

"And tomorrow and tomorrow and tomorrow," said D'Arcy.

The first one they talked to—Sue and Daisy gallantly stepping in to
help—was a wizened little pensioner, Sam Hayward. "Damn it," he
said querulously, "spoiling the afternoon. Been lookin' forward to seein'
those two pictures again. And then there had to be this ruction. I'm
sorry a man got killed, but keepin' us standin' there all that while—
Well, yeah, I got a look at the fellow when he was arguing with the
girl. I'd say he was about six feet high, kind of fat, and he had on a yellow shirt. Couldn't say I'd know him again, he was facin' away from
me."

The next couple were husband and wife, in the twenties, and they
said he was middle-aged, and she thought he had a mustache.

In the middle of that Whitwell called and told them about Cummings. "Beverly Hills!" he said disgustedly. "I don't know why they
took so long to relay, it happened two hours ago. No, they don't know
if Cummings will make it. And of course Lewis got clean away."

Maddox looked at Esther Price interestedly, aware of the small hostil-
ity in her eyes. She had just said to him, "Well, do you know who

killed her, and if it's somebody important how are you going to cover it up?"

"What gives you the idea we operate that way?" This was the usual comfortable, well-furnished, anonymous hotel suite: small living room, small bedroom, with bath between. It looked out on Highland from the second floor.

She really looked at him then, and sat down on the couch opposite and said, "That was a stupid thing to say, wasn't it? In fact, I couldn't care less if you did cover it up. But I remember now—what all the books say—this is supposed to be a very good police force."

"We like to think so, Mrs. Price. I only wish we had some idea who killed your sister. There's no evidence at all."

"It could have been anybody who knew her," she said wearily. "She wouldn't have changed any, so she'd have had people here who hated her too. No, that's too strong a word, isn't it? Resented. Disliked."

"Had you been in contact with her recently?"

"I had not."

"Did you dislike and resent her, Mrs. Price?" He had seen photographs of Jan Warden now, and he thought that this woman might be even more attractive, because there was character in her face, the lines of living. But she had much the same features, rather high cheekbones, wide mouth, large dark eyes. Her brown hair was short, casually styled; her clothes were quiet, smart without being high fashion. She wore a plain gold wedding ring, a small solitaire diamond, and an old-fashioned garnet ring on the other hand. She would, of course, be the older sister.

"I hope," she said, "that I'd got over hating her. It only hurts you to hate people. But for all the trouble and grief she caused, I am damned well going to get some of that money for Emily. Do you want to know about her, Sergeant? The real story on Jan Warden? Don't they say, the character of the victim is important to detectives? Well, I can tell you about her. I never knew her to do a generous or unselfish thing in her life. She couldn't even come home the Christmas Dad was dying, and she was his favorite—he kept asking for her. She had some bit part in a Broadway play that was more important. Oh, for heaven's sake—" She reached blindly for the box of cigarettes on the coffee table, and her hand shook on the lighter; he came and held out his. "Of course I know all theatrical people aren't cheap and immoral, there are a lot of fine people in entertainment, people with real talent and a—a vocation for it. Jan hadn't, she hadn't any real talent at all, she just wanted the excitement, and she liked exhibiting herself. That was all she was ever interested in—herself. The ultimate egotist."

"The me-first syndrome," said Maddox. "Some people in entertainment, and all criminals. Big and little."

"What do you mean?"

"The me-firsters are blind to anything but what they want right now. Consequences never enter in—or the imagination for anybody else's feelings."

"Oh yes, that was Jan, all right. Always sliding out from under any responsibility. Ah, Don was such a fool, but you couldn't tell him. He couldn't see anything but that beautiful face. He never understood that it just wasn't in her to love anybody but Jan, think about anybody but Jan. Don Becket, he was five years older—he'd always been mad in love with her, and they both got a little high one night and ran away and got married—she was seventeen." Esther Price laughed. "Dad and Mother were pleased—very pleased about it! The Beckets a nice family, Don's father owned a hardware store, he was such a steady young man! Of course in a week Jan was bored with it. And I know she'd have had an abortion, when she found out about the baby, if she'd known where to go or had the money. She hated Emily—hated the way she made her look and feel. She wouldn't even look at the baby, in the hospital. Poor stupid Don, he thought she'd settle down, she was just young. But of course nobody could expect Jan to dust furniture and wash dishes. That apartment was a pigsty—Mother took Emily or she'd have died. John and I were just married then. Nobody was surprised when Jan went off—just walked out, when Emily was a few months old. Don was wild, he hired a detective and found her in New York, begged her to come back. I don't know how she supported herself, she told Don modeling jobs—she never got anywhere on the stage until there was the big TV build-up, you know.

"Don's mother was an invalid, and Mother just kept Emily until it got too much for her, she and Dad weren't young when we were born, you see. And by then I knew I couldn't have any children, and John and I took her. That was about the time Don died. He'd started drinking when he first realized Jan wasn't ever coming back to him—he just went downhill and died. They'd lost the business."

She looked at Maddox steadily. "Emily's fifteen now. A pretty girl, but not too pretty, thank God. And clever. She's like our own, though we never legally adopted her. And I didn't care if we never heard of

Jan again. But then there was all the publicity, the photographs, great discovery, gorgeous new superstar on TV."

"About five years ago."

She nodded. Her mouth was bitter. "I swallowed a lot of pride that year. I could guess how much money she was making. We get along, Sergeant—John has a good law practice, we've got a nice house, and it's cheaper to live in a small town. But that year—we had to have a new furnace, and Mother had had another stroke, she was helpless and needed a lot of care—and Emily had to have braces. I wrote to Jan. I thought it was worth a try, she might be feeling so triumphant that she'd be—magnanimous. One of the articles in a TV magazine mentioned her agent's name, and I wrote to her there. I never had an answer. I don't know why I expected one."

"She had your address listed in her book. Why?"

She laughed shortly. "Mr. Shapiro was very polite about it, but he told me why she made that will. How he explained about leaving me a little something so we couldn't contest. She was so stupid in some ways —didn't she realize that Emily's a closer relative in law?"

"She may have thought you'd adopted her, and that that would make a legal difference."

"I don't know. It's quite possible that she'd forgotten about Emily altogether. It's queer, Mr. Shapiro was her lawyer, but I think he was pleased to hear about Emily."

"You could have taken her to law. Only living parent, well able to afford support."

"Do you think we'd have exposed Emily to all the dirty publicity? And Jan knew that all right! If she remembered there was an Emily! Shall we say that we followed her career with interest," and her mouth twisted. "All the rumors of romances and the glittering life style of the superstar. I wrote her again when Mother died. Duty. I didn't know if she'd be at all concerned. If she had any—memories at all, or wanted to."

"Did you send that to the agent?" It was an irrelevant question, and as he asked it he saw her eyes flicker. "I just wonder," he said casually, "if she did have any little lingering sentiment, kept the letter maybe."

"I should doubt it." Her eyes were angry now. "No, that was funny. I suppose it was morbid fascination, whenever there was an article about her in some TV magazine I got it to read. It was just about then one of them was gushing about her moving into Greg Ryan's beautiful house, and it even gave the address."

Maddox sat smoking placidly, and cast an idle glance at her feet in conservative low-heeled pumps. They could well be a size seven. And so she had known the address?

"When we heard about the murder, John said we had to think of Emily. I don't want Jan's damned money, if she abandoned Emily at least we've given her a happy family background, but it's only fair Emily should have some of it. John looked up law firms here. I'm only here to give them all the facts, all the papers, Emily's birth certificate, and they can get on with it. It'll take a while."

A very strong-minded, confident, capable woman, thought Maddox. And Emily her one ewe lamb. The husband an unknown quantity; but a lawyer. And she'd had a motive. Brooding on all the loot Jan was taking the last five years? Jan Warden could have skidded off the top ratings, lost all the money foolishly, and at thirty-three or so she'd had an excellent life expectancy.

Was it possible that Esther Price had done something about that? There were ways she could have managed it. There were ways she could have been there, waiting to destroy that selfish arrogant life, a week ago Wednesday night. He was thinking about some of them.

But there were other questions in his mind too, and after dinner he said to his two girls, "I'm going out for a while. Man about a dog."

Sue eyed him speculatively. "You're out of cigarettes? I know you don't like filters, but I could lend you a pack."

"No, I'm going out to a strip joint," said Maddox. This was met with unseemly hilarity, and he retreated with dignity.

The Can-Can strip house, just past the Sunset Strip, had its own parking lot, and there was a lot of raucous neon lighting the night. He found a slot after searching, and walked up to the entrance. The door beyond the ticket booth was opened and a pulse of the brassy beat of a combo vibrated out this far.

It was eight o'clock. He didn't know any exact times, but it would probably have been about this time, a couple of months ago, that Bill Wagner had stood here arguing with Andy Merton about paying six-fifty to see a few uninhibited females take it all off.

Bill, looking down to the side door of the building?

He stood there and lit an idle cigarette—just looking, and waiting—and ten minutes later that door opened and he saw, with the same surprise Bill Wagner must have felt, what Bill Wagner had probably seen.

CHAPTER 8

On Sunday morning, with Daisy and Ellis off, Maddox listened absently to what D'Arcy and Rodriguez had to say about the Martino homicide—nothing helpful—at the same time looking over the night report. There had, of course, been another heist, at an all-night market for a change. When D'Arcy and Rodriguez had gone out on the continued legwork, he sat staring into space for a while and then walked across the big office to where Feinman was finishing up a report from yesterday.

"Like to come and listen to me ask some questions, Joe?"

"What about?" asked Feinman.

"I really don't know. This is a funny one, and I'm not sure what it means at all—these lax permissive days—but I think we'll ask some questions." They took Feinman's Chevy, and on the way, Maddox told him about it.

Feinman said blankly, "But why should she—"

"I don't know. But you see what I mean."

At the little white-painted frame house on Finley Street they rang the bell, and presently she opened the door. "Sorry to disturb you on Sunday morning," said Maddox. "We've just got a few more questions for you."

"Oh—all right," she said shortly, and held the screen door open. "I told you I wasn't here, don't know anything. You might as well sit down." They sat together on the couch and she perched on a chair opposite. The house was silent; she said, "The kids went to Sunday School with the Roberts twins up the block. What did you want to ask?" She had on the shapeless green muu-muu, no make-up, and the scattering of freckles on her nose made her look young and vulnerable. Maddox didn't say anything for a moment and she asked sharply, "What are you looking at me like that for?"

"I was just thinking, you look a good deal different in the costume you wear at the Can-Can."

She went greenish-white, and the freckles stood out. "I don't know what you mean. I've got a job as a hostess at a restaurant—"

"Where they have floor shows so you have to be there late—a rather naïve story, Mrs. Dorn, when I thought about it. But you see, I saw you there last night. Just stepping out the side door to have a cigarette in the fresh air. You must have a break about then? Because Bill Wagner saw you there at about the same time, a couple of months ago, didn't he? Just by accident?"

"I don't know what you—" Her eyes had glazed a little; she got up and looked around the room vaguely, opened the top drawer of a chest of drawers, went across to a little desk under the side window and opened drawers. "I told you, I didn't know Bill Wagner."

"I think he mentioned it to you," said Maddox.

"I know I've got some cigarettes somewhere," she was saying distractedly. "Oh, my sweater pocket—"

"You're ashamed of the job, Mrs. Dorn? But it doesn't have to be anything but an honest job, if that's the way you want to play it."

"I really don't know what you're talking about," but it was a play for time. She flicked a lighter and lit a cigarette, and Maddox reached over and took it out of her fingers.

"A Murad. Pure Turkish. You can't buy these everywhere, it has to be a specialty shop. Not many people smoke them. We found the stub of one in the ashtray of Bill Wagner's car." She was shaking her head blindly. "There are a lot of scientific tests we use these days, Mrs. Dorn. We can run a saliva test and prove it was you who smoked that cigarette. Would you like to tell us where you got the gun—a Smith and Wesson .32 automatic?"

She began to cry, regular deep stomach-wrenching sobs. She put her head in her hands and huddled there sobbing and gasping, and then just breathing in deep irregular gasps with an occasional catch in rhythm. She groped in her pocket and found a handkerchief and choked into it.

"Would you like to talk to a policewoman, Mrs. Dorn?"

Blindly she shook her head. After another long minute, without looking up, she said in a dreary flat voice, "And what'll happen to Bobby and Rita now? I suppose—Mother or Betty—have to take them, and it's not so easy for Betty and Ray now, get along, with three of their own and just that little farm outside Delano. An honest job? An honest *job?*" she said violently, passionately. "Can't you understand how things *are?* When Gil and I bought this house, it was the first time I felt settled since we were married—a nice quiet street, the neighbors so nice and friendly, kind people and—and good. And when Gil died—he had cancer, he was only thirty, I couldn't believe it but he did —I wanted to keep the house, it's a good place to raise kids—didn't see how I could manage the payments, I had to get a job and I'm not trained for anything, I can't type or anything. I answered—that ad—I thought it was waitress work, I could do that—but when I found out what it was, they'd told me the salary—more than double what I'd earn waiting on tables. I hated the whole idea, but I thought—to keep the house, have things for the kids—and Mr. Hirschberg's been kind, he gave me lots of advice—and—and it's got so I can pretend it's somebody else up there doing all that. It got so I didn't mind—and the money's so good—I was getting along fine. But don't you think I knew—how it would be if everybody knew? I'd die if the neighbors knew, don't I know how they'd act, what they'd think! Nobody would ever talk to me again—and the Roberts wouldn't let the twins play with Bobby and Rita—and Mrs. Keeler's so nice, she'd never come near us again. We'd have to move away, I'd be so ashamed, so ashamed to have them all know—

"And Bill was waiting for me when I came home one night. Made me get in his car while he told me—how he knew. He thought it was funny—he laughed. He didn't exactly ask me for money—or he'd tell about it. He just said, all the neighbors would find it so interesting to know—how I did my hostess job. And I gave him some money the next day, I gave him a hundred dollars, not to tell anybody. But he'd be waiting again—three times it was—and he wanted more. I couldn't go on paying him, I've got the house payments and everything so expensive now—

"I was afraid somebody'd see us, even so late, we used to drive up to the next block. And the last time, I mean a week ago Friday night, I told him I couldn't give him any more, and he said—if I wanted to keep the secret I'd just have to—to make a little sacrifice to keep him sweet. So I—so I—saw that I'd have to—get—rid—of him—some way. I had Gil's gun, and of course I know how to use it—I'm a country girl." Her voice was dull, expressionless. "I gave him a last chance when I met him the next night, I said I'd get more money that Friday night, and I

met him Saturday night. And I told him he couldn't expect any more—
and he just said, I knew the rules. So I just pretended to reach into my
purse for the money, and I got the gun out and shot him." She came
out with one last dry sob. "He drove me to it—I never wanted to hurt
anybody—all I ever wanted was to keep on living my own life, take care
of my kids—I was getting along all right. But he had to find out."

The me-first syndrome, thought Maddox. Bill had been just a little
too anxious to start piling up that million.

"You'll have to come with us, Mrs. Dorn. We'll get a policewoman up
here to let you change your clothes and pack a bag."

She looked down at herself indifferently. "My clothes don't matter,
I'm all right like this. Maybe a policewoman could pack a suitcase for
me later. The main thing is, please will you send a telegram to Betty—
I'll give you the address—to come get Bobby and Rita."

"We'll do that. One more thing—"

"It's in a box on the closet shelf," she said. "Gil's gun. I didn't want
the kids getting hold of it." She rode downtown in silence.

She read over the statement Maddox typed up and signed it. He put
in an application for a warrant, and they booked her into the jail. It
had been a funny one. And just a fluke, Maddox pointed out, that the
truth had come out. "Also a fluke," said Sue wryly, "that Bill found out
about her."

"Well, yes."

Feinman went back to his report and presently a messenger came in
with the autopsy report on Wanda Bates. Expectably, it said she had
been raped and died of a massive skull fracture.

The D.A. had decided to let the little matter of the wedding party
drop. It would be impossible to find out who had stabbed Tony Scarola
in that melee, and the two feuding fathers were refusing to charge each
other.

Maddox called Beverly Hills and asked about Cummings. He'd had
surgery and was doing better; they were saying he'd recover, the doctors
thought. Those flyers were out county-wide, but Lewis hadn't been
spotted again.

And he couldn't reach Goldstein today, but Kelsey— He got the
number from Information and found Kelsey home, unexpectedly co-
operative and cordial. It was Arnhelm Productions, he told Maddox,
and they'd been renting space in the old Paramount studio, but opera-

tions would be shut down now. He could get hold of the director, Jerry Ross, through Arnhelm's office.

Maddox wandered over to the window and looked out to the big parking lot. A very funny thing, Bill Wagner and Amy Dorn; he felt absently sorry for Louise Wagner. A funny motive; but you never knew what notions females would get. He wandered over to Sue's desk where she'd stopped typing to deal with a rough fingernail. "If you were Esther Price building a plot to murder Jan, how could you possibly get hold of a key to that house?" He laughed; keys; either a feast or a famine.

"Yes," said Sue thoughtfully, peering at the nail. "Airline ticket for Mary Smith from New York. Lie in wait in a spare bedroom until she was asleep, kill her and get out. Why, Mrs. Price was just down with the flu a few days, been right here at home. Yes. Well, of course there'd only be one way. The parking lot at a big restaurant with parking attendants. Jan would have gone to a good many places like that— the more expensive restaurants—in her own car, I should think. For lunch when she was shopping."

"Frequently, I suppose."

"It's queer how people don't think about leaving a whole bunch of keys in a car, in those places. There were all those burglaries a few years back, the attendants taking impressions of house keys—yes. I'd have tailed her in a rented car until she went to one of those places, and parked, and quietly walked back to her car in the lot and got an impression of all the keys, to be on the safe side. In Plasticine or something. She carried them all together?—yes, so many people do. And then I'd have found a locksmith in some obviously poor section of town, who'd make copies for five bucks. But you know, Ivor—"

"Yes, love. It doesn't match. The conniving, and the murder."

"Mmh. It'd have taken some long planning, and Jan hadn't been running around amusing herself lately, she'd been working. If Esther Price got a key that way, it must have been months ago. Why did she wait to use it? And the murder—all I can say is, if she's clever enough to plan it out that way, she wouldn't have done the murder like that. She'd have been neater and surer. A gun, or a garrote."

"No," said Maddox, "the two ends don't match. Unless she's clever enough to pull a double bluff. And she's a clever woman all right."

On Sunday evening about eight-thirty Sheriff's Deputy Lew Curran was riding his squad car on routine patrol in a section of county territory in east L.A. The sheriff's department patrols all county areas, and throughout the urban sprawl of L.A. and environs a good many such areas exist, the lines unseen except on a map, unnoticed by most citizens. He was in the town of City Terrace here, with Boyle Heights to the west. He was cruising rather slowly down Eastern Avenue, when a car swung around him in a legally correct pass, came back into the lane ahead. His headlights lit up its rear license plate, and by God, it was that one on the A.P.B.—the one with Gary Lewis inside it, armed and dangerous. He reached for the mike, and the wanted Mercury slid into the on-ramp of the San Bernardino freeway up ahead.

"Oh, hell," said Curran. He punched buttons and got on the Highway Patrol frequency. The Highway Patrol is responsible for freeways. "Sheriff Z-14 here. I've got that Merc with Lewis in it right ahead of me. He's just got on the San Berdu freeway from Eastern, going west. Doing about fifty."

The line crackled for a few seconds and then a Highway Patrol squad responded. "Got you. Just keep him in sight. We'll deflect a couple of squads to join up as you keep informed. I'm four miles east of you on the Long Beach freeway, will try to catch you in eight or nine minutes minus siren."

Curran kept pace behind the Mercury, but he had a foreboding of what could happen. By what they had on Lewis, he was from out of state and unfamiliar with Los Angeles; and even long-time residents sometimes get confused at the Stack. The Stack was coming up just ahead, the great spider web on different levels where all the freeways came together downtown. If you didn't know just which lane you wanted—

The Mercury veered into the extreme left lane. Recklessly so did Curran, right behind it; it might spook Lewis if he noticed a black-and-white on his tail, but his attention was probably taken up with the menace of the Stack. Round and round went the Mercury, off-ramp, on-ramp, and willy-nilly whether it was where he wanted to be or not, Lewis was on the Hollywood freeway. Curran reported rapidly on the radio.

"O.K.," said an unexcited voice. "We hear you. Bill, are you anywhere near the Stack? . . . Freddy, give me your position. . . . O.K. I've just passed Echo Park, I'm ahead of you, Sheriff. Lewis should pass me in about one minute, I'm doing forty. If he passes me, fall behind and I'll take over. Bill, you get in line behind the sheriff when you catch up."

By the time Curran was in Hollywood, the operation was complete. There was a Highway Patrol squad ahead of him and one behind, with the Mercury still up ahead. The man in the first car kept them informed as they swept through town. Above Hollywood Boulevard the Hollywood freeway curved up in an arc that followed the old line of the Cahuenga Pass over into the valley—there were just a few senior citizens around who remembered when it used to be Dark Canyon Road. The freeway swept past the Hollywood Bowl, and cut the edge of Universal City, and now the Mercury was well out into the San Fernando Valley. At this time on a Sunday night, there was moderate to heavy traffic. So far, so good. If Lewis stayed on the freeway, or got deflected off to the Ventura freeway, which would shortly be coming up, he'd be getting out into the lonelier open spaces, traffic would thin out, and they would feel easier about trying to take him without a lot of innocent citizens around. As it was, the other traffic was providing cover for them; obviously he didn't realize he had an escort.

But his very unfamiliarity with the town blew that one. As the interchange came up, the Mercury veered into the right lane, and they all heard the first Highway Patrol man utter an involuntary dirty cussword. "He's getting off—that ramp'll take him right onto Riverside." There was a brief pause while he pushed buttons to change radio frequency. "Any unit, any unit LAPD, do you read? Lewis will be on Riverside in North Hollywood, one minute, going west."

In three seconds a new voice: "X-92, Magnolia and Teesdale, turning down Coldwater Canyon to intercept."

All over the county, where dispatchers sat in Communications rooms and the uniformed men rode the squads, the pursuit was being followed, the tense, calm exchanges listened to. Everybody was thinking now, once he was off the freeway the cover would be blown, and that was a fairly busy area of town; they just hoped nobody was going to get shot.

As soon as Lewis was away from the broad freeway with its great arc lights and busy traffic, he spotted the first black-and-white behind him and the Mercury took off like a scalded cat. It went jinking and turning at random, cutting from lane to lane in the fairly heavy traffic, and all three lawmen cussed and switched on red lights and sirens. Traffic stopped, and the chase speeded up. As the Mercury swept left in a wide turn onto Burbank Boulevard from Laurel Canyon, Lewis leaned out the driver's window and fired left-handed at the Highway Patrol car; a couple of slugs hit the left fender. "O.K., let's make it now." The second Highway Patrol car came level in the next lane; they meant to box him; and the driver of the first squad, in the right lane, unhurriedly leaned out his window and got off four shots at the rear end of the Mercury; but he was left-handed, and he got a tire.

The Mercury shot out of control a block further, hit the curb, and came to a smoking stand. It was no more than one minute before they were up to it on foot; but Lewis was gone. Lew Curran looked a quarter block up and said angrily, "Hell and damnation!"

The end of the college year had come last week, and up there the huge sprawling campus of Los Angeles Valley College was all dark. Forty acres of it, with seventeen buildings and parking lots and gymnasiums and playing fields— If Lewis was there, he could dodge a regiment of cops this moonless night.

On Monday morning, Maddox spent an hour or so trying to contact the TV people before he got through to anybody in authority. He finally went out, taking Rodriguez and D'Arcy with him, to try making contact in person. Dabney and Rowan were out with Lyons' team on the new leads, and Feinman was looking for a hot heist suspect.

Sue and Daisy were alone in the office when a new call went down at eleven o'clock, and so they went out on it. They alerted the lab before they left, because it was reported as a homicide, and Franks said disapprovingly that one of the men ought to be with them. "We're both big girls now," said Daisy. "We'll meet you there."

They took Sue's car, and as she thrust the key into the ignition she glanced at Daisy and asked, "Are you ever sorry you went in for this?" She happened to know that Daisy was fifty-two, which was just her mother's age, but you'd never think so: Daisy was slender and blond and still pretty, if she did have three lively grandsons.

She looked at Sue and said seriously, "No, not really. It was Albert's whole life, and when that punk shot him, I felt it was a way I could— live it out for him." Her husband's name was one of those on the Honor Roll in the lobby at Parker Center, LAPD men killed in line of duty. "It's a useful sort of job," said Daisy, "after all."

Sue thought of Mrs. Katharine Gorman. "Yes," she agreed, "but it's also useful to raise the next generation right. We'd like two, and that damn doctor is still saying just relax and don't worry about it and it'll happen."

"Quite right," said Daisy.

"But it doesn't seem to."

The address was an apartment on Edgemont, an old one of four stories. Patrolman Rinehart was waiting for them, and the lab unit rolled up behind the Chrysler. "It's upstairs," said Rinehart. "Number nine, right front." Up there was a rather pretty dark girl looking agitated and tearful, and a stout elderly woman looking shocked, outside an open apartment door. "Girl who found her and the manageress," said Rinehart.

Daisy introduced herself and Sue. "We'll want to talk to you, but it'll be a little while. Suppose you wait in"—she looked at the manageress—"your apartment?"

"That's a good idea, I'll make us a cup of tea. It's first left downstairs. Come on, honey, we've both had a shock."

It was a pleasant apartment, the rooms larger than in newer ones, shabby and mismatched furniture but everything neat and clean. The body was in the living room, in the middle of the carpet between coffee table and china cupboard, the body of a tall slim girl with blond hair, lying on her left side as if she slept there. But there was thick crusted blood on the right side of her head, where a heavy weapon of some sort had smashed in her skull.

Franks came in behind them with the camera. After a minute he said, "That didn't happen yesterday. A couple of days maybe."

They looked around a little while the men got busy; the kitchen was neat, the bed made up. "In the evening sometime," said Daisy, and Sue agreed. The girl had been wearing a tailored housecoat.

They went downstairs to the manageress' apartment. She was Mrs. Harriet Beaton, and the girl was Nora Cooke.

"I've got to call in, if that's all right," she said. "To work. They'll think—you see, when she didn't come in this morning we tried to get her on the phone and couldn't, and she's always on time, she wouldn't take off without letting somebody know. And we thought she might have been taken sick over the weekend, too sick to let us know, so I came over on my break. I didn't know her awfully well, but we'd been out to lunch together. We got her address from the files—"

"You haven't told us her name."

"Oh, I'm sorry, I guess I'm not thinking straight. It was just—when there wasn't any answer I thought maybe she was in there with appendicitis or something, I went and found Mrs. Beaton and she had a key

—oh, dear, I can't believe this is happening—somebody you know—to see her like that—" They got her quieted down finally and she was more coherent, gave them names and details.

"And I can tell you a little something," said Mrs. Beaton significantly. "She was a nice girl, Karen, and she'd lived here ever since she came down to L.A. Came from up in Vallejo, I guess a small town, and her mother and sister still live there, she hadn't any relations here and she wasn't a girl for running around and having a lot of friends. She'd come in here and sit and talk when she came by to pay the rent, and sometimes she'd tell me things. I liked her, I guess she could see that. And I do know that she'd been awful upset about having a fight with her boy friend. She said a little about it."

"Do you know his name?"

"Tom Wiley, he works in the men's department in the May Company. She liked him fine, but she said he'd got to drinking too much lately, he was likely going to lose his job and they had a fight over it, she told him she wouldn't see him again and he was mad. That was last week."

"Oh, *dear*," said the girl. "I do feel queer. But I've got to get back—" Sue explained about signing a statement, and she said she'd come in after work tomorrow.

There wasn't much else they could do until the lab men were finished; they did find an address book, with Tom Wiley's address and number in it, and family addresses up in Vallejo. It was past twelve-thirty and they stopped for lunch on the way back. Daisy was just starting to type the initial report on it, and Sue was telling Feinman what it looked like, when a stocky dark man in a rumpled navy suit came in purposefully and said, "I may have some information somebody here wants. Gene O'Hara, Welfare and Rehab."

They looked at him enquiringly. "Is it on the grapevine," he asked seriously, "that the Hollywood fuzz is interested in hearing about an Aggie and Joey, something about some kids? Because—"

"Yes, yes, yes!" said Sue. She and Daisy practically fell on him, sat him down in Maddox's desk chair. "What have you got? Where did you hear—"

"Take it easy, girls, I came on purpose to tell you." His dark eyes were amused. "Look, would you settle for a Mrs. Nagy and her husband Louis? Because that's what I've got. From one of my little flock." The Welfare and Rehabilitation office downtown housed all the parole officers. "Natty Dukes. I like Natty. He's an old-fashioned burglar, that's his trade and he's not ashamed of it. He takes the prospect of the slammer as one of the hazards of the job, the way a politician rates bronchitis. Not a genius, and he's knocked around some in fifty-odd years, but in his own way he's quite a nice guy. He's been in Folsom for the last nine years, and I'm supposed to see that he takes an honest job and doesn't backslide. Well—" O'Hara laughed. "On that I'll take no bets, but at the moment he's working at a gas station and reporting to me faithfully. And when I saw him this morning he had something to tell me. He said he'd been thinking about it awhile, because he wasn't no snitch and his sister Naomi had been awful good to him all their lives, but this time when he gets out he finds she's took up with a new dude, married him and all, and he's a nogoodnik, got her into something real bad. He says Naomi's hitting the bottle some too, he don't approve of that, and the pair of 'em in a real nasty caper. He says, says Natty, there's things he don't mind and things he don't hold with, and he hates to blow the whistle on his own sister but he gets it on the grapevine the Hollywood fuzz are after 'em anyway. He thought maybe he could do something without bringing in the fuzz, the time he did the favor for the little girl—"

"The man who mailed the letter!" said Sue and Daisy together.

"For heaven's sake, did he tell you where they are?" demanded Sue.

"So you do know something about it. I couldn't make it out, he wasn't saying much. Something about a letter, sure, thrown out a window at him. It's an address down Vermont, around Exposition Park. What's it about?"

Sue told him what it was about while Daisy got onto Central. "It may get a little rough if they're there, and possibly some johns," said Feinman, getting up. "You going to join the party?"

"I'm LAPD too," said O'Hara, hurt. "My God, what a hell of a thing—yeah, sometimes the damn-fool kids ask for trouble, but this— I just hope Natty knows what he was talking about."

It was an old two-story frame house on Thirty-first just around the corner from Vermont. There were three squads from Central waiting to meet them along the main drag; Feinman double-parked and they discussed operations for a minute, and then they all converged on the place at once, left the cars all over the street, and started in. Feinman said, "You stay here till we see what we've got," and he and O'Hara ran after the six uniformed men.

Sue and Daisy, of course, did no such thing. When they got over there, a trial ring at the bell had produced no result, and the biggest man drew back carefully, and aimed a powerful kick at the door below the knob. The door burst in, and they all crowded in together, the girls behind, to a bare hall, a sparsely furnished living room to the left, steep stairs. A couple of the men started for the back of the house; the rest of them pounded up the stairs, Feinman and O'Hara ahead. They were old uncarpeted stairs, and at the top was a long narrow hall with doors on either side. The first two were unlocked, giving on bedrooms barely furnished; the next showed an old-fashioned bathroom with a claw-footed tub. Sue flew to the other side of the hall. The rear door there was locked.

"Oh, please—quick!"

Feinman obliged by kicking it in, and it crashed open to reveal a room about ten feet square, with a double bed, a chest of drawers, a window with bars, and two girls, one fair, one dark, in dirty nondescript clothes.

"Sally Rittenhouse?" said Sue.

The fair girl let out a scream at the sight of the uniform and began to weep. "Somebody did come, Marge! I guess Daddy and Mother don't care what happened anymore, but *somebody did come*—because we prayed and prayed *so hard!*" She fell into Daisy's arms, sobbing, and the dark girl collapsed on Feinman's chest.

"Darling, your daddy and mother have been worried sick—they've been calling and calling us, and we've been trying to find you, we just didn't know where to look till now, but it's all right, you're all safe now—"

There were four other girls in the other two rooms; aside from that the house was empty. The Central men called in and were put on stakeout to wait for the proprietors, so they went to get the squads out of sight. Sue and Daisy commandeered one to ferry the girls back to the station. They were all minors; they'd be taken to Juvenile Hall for the night, and it was possible that a couple of the other four were on Missing lists somewhere. They'd sort it out. The girls all seemed eager to cooperate.

They all talked at once on the way in. "Nobody would take my letter—such awful, awful men—I saw that one in the side yard getting into a car, I just thought maybe—" "Listen," said one of the others in an aggrieved southern drawl, "if I'd 'a' wanted to be a hooker I dint need come all the way to California—" "I haven't got any money but my mother'll pay for the call, I got to call Mother, it's Phoenix, please could I—"

At the station, Sue called the Rittenhouses and Sally managed a few words to them before she started crying again. The Rittenhouses said they'd fly right down with Marjorie's parents.

It was borne in on Maddox that this had been an exercise in futility too. He'd had a good deal of trouble reaching Jerry Ross, the director, and persuading him to get everybody together, all the people on that TV series Jan Warden had been doing; it had been set up in their working quarters at one end of the old Paramount studio, and when he walked in there with D'Arcy and Rodriguez at one o'clock, they were all a little startled by the crowd and the place. It was a drafty, dusty, dreary place with three sides of a rather opulent living room in the middle, and all around that booms, cradles, cameras wherever you looked, a lot of wooden folding chairs, hundreds of feet of electric cable all over the floor, and lights suspended in unlikely places. There must have been sixty people milling around there, talking excitedly.

Jerry Ross was a cheerful-looking short man with a paunch and a beard. "You're going to be very unpopular," he said to the detectives. "They think they're due for some news." He hopped up onto an extension ladder leaning against one wall of the living room and raised his voice to a bellow. "Boys and girls! Quiet down now! You're all together again in this million-dollar set to talk to the fuzz—they want to know which one of us murdered Jan!"

There was one concerted groan and catcalls and whistles. "Hell with the fuzz, what's going to happen to production?" "Who cares who did it, who's coming in and when do we start shooting again?"

"Now be nice to the Man, boys and girls, they don't know the stark facts of life like we do—"

"Have you seen Arnhelm?" "What's Arnhelm saying?" "What's Arnhelm *doing?*" "Don't you know *anything* yet?"

"Now, boys and girls, I give you the Man. You take it," he said to Maddox, hopping down. "Hell. I've been in the business a long time, and things happen, but this is the worst yet. *The* worst. And Arnhelm sitting there with those damn P.R. men adding up figures—will he drop more by closing down or reshooting? Hell, hell, hell." He sat down and lit a cigar.

"We'd like to question people individually—I didn't realize there'd be so many."

"How the hell do you think a TV show gets shot? By magic? You said everybody. The cast numbers, lessee, nine. Then there are camera men, assistant cameramen, the assistant director, he's not important, make-up people, script girls, hairdressers, prop men, electricians—"

"Well, we want to talk to the cast anyway."

Just talking to the cast revealed to him that all these people were seeing the murder of Jan Warden from a completely different angle than anybody else, certainly the press or police. "Oh, she wasn't as bad to work with as some I've known," said Clarissa Clifford, "but they've just raised my rent and if this thing gets scrapped it's a whole season lost— you don't know what I'm talking about, do you? Facts of life like Jerry says." She was only about twenty-two, a dark gamin type. "Everybody's tied up or not tied up this time of year, it's when we make next fall's shows, and if this thing is out, sure, we got contracts, but it'd be a year off the screen and that much harder to get work next year, you get forgotten fast in this business. I just hope to God you catch whoever killed her—making all this trouble—"

"They're all alike," said Dennis Stanton indifferently. He was the romantic lead by his looks. "At least she didn't fight with the director. But what the hell's going to happen to production—if it's canceled, I told my agent, we break the contract, I said. That is it! I can't be expected to have my career damaged, I didn't need to have got into this spin-off at all, Arnhelm had to argue me into it—"

"All publicity!" said Bertram Halliday, the elderly character actor with the clever monkey face. "Now when I came into the profession, you had to have something to get anywhere. These pin-up girls, tchah, nothings. Where do they come from, what do they have? Do they last? No, because once the face and figure's gone they got nothing. Arnhelm's no fool, he knows anybody could replace her—" His trained voice carried and instantly the orderly routine of detectives talking to individuals was broken.

"If we start shooting tomorrow, it'll be twenty hours a day to do enough episodes, there are nearly twelve in the can now, and if anybody thinks I can be expected to work my tail off *unless* I get a new contract and a raise—"

"But we could do it, Denny! If he got somebody with her coloring, we can still use the long shots, and we'd have something to go on—"

"Now I know the very little lady could really carry the part and make it go, and after fifty years in the business I ought to know what I'm talking about— I put it to Arnhelm, I said, that little girl will go places and we ought to get her under contract—you know the one I mean, the Foyle girl, did the music teacher bit in the third episode of 'Newcomers'—a vignette, and a nice job—"

"All I say is"—the beautifully modulated tones of Eva Winkler cut across that—she was fat and white-haired and arthritic, but her voice reminded you that she had started in pantomime in London and in her time played Rosalinds and Portias—"is that I'd like to go home. This is a waste of time and I'm tired and I want my tea. Either Arnhelm's going to cancel or he isn't, and personally I don't give a damn if he replaces her with a witch. Where's my handbag?"

None of these people, realized Maddox, had cared very much about Jan Warden one way or the other. She was the center of the production, the reason for its being; and her sudden removal had brought the threat of economic and career damage to everybody involved. If any of these people had hated Jan Warden enough to murder her, they'd have restrained themselves until after the season's episodes were shot. They had already nearly forgotten her; what they were madly concerned about was the production.

"Look," said Ross, "I'm sorry, but I've got an appointment set up with the lord and master. Maybe he's decided one way or the other." He hopped up on the ladder. "Now hold tight, boys and girls! I'm on my way to see Arnie now and you'll be the first to know what the great man ordains! Cheers, dears, and keep your peckers up!"

They groaned at him again.

About five o'clock on Monday afternoon a disheveled young man burst into a drugstore on Highland Avenue and demanded a dime from the nearest clerk. "I've got to call the police—I've been kidnapped! Damn it, if you won't give me a dime call 'em for me! Somebody ought to chase that wild man—"

He convinced them to make the call, and after hearing his first sentence Rinehart ferried him back to the station in a hurry.

"I don't know if he was doped up or just crazy," the young man told Maddox and Rodriguez. "I wasn't about to argue with that gun. Damn it, I've just had a baby and I'd like to live to see him grow up. I mean, for God's sake, my wife just had a baby—yesterday—a boy, nine pounds,

John Patrick—and I'd been to the hospital to see her—the Riverside Hospital in North Hollywood, we live in North Hollywood—"

"Just take it easy," said Rodriguez, smiling at him. "You might tell us your name, sir."

"Oh, I'm sorry—it's Dobson, Michael Dobson. I came out of the hospital when visiting hours were up—my God, I'd better call the boss, I used my lunch hour to go to the hospital—I work at Power and Foster Engineering—anyway, I just got back to my car when this wild man shows up with a gun. I was at one side of the lot, nobody around—he gets me in, holding the gun on me, and starts to drive. Oh, first he robbed me, he took my wallet, every dime I had, my watch, even my wedding ring—and my God, he doesn't know the town, he kept going every which way. I tried to tell him I could give him directions, if he'd say where he wanted to go, but he just told me to shut up. Look, I never understood before how anybody could get picked up like that, my God, the guy's driving, you'd think you could just grab for the gun or jump out or something, but I tell you, I wasn't about to start a hassle or jump out when he's doing sixty on the freeway—"

"Mr. Dobson, your car—"

"And then, thank God, he gets shunted off the Hollywood freeway onto Highland, and I know he's not crazy enough to run lights, call down cops. He got one at Fountain, he stopped for it and jabbed me with the gun—so the next time he got one I took the chance, I had my hand on the door latch and I just shoved the door and rolled. I don't know if he fired at me—I didn't look, I just lit out. After I called you, of course he was long gone."

It was about thirty blocks from the Los Angeles Valley College to the Riverside Hospital, but that had probably been Lewis.

"What's the car?" asked Maddox. "Do you know the plate number?"

"What? Oh, it's a Monte Carlo, gray, three years old. It's a vanity plate, our name—DOBSON."

Rodriguez went over to Communications to put that on the wire. They were still behind Gary Lewis, but maybe getting a little nearer.

Sue had left, and Maddox was just going out when the hall door to the front desk opened and a couple came in. "He said to come back here," said the man. "I'm Ray Egbert and this is my wife Betty. The sheriff came and told us about Amy." He was a thin, tired-looking man in old clothes; she was small and dark like her sister, and looked tired too. "How she asked us to take Bobby and Rita. We'll be glad to, we came right down, just got into town. Until we know what's going to happen to Amy. Could you tell us anything about that?"

"I could make a guess," said Maddox gently. "I think they'll call it Murder Two or voluntary homicide. She might get a five to ten, and be out in about three years." And if that seemed a little price for a man's life, on this one you had to look at it from both angles. Bill Wagner, too interested in money, stumbling on Amy's queer little secret, really needn't have gone in for miniature blackmail.

"I want to see Amy," said Betty.

"Yes, you can see her." He told them about visiting hours at the jail, how to get there. "The children are in Juvenile Hall." Sue had seen to that yesterday. Looking at them, he wondered if they had enough money to get a motel room, buy meals here. But they just thanked him politely and went out.

He got up again; it was ten past six; and the phone rang. It might be something important. "Maddox."

"Well, I didn't know if I'd catch you. I've got this bird," said Barney McCaffrey. "I'm sorry to get you at end of shift, Maddox, but I'd like to get him out of my hair. You've got him for exposure, vandalism, uttering threats, and attempted rape."

"The flasher," said Maddox. "Who is he and how did you get him, Barney?"

"I didn't get him," said Barney, sounding amused and resigned. "I'd been worrying about it, trying to figure how to set up a stakeout. He went after one of the maids a couple of days ago, she got away from him but he'd marked her up—by the time we got up there where it happened, of course he was gone. He never pulled anything at regular times or places, and I couldn't figure how to set any trap. We've had more linen cut up, obscene notes, this assault, and the complaints about the exposure. The same kind of ladies, you know. Middle-aged and up."

"So what happened?"

"So," said Barney, "we've got a lady staying here, a Miss Ophelia Widdemer-Jones her name is, and I understand she's an archaeologist from Oxford University. She doesn't—well—look like it. She's a little old lady with white hair in a bun on her neck, and she wears plain black dresses and flat heels—you know. She told the manager she's here to study something called Minoan B tablets from an archaeological collection that's at the Exposition Park museum. She's been a little trouble, she wants a hot water bag filled and the maids never saw one before—and she has her own special brand of tea and has to have it made just so."

"I see her," said Maddox. "Don't tell me the flasher—"

"Well, it was a mistake," said Barney, "he picked her. He knocked on her door about fifteen minutes ago, there he is with his pants open and his newspaper, and she clobbered him. She knows some jujitsu, and she put him down and out and tied him up with the belt of her bathrobe and called the desk."

"I'd like to meet her. Quite a lady."

"Well, yes. And I recognized him. A little load off my mind, I can stop worrying about our own staff," said Barney. "He was one of the painters. We had most of the ground floor painted a couple of months ago—including the manager's office. He was one of the crew. He's come to now, I've been talking to him. His name's Clarence Teed. He says he used to work in a hotel once, so he'd know where to look for the manager's master key and get it copied. He had it on him. He's a nut and I'd like to get rid of him," said Barney.

"Bring him over. The night watch 'll be coming in."

Brougham and Donaldson had just got there when Barney delivered the flasher. He was a mild-looking young fellow about twenty-eight, medium-sized, and he sat and smiled at them. "Are you going to send me back to Camarillo? I don't mind. It's a very nice place. They're very nice to me there. My doctor's Dr. Willoughby, I think, he's a nice man."

CHAPTER 9

Maddox got in before anybody else on Tuesday morning. There was an in-depth meeting scheduled at the D.A.'s office this afternoon, on Warden, and he had to get out a complete summarized report of what they had on it so far. The press would have been on the D.A.'s neck too. He had a cursory look at the night report; it had been a quiet night, the only thing for the detectives a felony drunk driving with two people killed.

He had made a fair start on the report, automatically cussing the recalcitrant carbon paper whenever he finished a page, when everybody else started to drift in.

"The busy bee," said Rodriguez, sitting down at the next desk. He was as dapper as usual, in a sharp gray suit, his mustache newly trimmed. "After that interesting little experience yesterday, have you any more bright ideas on where to go on the superstar?"

Maddox knocked off for a few minutes, swung the desk chair around and lit a cigarette. "Yes, in a way, and nobody's going to like it. It's what's going into this damned report for the D.A. All the facts we've got on this, and the lab evidence, and the autopsy, send me right back to some of my first ideas. I don't think that murder was intended, César. It happened more or less by accident. And that takes us right back to the burglar, and all those thrice-damned keys. There are a hundred ways it could have happened, you think it out. Somebody who once worked there—for Ferensky, Medford, Guardeau, Ryan—coming across a key and casually mentioning it. Somebody honest, but with a grandson having a habit to support. But also I've had a new idea about that, which is even more simple and, hell take it, very, very likely." Ellis and Feinman had drifted over to listen, with Dabney and Rowan behind them. "And that is, a key like that one Von Bazen came across. A key with a neat little tag attached to it with the house address on it. Found in the effects of somebody dead—left in a kitchen drawer in an empty apartment—overlooked in a handbag or jacket pocket and ending up in a Goodwill thrift shop anywhere in this damned town."

"That," said Ellis, "is the kind of thing that's all too damned likely, Ivor. And there's no way to check back on those keys, even to guess at random. We're back to the burglar?"

"The way I outlined before—it'd be worth a drive past the house, wouldn't it, and anybody'd know there was loot in that place. He didn't even have to know who lived there, but he'd case the place a little and find she lived alone. If he saw her leave that night, with a date, he could assume she'd be out to all hours— Let Gunther settle down, he could have just got up to that bedroom when Warden came home. He slid into the closet, and he'd have been, um, annoyed—no chance at any loot at all. It's also very much on the cards that he was an amateur, and damned scared. And she heard him when he tried to get out. Those stabs were made in the dark, in panic—he just wanted to put her out of action while he ran—and he slashed that artery just by chance. Then, of course, with all the blood, he realized what he'd done—had to clean up, get the worst off, in a hurry. And there's no possible way even to get a smell of a lead on it. On who, or how he came by the key."

"Yes," said Ellis. "The simpler a thing is, the harder it always is to work. I'm bound to agree that's where all the evidence points. The press is going to be calling us some names, and the D.A. isn't going to like it one damn bit." He laughed. "Maybe five years from now some punk confessing to a burglary or heist 'll blurt out, by the way, it was me killed that Warden dame. It happens. But meanwhile—"

Maddox said shortly, "Yes, frustrating." He had time to finish the report; he turned to rummage in the top desk drawer for a fresh pack of cigarettes, and noticed the report in Sue's neat typing on the other side of the blotter. He picked it up to see what it was about. Ellis and Feinman had drifted to their desks. "What the hell?" he said to himself, glancing down the form. "What's this? This new homicide that went down yesterday—" Nobody knew; the girls had gone out on it alone, and they were now down at Juvenile Hall dealing with those minors. Maddox went over to the lab and asked Baker about it.

"Oh, that," said Baker, looking up from a microscope. "Just what I heard, it looked open and shut. There wasn't a break-in, she'd let him in, whoever did it, and Sergeant Hoffman found out she'd had a fight with her boy friend."

"Yes, I saw that."

"We picked up some good fresh latents off the coffee table, besides a lot of hers, of course. I'll have photos for you this afternoon. I just sent the prints downtown before I went off yesterday."

It was, of course, the name that had caught Maddox's eye. Karen Hansen. One of the tellers at that bank where, probably, the first bogus checks had been cashed. That batch was down in Questioned Documents now with all the others; that office took their time about reports, and probably wouldn't come up with anything significant anyway. But, for God's sake, he thought, the bank had nothing to do with the bogus check caper, hardly the only bank involved. And bank tellers had private lives like everybody else, and it wasn't unprecedented for an estranged boy friend to murder an ex-girl friend. But it was queer that they should just have run into her, however much on the fringes of that case, just recently. Karen Hansen.

He went back to the office. Rodriguez was looking over a sheaf of statements, and swearing in Spanish under his breath. "Speaking of things right up in the air, we had better just forget about that poor ticket collector at the movie house. My God. There's hardly any agreement about a description of the knifer, except that he was big and wore a yellow shirt. And the girl was a lot younger, and blond. ¡Carape! It can go in Pending."

"Yes," said Maddox. He took Sue's report over to Ellis. "I'm busy. I suppose we ought to do something about this sometime."

Sue and Daisy were having a busy morning clearing up the aftermath of the sex-slave ring. The Rittenhouses arrived about ten o'clock, and Marjorie Burns's parents were with them. There was a tearful reunion.

"Oh, Mother, you don't know—how glad to see you— Oh, oh, oh," sobbed Sally, "we were sorry we ever did it by the time we got to Hollywood! But we only had about fifteen dollars left, not enough to get back home, and we thought we'd have to get jobs and earn enough —and the woman right there at the bus station, she *looked* all right, she acted nice, and she said she knew where we could get jobs cleaning rooms in a hotel, and we thought we could do that O.K.—but she took us to that place, and that horrible man locked us in—and—and—oh, Mama, what they made us do—all those awful men, some of them drunk and— Oh, Mama, did you get the letter?"

"Yes, darling, we did. That's why—"

"*Oh*," said Sally with a great sigh. "It was just a—a sort of desperate venture. Marge had some Scotch tape in her purse—but all those awful men, no use to ask—and then I saw that one in the side yard under the window, he had a kind of funny face when he looked up, sort of like an old prizefighter, but he did pick it up—"

Sally and Marjorie owed something to Natty Dukes the pro burglar, but they'd never know it.

And before they took the girls away, Mrs. Rittenhouse said anxiously, "It's a terrible thing for such young girls to get over, if they ever can. Do you think they can, ever?"

"Well, they are young," said Daisy. "Let's hope it'll fade into a nightmare, the bad kind you forget when you wake up."

"We just don't know how to thank you for your help."

"You needn't thank us," said Sue soberly. "We felt pretty helpless there for a while, but finally we got a lucky break."

The other four girls were from different backgrounds. The girl from Alabama had run away from a foster home where, she said, the people just wanted somebody to do all the housework. She was fifteen. They had to talk to the social services department in Montgomery, arrange for her to be sent back, and Sue told her if she talked to the social workers they'd probably find her a better place. "I don't reckon," she said stolidly. "Most places are like that. I guess I just got to stick it out till I'm eighteen. It ain't nobody's fault, Pa getting killed in that huntin' accident and Ma goin' to die pretty soon, in the T.B. sanatorium. I'm pretty tough, I guess I can last out."

Two of the others, from Phoenix and Colorado Springs, wanted to go home; those parents were contacted and money wired. The fourth girl just stared at Sue and Daisy and said bitterly, "Home? With them getting drunk and fighting all the time? If you send me back, I'll just run off again, and next time I'll know better how to stay out of trouble." She wouldn't tell them who she was, but in her otherwise empty handbag they found a grimy official card from the Aid to Dependent Children Bureau in Indianapolis, and eventually arranged to ship her back. That kind of thing made them feel helpless too. There'd be a lot of paperwork.

In the middle of all that, Sue thought to call the Vice office downtown, to ask if they'd picked up Naomi Nagy and her husband. The Sergeant Lightner she talked to had a pleasant baritone voice. "Oh, yes, they came walking into the net about an hour after your party got away with the prisoners. Couple of nasty little people. We'll hope to put them out of circulation for a while."

"Thank goodness," said Sue. "We're just getting the prisoners sorted out."

"And isn't it lucky we're both on day watch, dear—you do have a charming voice. What about dinner some night?"

"I've already got a sergeant," said Sue demurely. "All tied up for keeps."

"Well, isn't it a pity I always run into the nice ones too late," said Lightner gallantly.

They wouldn't be seeing an autopsy report on Karen Hansen right away, but Daisy's report said that she'd probably been killed on Friday or Saturday night, and of course it looked like an open and shut case. Ellis and Feinman went over to the May Company—a guess said it was probably the Los Angeles store, nearest, and it was. Tom Wiley was about twenty-six, a big young man with sandy hair and boyish good looks. By the time they got him back to the station, there had been word from R. and I. downtown. The prints lifted from the Hansen apartment were his, and he had a small pedigree of assault, D. and D., and drunk driving.

"Well, there you are," said Feinman. "Simple."

He claimed he didn't know Karen was dead. "Oh, my God, I wouldn't hurt Karen," he said there in one of the little interrogation rooms. "She was a nice girl. I—I even wanted to ask her to marry me, but what did I have to offer her, she was making more money than me. Oh, God, how could she be dead, nobody'd want to hurt Karen! Yes, sure, we had a fight, I mean she just told me she was through, and I was sore about it, but—but I wouldn't—"

"You've got a little record of violence, Tom," said Ellis.

"Oh, my God. I know I shouldn't take a drink, it always gets me to picking fights. But I get to feeling damned low, stuck in that dead end job—I was a goddamned fool to drop out of high school, it seemed a good idea at the time but— So I take a few drinks to feel better—"

He said on Friday night he'd stayed home alone watching TV. He had an apartment on Berendo. Saturday night he was home alone too, and admitted he'd tied one on. "Feeling sorry for myself."

Of course he had been in her apartment, picking her up for dates, and his prints could have been there for a couple of weeks. It was all inconclusive, unless they got something to tie him in closer. Both Ellis and Feinman thought he'd done it, but there would probably never be enough evidence for a legal charge.

"Well, that is a lovely handful of nothing," said the deputy District Attorney. He was a man about thirty-five, stocky and good-looking in a Nordic sort of way, with tawny fair hair and a high-bridged nose. His name was Peterson. "You know what the damned press will be saying."

"Well, you know as much about evidence as we do," said Maddox untactfully, and Rodriguez coughed.

"My God, all those damned keys— Yes, I see your position, Sergeant. There's nowhere to go."

"We'll go on worrying at it, sir. Talk to Gunther again, ask who was at the house lately, if Warden had mentioned any quarrel, but I don't suppose she confided in the housekeeper. And in any case, as I said in my report, we've come back to thinking that it was the impersonal thing—the nervous burglar, and no intent to kill."

"Yes, the facts seem to point that way, don't they?"

"For one thing," put in Rodriguez, "nobody who had any reason to be jealous of her, dislike her, stood to gain any advantage by her death. All her death accomplished was to stop production on that TV series, which seems to have made everybody concerned good and mad. None of those people seem to have had anything but casual relations with her, even the rest of the cast."

"Yes," said Peterson. He went over to the window, hands in pockets, and looked four floors down to the traffic along Temple Street. "This sister. I understand she's contesting the will."

"Yes, and she'll undoubtedly get something, she and the daughter being the only living relatives. I don't know how the law will see it, I suppose a court might consider Warden's intentions and split it down the middle."

"A nice piece of change in any case."

"Well, that's nothing to do with the murder, unless the sister did it, and I can't buy that. As I say, the one conclusion we have reached is that this wasn't a planned murder. It was done almost by accident, I think."

"Yes. On the facts I'll have to agree, and don't we both know, that kind is always a bastard to work. It can't be helped," said Peterson. "We'll go on handing out the standard press releases, the investigation still proceeding, and maybe some other superstar will announce a baby or have a diamond bracelet stolen, and take a little pressure off."

Rodriguez grinned. "Oh, any day we'd rather deal with the regular street people. They're a hell of a lot more predictable, just from what we've seen of the other half on this case. You know where you are with the hookers and dopies. And the press couldn't be less interested."

"Damn the press," said Peterson without rancor. He wandered around the office whistling softly, and ended up back at the window. "Sometimes I wish I'd stayed in Marysville to practice. Not as much money, but a hell of a lot more peaceful life."

The old Bijou Theater on Larchmont Avenue was slowly going out of business these days, the management able to book only the oldies, and it didn't open until six o'clock. The projectionist, getting there a little late that night, came down the alley to the back door as usual, and shied away at the sight of a woman's body lying up against the fence on the other side. He had a nervous stomach, and he didn't like dead bodies. He made a wide berth around it, not looking back, went into the theater and called the police. Let them deal with it. That was what police were for.

The police, in the form of two plainclothes detectives, interrupted him later to ask questions, but he didn't know anything, and he got so upset at the idea of going to the morgue to look at the body that they quit bothering him.

The body was very anonymous, a girl in the twenties with dark hair. There wasn't any blood on her, and Brougham and Donaldson deduced that it must be an O.D. of some kind. There wasn't any handbag near her. The only interesting thing there was, was a queer mark on the back of her left hand: not a tattoo, but something like those decals kids liked to use. It was blue, and it looked like a blurred star.

"It seems to say something to me," said Donaldson, "but I can't put a finger on it." Neither could Brougham; and later on they got called out to three different heists, and it went out of their minds.

Unexpectedly for the middle of the week, there had been three heists on Tuesday night: a bar, a Seven-Eleven store, and a market. At the Seven-Eleven, the manager had been shot, and was unconscious when Brougham got there. "Damnation," said Maddox. "Women's work isn't to be compared. Always something else coming along. César, you might get onto the hospital and see if we can talk to this Fryer." He handed over Brougham's report. On the other two, witnesses had given fairly good descriptions, but it just posed a lot more legwork, looking for the men with suggestive pedigrees, hauling them in.

Then a messenger came in with a manila envelope, from Bergner's office: the autopsy report on the Hansen girl. Bergner had got right on the ball. There wasn't a great deal in it: she'd died of a massive skull fracture, and there was no indication what the weapon had been. In lay terms, it said that unless the blow had been struck by a powerful man, it had probably been a fairly hefty weapon. Digestive process about two hours completed after a meal. She had been a virgin. The estimated time of death was anywhere between 6 P.M. last Friday and 6 P.M. Saturday. Of course they hadn't got to the corpse right away.

Daisy had come to read over his shoulder. She said now, "Friday. Both Sue and I said, sometime in the evening."

"Why?"

"And you a married man, but of course you didn't see the body. A girl comes home from work, unless she's going out again somewhere, the first thing she does is get undressed. Get more comfortable—put on a housecoat. That's what she'd done. So it wasn't Saturday evening, it had to be Friday."

Maddox looked up at her over his shoulder. "She was a nice respectable girl. Would she have let the boy friend in, dressed like that?"

"Well, she was covered up better in a long robe than in street clothes. Or, of course, he might have just pushed in when she opened the door."

"Um. We'd better talk to this Wiley again, though"—Maddox laid down the report—"if he killed her, he brought the weapon with him, which would say he planned it. He's got the right record for it, by what George had to say. Belligerent with a few drinks in him."

Rodriguez put the phone down. "Fryer's conscious. I'd better go and see if he can give us anything useful."

The Seven-Eleven chain store manager, Earl Fryer, had taken a bullet in the side and lost a good deal of blood, but the redheaded nurse who led Rodriguez down the hall in Emergency said he'd be fine in a few days. "Did anybody tell you to send the slug over to our lab?" asked Rodriguez.

"I wasn't here, it was the night shift," she said. "I'm sure they did whatever the police asked them to do. Here's a visitor for you, Mr. Fryer," she added brightly. "It's the police."

Fryer was sitting up in the high hospital bed, but he looked white and ill; he wasn't a young man. He said to Rodriguez, "I guess I was out like a light last night, reason I couldn't talk to the officers came out. I don't even know who called the police—I never had a chance."

"No, sir. Your store is next to a drugstore, and the owner was there working on his books. He heard the shots and called us."

"Oh. Old Daggett, eh? Lucky for me he was there, I might have bled to death. And serve me right if I had," added Fryer candidly. "It was a damn-fool thing to do. You'd think a man sixty years old would have acquired some common sense, wouldn't you? Well, live and learn —it seems I haven't. My wife's never going to let me forget this—thank God she's down in San Diego with our daughter right now. Trying to play the hero, me."

"What happened, Mr. Fryer?"

"Well, like you know we're open 7 A.M. to 11 P.M. I don't like to ask the girls to work night hours, there are too many nuts and wild ones around. I generally take the evening shift myself. And I was just about getting ready to shut up shop—business had been slow—when in he came. He was a great big fellow about forty, needed a shave, barrel chest on him, and he had a gun. He says to give him the money, and I did, and at the same time I was feeling so mad—the crime rate going up, people think the world owes them a living— And when he went out I chased after him. A hundred and twenty dollars he got, and I was mad. I thought he must probably have a car, and maybe I could get a look at the license plate for you."

"No, that wasn't very smart, Mr. Fryer. A lot of these hoods might be hopped up, and trigger-happy."

"I know it wasn't, now. That's when he shot me. I saw him getting into a car, it was the only one on the lot out front, and he saw me come out, and fired at me three times. I guess I'm lucky to be alive. But," added Fryer casually, "I saw the license plate all right. Last thing I remember, him gunning out of the lot."

"That's very good, sir, if you can recall any of it." A partial plate number was no use.

"Oh, I can tell you what it was. It was one of these vanity plates, and it said DOBSON on it."

Rodriguez made time back to the station and that went out county-wide. With all those flyers out, and every lawman within fifty miles on the lookout, it was a little queer that Lewis hadn't been picked up by now. But, remembering what Francie Keach had told them, Rodriguez wondered—could he be holed up somewhere out of sight, just coming out to replenish the money supply and get food? Francie had said, an empty house. There'd be some around, and some in places where neighbors wouldn't notice or care.

He passed on the news to Maddox and D'Arcy, and they were still talking about it, kicking that idea around, when Sergeant Whitwell buzzed to say he was sending somebody in.

It turned out to be two somebodies, looking uncertain and nervous: a couple of late teen-agers, a boy and a girl. "What can we do for you?" asked Maddox, smiling at them.

"Well, I don't know, we thought we ought to come. I'm Bob Dinsdorf and this is Cheryl Coburn. It's about that man that was killed at the movie theater." They were a nice-looking pair, as teen-agers went these days: the boy's hair not overlong, the girl in a dress instead of pants. They both looked clean and tidy.

Rodriguez set chairs for them hastily. "What do you know about it?"

Dinsdorf seemed to be the spokesman; the girl just smiled back at Maddox. "Well, see, we never knew anything had happened there that day. Cheryl's kind of a Disney buff and wanted to see those pictures again, and we got there early but there was already a little line. I guess we were about fourteen or fifteen people down the line. And I got the tickets and we went in and saw the show, and that was that." By the time they'd come out, of course everything was over: the squads gone, the lab men, who had only wanted photographs, the morgue wagon. "We never heard anything about it till last night, I mean Cheryl found out last night and called me. And it was funny how she did. She was at the library, and she and this woman reached for the same book, and it turned out—"

Cheryl opened her small mouth and said, "*The Art of Walt Disney.* It's a new one."

"—Turns out that this woman's a Disney buff too, they got talking and the woman told Cheryl about the thing at the theater. She was there, back in the line, and the police talked to her, and what she said, well—"

"They were just behind us," said Cheryl softly.

"They, who, you mean—"

"She said it was a fat man in a yellow shirt, all she could tell the police. They were right behind us in line, and we'd talked to that girl."

"¡Santa Maria!" said Rodriguez to himself. Naturally they'd questioned the people closest behind in that line, facing toward the ticket booth.

"So I called Bob and said maybe we ought to come and tell you."

"So what can you tell us about them? You talked to them?"

"To the girl. She was about fourteen, maybe. The man was her father. She liked Disney too, but I thought he looked kind of bored." The girl had found her tongue now. "I don't remember much about him, we just talked to the girl. But they both had on yellow T-shirts, with the same thing on them, on the front you know. It was a picture of a horse's head, and all round the top it said *Manorview Stables.*"

"I only wish," said Rodriguez to D'Arcy, "that we'd get a break like that on an important case, you know. Such as the superstar. Because this doesn't amount to more than manslaughter, probably."

"Probably," agreed D'Arcy. He was driving. They had found the address in the phone book; it was just over the hill into the valley, this side of Studio City. With the bridle trails in Griffith Park, there were stables scattered here and there, and on some property it was legal to have private stables.

But the stable called Manorview was a public one, not very large, with a corral beside it, just off a secondary road. There was a party of four young people standing in front of the stable door, and two horses saddled and bridled. As Rodriguez and D'Arcy parked and got out, two men came out of the stable with two more horses; and one of the men was tall and broad, a little too heavy, with a yellow T-shirt stretched across his chest exactly as Cheryl had described.

They waited until the four had mounted the horses and ridden off to approach the two. Rodriguez showed the badge. "I think we'd like to ask you some questions, Mr.—?"

The other man looked startled and alarmed. "What the hell do the cops want, Bruce?"

"Nothing. They've made some kind of mistake, is all. You better go see to that mare," said the bigger man roughly. The other one shrugged and went back into the stable. "I'm Bruce Stroud. What the hell do you want?"

"Answers about that knifing in front of the theater in Hollywood," said Rodriguez.

"I don't know anything about that. I'm busy, I got no time to talk to you guys. You must want somebody else."

"Oh, I don't think so, Mr. Stroud," said D'Arcy. "Do you work here?"

"I own the place, and I can say who I want on my property. Now I'm busy, and I already told you—"

A brown horse came up the side of the road behind him. A blond girl about fourteen was riding the horse bareback, and as she slid off handily she glanced casually at the two strangers. "Daddy, has Miss Lusk come for Robin yet? I wanted to—"

"Ah," said Rodriguez pleasedly. "We have a couple of witnesses who can identify this young lady without any trouble. Mr. Stroud, we're taking you in for that knifing. Come on."

The girl put her hands to her face and started to cry. "Oh, it's all my fault because I pestered you to take me to that show— Oh, Daddy, you said they'd never find out!"

This time Stroud didn't lose his temper; he just looked despondent and surly. He looked at them, and at her. He said, "Debbie, you go call your mother to come get you." And he went over to D'Arcy's car stiff legged.

He didn't try to argue, listening to them in an interrogation room at the station. When he knew what they had, he just nodded shortly. "I know I got a quick temper," he said heavily. "If I hadn't 'a' had that knife on me—but I did, I got in the habit of carryin' one when I used to live in Mexico. I didn't know the guy was dead. I was just mad at that girl for shortchanging me, she give me change for a five instead of a ten, and when he butted in— I knew he was hurt bad the minute it happened, and I— Well." He stopped and shrugged. "I remember Debbie talking to those two, but they'd gone on in and I didn't figure they'd remember anything."

They put in an application for the warrant, and took him over to the jail. The Metro squad was still out in the streets, but not operating quite so briskly now; they had done their job, and the streets had largely begun to empty of the undesirable ones.

It had gone up to eighty-three today, unusual in May, and possibly a portent of a long hot summer to come. They were nearly into June, and in another month the fierce season would be on them, the long time of the unbearable humid heat, when the blacktop in the streets was sticky where it melted, and air conditioning was a necessity of life (and what it was going to cost to cool that big two-story house they would find out), and inevitably tempers frayed and passions flared and the crime rate soared.

At least, one blessing, the Metro operation was almost finished. They had been hassling the hookers and pimps roughly for over a month, and the usual satisfactory results had been obtained; the cockroaches had crawled back into the woodwork, going underground, not bothering the respectable citizens, and at least some running out of their territory temporarily, until the heat was off.

Maddox went out to a solitary lunch—it was Sue's day off and Daisy was down at Juvenile Hall again on the follow-up work on those girls. Just after he got back, Lyons called.

"Keeping you up to date," he said tiredly. "We've located nine of those men, and the fired maid, from Mr. Tabor's list. These looked like promising leads, Maddox, but several of these fellows are near illiterates, and none of them look like the type to plan a caper like this. We've got search warrants, but nothing's showed—no phony checks, no VISA cards, nothing. The woman's Doris Canning, and she doesn't look too bright either."

"There could be someone connected with one of them, had the bright idea. Because that has got to have been the beginning of it. That's obvious," said Maddox.

"Well, I think so too."

"I did have one thought. You said Simms's Sears charge card was originally issued in 1950. All our witnesses say she's anywhere between thirty-five and fifty. Split the difference, in 1950 she'd have been about twelve."

"I hadn't thought of that," admitted Lyons. "Well, so somebody else is using Simms's card. We'll just have to go on poking around."

Maddox agreed. Also go poking around on their superstar, he thought glumly. He finished his cigarette and reluctantly dialed Shapiro's office. He was put through, and asked if Miss Gunther was still at the Nichols Canyon house.

"Yes, she's agreed to stay on as caretaker. The realtor's charging it to Ryan. Miss Warden's possessions can be stored until the estate is settled."

"And that will take months and months, with you lawyers running up the bills on all parties."

"You know, I very much doubt it," said Shapiro seriously. "Against the blood relatives' claim, and the—er—tenuous relationship to the other two on Miss Warden's part, there's not much to appeal to a judge even with that clause in the will. Unless Wells and Maximilian want to make a real court fight, which would be expensive and risky, I think the major part of the estate will go to the relatives without much trouble."

Well, that was good news, at least· something calvaged for somebody out of the random disorganization of Jan Warden's life.

He tried Wells's office, and then the condo. Neither answered. Was he still cogitating in Acapulco?

Feinman and Ellis came in and asked what he thought about the new body. He hadn't heard about it. "We'll see an autopsy report eventually," he said. "You'd better hear the latest from Lyons' office."

After the hectic night they'd had last night, with the body and all the heists, Brougham and Donaldson didn't get a call until nine-fifty. All the paperwork was caught up, and they didn't have anything to do. "I wish I'd brought a book," said Brougham, yawning. "Damn, Ken, I'm like you—there's something about that mark on that girl—I wish I could think what's trying to get through to me. There's something, sort of, right on the tip of my mind about it—"

"Don't reach for it, it'll come to one of us when we're thinking of something else." They sat around until nine-fifty, and then they had a call.

It was Patrolman Carmichael, and he said, "You can come and pick up your ape-man rapist. He's right here waiting for you."

"What?" yelped Brougham. "When? Where? How'd you drop on him? For God's sake, you mean you've got him? In cuffs?"

"He doesn't need any cuffs," said Carmichael. "It's a laundromat on Melrose," and he added the address.

"That's the same one where the Unger girl was attacked. What the hell do you mean, he doesn't need cuffs? Did he get another—"

"Oh, no," said Carmichael. He sounded as if he was looking over his shoulder, away from the phone. "No, she had a puppy dog with her. Mrs. Joan Reeves. The ape man didn't know that until he got in. He's pretty well chewed up, you'll be taking him to Emergency first. We'll all be waiting for you."

Brougham and Donaldson got out there in record time. At the laundromat, Carmichael was standing by the door. "Isn't he pretty?" he asked.

The ape-man rapist, Russell John Barlow, was so scared that he was huddled into a sobbing heap against one of the washing machines. His throat was gashed open and bleeding, his left arm was in bloody shreds, and one pant leg was torn clean off and there was a bloody slash down that leg. He was moaning in abject terror. Across the room a pretty young woman was watching him gravely. And five feet away from him was standing a great big dog. There was a look in the dog's eyes—if Brougham knew anything about dogs, the one thing in that dog's mind was just what part of Barlow's anatomy was going to get attention next.

"All right, Mrs. Reeves," said Carmichael. "You can call off your pet security guard."

They called an ambulance and sent Barlow over to Emergency. They got there five minutes after the ambulance and waited half an hour to see a doctor. When they finally did, he told them, "Well, he'll live. We've patched him up and given him a tetanus shot and you can take him to jail. Tell your doctor to keep an eye on that leg, there was a tendon slashed and he may have trouble with it. What the hell kind of dog was it, like three parts wolf?"

"I don't know," said Brougham.

When Barlow was ushered out to the hall on crutches, with bandages here and there, he looked oddly shrunken and gray. The big brawny ape man, the lightning attacker, had met his match.

"Well, Barlow, it's going to relieve our minds to have you tucked away all safe and cozy in jail," said Brougham. "Even if we did need a little help from a puppy dog."

Barlow wet his lips and said huskily, "That isn't no dog. It's a—a—a monster. It roared at me, and I tried to run—but it didn't give me time. It roared like a dragon. It like to nearly killed me. People shouldn't be let to keep things like that."

When they'd booked him in, Brougham called Maddox. "Well, I will be damned!" said Maddox. "A dog?"

"Well, yes, a dog," said Brougham. He told him the rest of it, and what their big dangerous ape man had looked like, and what he'd said; and Maddox roared too. "We found his car around on the side street, and asked Sacramento. It was stolen in Bakersfield three months ago."

"Well, it's all very gratifying," said Maddox. "Listen, Dick, just leave a note—it's my day off, but I'll go and get the woman's statement. I think I'd like a look at that dog."

"Oh, it was just a great big dog," said Brougham.

In a way, of course, it was an anticlimax, thought Maddox: after their hunt for the ape man, all the paperwork, and the luck of getting his prints, and the frustration of never getting nearer—and of course Wanda Bates—to have a mere dog bring him to grief

It was a neat white stucco house on a good residential street nearly into West Hollywood. The air conditioning was on; the front door was closed. He pushed the bell.

From away inside the house came a single emphatic bass utterance. It wasn't so much a bark as a bay, he thought; well, a roar. Thinking of Barlow, he grinned to himself. The door opened, and he held out the badge. "Mrs. Reeves? Sergeant Maddox. I think the detectives explained to you last night about making a statement for us. I just thought I'd save you some time, I can take notes and get it typed up and you can come in any time to sign it. You know the precinct station? —Fountain and Wilcox."

"Oh yes," she said. "Of course. Come in." She was in the late twenties, a pretty dark young woman with very white skin and a nice figure in a navy pantsuit. "Oh, don't mind Kaji. It's all right, the man's not a burglar." She shoved the dog aside with one knee, holding the screen door open, and Maddox went in. At her gesture he followed her from a small entry hall down a step to a big square living room; she sat down on the couch and he sat in a chair opposite, and the dog firmly planted itself directly in front of her and looked at Maddox.

It was a very large heavy dog with a stocky body, a massive broad head with prick ears slanted sharply forward and a thick bushy tail curved over its back. The dog looked at Maddox very thoughtfully. It had a short thick furry coat, reddish-brown, but its face and ears were black, which intensified the thoughtful appearance. The expression was concentrated and sinister, and it was obvious that the one consideration in the dog's mind was whether to spring first at throat or arm.

"So this is the, um, security guard," said Maddox, careful not to move.

She laughed. "I was sorry for the man until the other officers told me about him. I hadn't thought twice about going down there, of course. The washer went on the fritz on Saturday and you know servicemen now, I was lucky to get one up yesterday and he says the darned thing needs a part it'll take two weeks to get. Well! I had four loads already, all the sheets and towels, and my husband's building a raised brick bed in the patio and he gets filthy. I'm afraid I was so startled when that man burst in—I was bent over putting things in a washer, and I never saw him coming. I just heard Kaji sound off, and by the time I turned —I'm afraid I didn't call him off until he'd done some damage."

"Yes, indeed," said Maddox. The dog's inscrutable menacing eyes had never left him. There was a deep furrow between the dog's eyes. "Is he a trained attack dog?"

"Heavens, no. Just a family pet, though of course they're naturally very protective. My husband's parents breed them, Kaji was a wedding present, weren't you, boy?" She whacked the great dog on his shoulders. "You've probably never seen one, Sergeant—they're still fairly rare in this country, they only got recognized by the American Kennel Club about seven years ago. He's an Akita-*inu*, the Akita dog of Japan. The national dog of Japan. They used to hunt bears with them, and of course they're a little like bears themselves." She pulled the dog's ears. The dog continued to fix Maddox with the sinister stare, which, he now realized, held an oriental cunning.

"Um. Rather a responsibility to have around. I hope you've got a high enough fence."

Joan Reeves began to laugh. "Lord, I'm so used to him I always forget the effect on people who don't know. I suppose you could say it's their one big asset as a watchdog, they look so fierce that a lot of people are scared of them. Of course they're big strong dogs and if they have any reason to attack—like that man last night—they can do some damage. But they're pussycats to their own people, like any dog. Kaji, boy. The man over there's a nice man—a friend—see? You go and shake hands, that's a good boy."

The dog looked up at her and swiped her hand with a long pink tongue, and got up and stretched, and opened his mouth in a wide happy smile. He came over to Maddox and offered a paw gravely. It was a very large paw, and when Maddox took it the dog swiped his hand with the tongue, carelessly, and moved the bushy tail. Maddox laid a hand on the massive broad head and said, "You're quite a boy, aren't you?" The dog smiled at him and went back to Joan Reeves and tried to climb into her lap.

"Hey, you big clown, get down! Well, you see what I mean."

Suddenly Kaji remembered his dignity and fixed Maddox with the stare again. It was that deep furrow between the eyes that gave the sinister oriental effect, of course. "You know," said Maddox, "if I had something like this at home I wouldn't fuss about my two girls. They want to get a dog. Are all of these like this one?"

"Well, they're natural protectors, yes. But they're awfully expensive, being such a rare breed." She looked at him, amused. "I thought you wanted to take a statement from me."

"Yes, I do." He put out a hand, and Kaji shut his eyes blissfully to have his ears scratched. "I suppose they eat a lot, and exercise—"

"Well, actually they don't. They're such big heavy dogs, they're lazy monsters really—" She laughed. "You like my monster, don't you?"

"I'd like one in the back yard. Where could I get one?"

"Three hundred dollars for a pet quality puppy," she told him. "But of course there's the Rescue League."

"What's that?"

"Oh, they find any Akitas that are abandoned or lost, take care of them, try to find homes. There's a donation if you adopt one, I don't know how much."

"You," said Maddox to Kaji, "are just a great big actor, aren't you? Well, Mrs. Reeves, about last night. How long had you been in the laundromat when Barlow came in?"

"Is that his name? Well, I had to get the laundry done, and Mike was working on his ship model. Neither of us gave it a thought, my going alone, because I had Kaji—"

Kaji opened his mouth in a huge yawn, turned around five times, and lay down with a thud on her feet.

Sue had just got back from Juvenile Hall downtown, making the final arrangements for that girl from Indianapolis. She felt very unhappy about that girl, but of course there wasn't anything she could do about it. The office was empty, all the men out somewhere, and she sat down and lit a cigarette and started to talk to Daisy about it, when Sergeant Whitwell buzzed them and said there was a lady with something on her mind; he'd just sent her in.

Sue got up and went to meet her at the door. "I want to talk to Sergeant Maddox," said the woman.

"I'm sorry, he isn't here, it's his day off. Can I help you?"

The woman looked at her. "I suppose it doesn't matter. Any of you. It's just, it's all come to an end. With killing. I haven't been able to sleep since last Friday night, and I'd better just tell you and then maybe I can sleep."

CHAPTER 10

She was a pleasant-looking, ordinary-looking woman in the forties, neatly dressed, and she spoke quite coherently, but she was obviously speaking in a daze, from the depths of exhaustion.

"You see," she said politely, "it shouldn't ever have gone so far. I really don't know why it went so far. It started with just the one check, the little check for a hundred dollars. Really just the sort of thing Mr. Tabor would do. And then it came to murdering Karen. He had to bring me into it, of course, on account of the checks—the chief teller doesn't have anything to do with that. And of course it was a clever idea. Money, money, money. He had such terrible bills, he said, when his wife was ill—when she died, he owed over twenty thousand dollars."

"Please," said Sue, "what's your name? Can you tell us—"

"And I have a spastic son. In a wheel chair, you know. The doctor thought that special therapy might improve his co-ordination, and it has, but the therapist is thirty dollars an hour. My husband didn't leave any insurance."

"Sit down here," said Daisy kindly, and obediently she sat down in D'Arcy's desk chair.

"It was wrong, of course—but I didn't know then—how wrong it would go. Killing someone."

"Your name," said Sue gently.

"Ever since, I couldn't—couldn't—I called in and said I had a cold, haven't—been in—"

"Your *name*," said Daisy clearly, and the woman looked faintly surprised.

"Oh, I'm Mrs. Lederer. Mrs. June Lederer. And I'm—awfully tired—"

She slid slowly off the chair to the floor, and they leaped for restoratives. Daisy propped her feet up, Sue brought a glass of water, but three minutes later Daisy said suddenly, "It's all right, Sue, it's not an O.D. or a heart attack—she's just asleep."

She was, quite peacefully, on the polished gray tile of the floor, and Feinman and D'Arcy, coming in together, stopped and stared.

He faced them quite cool and steady, in the little interrogation room crowded with Maddox, Lyons, Rodriguez; his hands folded on the small table, he said urbanely, "Of course it will all have to come out now. I can't say how sorry I am that it has all come to this." He was still the neat, unobtrusive, formally dressed bank teller, and it was easy to understand how, on the one hand, the busy clerks had trustingly accepted his I.D., and on the other, hadn't remembered clearly what he looked like.

He looked down at his hands and sighed. "When we heard about Karen, and Nora Cooke mentioned that she'd had a quarrel with a boy friend, I took it for granted—it never entered my head that Mrs. Lederer had anything to do with that. I suppose Karen had—suspected something."

"We'd like to hear all about it, Mr. Corbett," said Lyons.

"Yes. Of course it's a classic example," said Corbett thoughtfully, "of giving in to temptation. Even a year ago, I don't think I'd have been capable—" He reached to adjust his glasses in a habitual gesture. "I've worked for banks for forty-one years, and I've never stolen a penny or had the impulse to. But I was so deeply in debt after Myra died— Oh, it's no excuse, I know. It started, you see, in such a little way. Tabor came in to cash a check, and carelessly tore off two instead of just the one on top. I noticed it, and the thought just came to me, he would never know it was gone, if I could make a passable copy of his signature—take a hundred, a couple of hundred, and he'd never notice. Well, I did. And I knew I could go on taking a hundred or two every month regularly, and he'd never realize—he never checked statements, and the account was so large—" Corbett brought out a pack of cigarettes. "If, you see, I just had the blank checks." Maddox shoved the ashtray toward him. "Thank you," said Corbett politely. He drew strongly on his cigarette. "I thought about it very seriously. I didn't know Mrs. Lederer well personally, just as a fellow employee, a nice woman—she'd been at the bank twelve years. It was a terrible risk, you can see that. If I had—approached her—and she was the simple honest person she looked, I'd be dismissed from the bank and probably never get another decent job. But I knew she had that crippled boy, and everybody's finding it difficult to make ends meet now—worried about money, who isn't—and it would be so easy, you see. Just a little extra—it couldn't be too much, just a little. A hundred a month for each of us. You see, Mrs. Lederer was in charge of New Accounts, the department which orders all the checks printed."

"Oh, I *see*," said Lyons. "That never—"

"Any client needing more checks would just ask her to put the order in. It's a big printing company, they make up checks for most of the banks anywhere around, millions of checks—private individuals, companies—and it's all a computerized operation, just send a sample blank check along with the order for a hundred or five hundred to be made up, it's automatically fed in and so many copies made. Or, of course, make out an order blank indicating the print style, company name, address, and that goes through automatically too. Nothing for anyone to notice, with the enormous number of blank checks made up every day. The various orders are sent by mail, back to the ordering banks, and of course at our bank Mrs. Lederer was the one to unpack the orders and mail them out to clients."

Lyons said, "My God. So simple when you know. And we've been beating the bushes for a crooked printer. They looked so damned authentic—"

"They *were* authentic," said Corbett with a faint smile. "At least, we couldn't get real checks from the various companies to copy exactly, she simply chose a businesslike-looking style from the print samples, but it was a first-class printing job."

"So you took the gamble," said Maddox. "Did you have any trouble persuading her?"

"She shied a little just at first," said Corbett. "I was nervous about it, naturally. I—approached her in the parking lot one afternoon—we were both late, and it would just look as though we were exchanging small talk, if anyone— But she's an intelligent woman, and she understood the awful temptation, really Tabor almost invited it—and when she said, it wouldn't be much, a couple of hundred a month, nothing to him and it would mean so much to us—I knew it would be all right.

"She just ordered a couple of books of his regular checks, and slipped them out of the order when it came in. But you see, we couldn't put through too many checks. Even Tabor would eventually wake up, and all the checks were going through our branch—I did them at home and just slipped them into the day's accumulation at closing time. There's no indication on a check which teller took it in."

"And you began to get greedy for more," said Rodriguez softly. "Of course you would."

"She was the one who had the idea," said Corbett evenly. He put out his cigarette. "We used to meet in the old Hollywood Cemetery, no one ever goes there and it was absolutely private. And"—he laughed suddenly—"to this day, we never got to using first names. It was her idea, the big department stores, markets, drugstores—names everybody knew. It was so easy for her to get the blank checks, you can see that. She always made up those orders herself, it was part of her job.

"We worked out the idea for the identification together. Of course we both know what kinds of I.D. would be most acceptable anywhere. Her mother, Mrs. Simms, had come to live with her a couple of years ago when she got beyond looking after herself—she died roundabout that time, and Mrs. Lederer had found her old VISA card and the older Sears card among her things. Old ladies hang onto useless objects. They were both years out of date, but that didn't matter for identification purposes. And she thought of Standish, for me, because he knew so many people, so many would know he had carried a VISA card and could have applied for the new one. His estate wasn't settled yet, and it wasn't likely that VISA headquarters knew he was dead. The apartment in Seal Beach cost a little something, but the investment was worth it."

"By God, I believe you!" said Lyons.

"I rather enjoyed myself," said Corbett reflectively, "making those checks look so good." His smile was slow and nostalgic. "I'd been bored and at loose ends since Myra died—we never had any family. If you've ever noticed, most checks on big companies show the most execrable signatures—an oversized capital and a long squiggle with a flourish at the end, and *Wrigley T. Zilch, Chief Accountant,* or something like that." Corbett was, Maddox felt suddenly, revealing more of his essential personality than he ever had to anyone, those long correct years of routine days at the bank, handling other people's money. "The main thing, of course, was that they had to be cashed in other areas. Not that either of us was well known, or active socially, but we couldn't risk going anywhere in the main Hollywood area where these people might possibly be coming into the bank, to recognize us. I cashed a few at a Thrifty a long way down on Vine, but the rest—" That had been enough to bring in the Hollywood precinct. "We used to spend Saturdays driving around with them—after I'd handed over her share, in the cemetery."

"You got around all right," said Lyons grimly.

Corbett took off his glasses and began to polish them on his handkerchief. "It was like going on a drunk. I imagine—I never went in for that. It was all so easy—it went like clockwork, once we had the I.D. It was"—he held the glasses up to check for spots—"exhilarating. All the money. But it was then I began to realize that we couldn't spend it. It isn't easy to spend money without having it known. I couldn't pay off all those debts at once—a bank teller doesn't earn a high salary, and everybody would wonder. Most of my share is stacked in the spare-room closet at home. I bought a couple of new suits, and more expensive steaks occasionally, that's about all. We never discussed that, but she's a very sensible woman and I expect she figured it about as I did. I'm due to retire in three years, and I thought I could build up a fat little nest egg to augment the pension—insurance to make life easier, unless the whole economy collapses."

He looked at his new cigarette, and up to the men who had just arrested him. "Temptation," he said. "Just that one careless check of Tabor's—and it snowballed. My God, how it snowballed!" And he began quietly, infectiously, to laugh and laugh.

And that was Lyons' business; but Karen Hansen belonged exclusively to Hollywood.

Mrs. Lederer slept for twenty-four hours, and awoke her usual competent, sensible self, and was transferred from the hospital to the Wilcox Street jail. She told Daisy that the regular practical nurse would be with her crippled son, and asked that someone go and arrange for him to be taken back to the convalescent home where he'd spent periods before. And then she asked for a Bible. "It's bad enough to put the sin on my own conscience," she said, "but I needn't have made life worse for Johnny, and of course it will be, now."

When Maddox and D'Arcy had her brought into one of the interrogation rooms at the jail, that afternoon, she looked ten years older. "We'd like to hear just what happened, Mrs. Lederer. We have to know, for the court and the District Attorney."

"I'll tell you anything you want to know," she said, "but I think—I think I'd like to have that nice young policewoman—here too." So Sue sat in on that, as she told them just how it had been.

"You see, once we started, it was as if we couldn't stop—it was a kind of madness. All that money coming so easy—even if we couldn't spend much of it. Just put in an order for the checks to be printed up, and when they came in the mail put them aside to pass on to Mr. Corbett. I suppose I'd got careless about that—well, it wasn't often I had to put in an order, you know. I'd get fifty or a hundred at once, more, and after a while Mr. Corbett didn't have to use so many to practice on. Because, you see, it was the checks that Karen noticed. The tellers do sometimes come over to my side of the bank, for one reason or another, and that day"—she looked at Maddox—"it was the day you came, about those checks of Mr. Tabor's—the mail had just come that morning, and there were quite a lot of boxes of checks for regular clients, and in with them was another box of Robinson's checks. When I came across those, I put them aside and when I was finished unpacking the big box I took those back to my desk and just opened the box to check on the printing job, and put them in my handbag—and when I looked up, Karen was right there with a queer look on her face, she'd come across with a check on somebody's VISA card, to check the account number. If I'd thought of it, I'd have said right away that they were my own checks, I'd run out the week before and reordered—but I didn't think of it, and I could tell she was suspicious. The rest of that day, every now and then I saw her looking at me that queer way, and I was afraid—oh, I was terribly afraid! If she'd seen anything to prove—it would all come out, and we'd go to jail, and nobody to take care of Johnny—I knew I had to do something. And I knew too she wouldn't find it easy to believe I was a criminal—she'd known me so long, I'd been at the bank so long, and in charge of a department too. I had to find out—if she knew anything definite. I managed to leave at the same time, when the bank was closing, and I followed her to her car—it was on one side of the lot, no others right there. And I tried just to sound ordinary and friendly, I said I'd seen her wondering about the boxes of checks, as if she thought it was funny I was taking them, but they were my own, I'd just ordered some. And she looked at me—as if she'd never seen me before—and she said, 'Mrs. Lederer, those were checks for Robinson's Department Store, I saw the top one, and they don't have an account here.' So she had—"

Mrs. Lederer hugged herself as if she was cold, looking back to that minute. "You see, she wouldn't have known anything about—all the forged checks cashed all over the city—and you'd just come that day about Mr. Tabor's checks, she wouldn't have suspected any connection. But she knew there was something wrong, and I knew she'd think it

over and do something about it. On Monday. Go to Mr. Dewberry."
Mrs. Lederer drew a long breath.
"Take your time," said Sue. "There's no hurry."
"I was so frightened. So frightened of what she could make happen.
I just seemed to think like lightning. I knew she hadn't any family
here, and probably lived alone. And I pretended I'd forgotten my keys
and went back, and Mike—the security guard—was just locking up and
let me back in. I knew just where to look in the personnel files, it
didn't take me a minute to get her address. And that night, I found a
big heavy wrench in the garage, and it just fit into a big summer tote
bag—and I went there—and she let me in. I said I wanted to explain to
her about the checks, that there wasn't anything wrong, and she said
she'd be glad if I could do that because she'd been worrying about it.
I'd brought a letter from my sister, her writing is terrible, and I handed
it to Karen and said read that, it'll explain everything. We were standing in the middle of the room, she hadn't asked me to sit down. And
she took the letter. And that gave me time to get out the wrench and
hit her as hard as I could." Mrs. Lederer was silent for a moment and
then went on. "I made sure she was dead. So I was safe—everything
was safe again. I came away. And it wasn't until I was back in my car
that I began to realize it. What had happened. What I'd done." She
raised her eyes to Sue's. "Murder. I'd done a murder. And we couldn't
spend much of the money at all. And ever—since then," said Mrs.
Lederer painfully, "I've been wishing that I'd killed myself instead. It
would have been—more sensible."

They would both probably be arraigned, Mrs. Lederer on the two
counts, sometime next week. Barlow, still on crutches, was coming up
for arraignment on Monday. And at least the Metro Squad was gone.
Now they could wait for the cockroaches to start crawling back out of
the woodwork. The paperwork on the bogus-check caper was all for
Lyons' office, but there would still be some for Hollywood to do to as-
semble all the background facts on the homicide, for the D.A.'s office.
Karen's family in Vallejo had been notified on Tuesday, and on
Thursday somebody had come for the body; it had been sent back to
her home for burial.
The girl found in the alley hadn't been identified yet, but they had
had an autopsy report: she'd had an overdose of barbiturates.
Lewis had evidently, belatedly, realized that he was carrying a no-

ticeable license tag. Dobson's car had been found parked in a lot on Sunset. There had been two cars stolen within a radius of six blocks in the next two hours, but also six others within a radius of a couple of miles by four hours after that, and they had been set back a long way on that hunt: now, they just didn't know what he was driving. The flyers with his mug shot were still out county-wide; that might help.

They cleaned up two more heists and shoved two more in Pending by that Monday.

And on Tuesday afternoon about three o'clock Rinehart brought in a UPS driver, Ed Busch, and two teen-age girls. Busch was sneezing and coughing and blowing his nose, and he told Sue and Rodriguez that he felt like hell, he was coming down with summer flu, so he brought the truck in early and went home. His wife worked too, and when he came into the house he'd found these damn kids just getting out a bedroom window with some of his wife's jewelry and a transistor radio. Girls yet, he said, sneezing explosively. He'd grabbed them and locked them in a closet and called the cops. He signed the complaint form and went out coughing his head off.

The girls were Dorinda Lynch and Paula Barker, and they were both juniors at Hollywood High. They looked at the detectives both defiantly and sullenly and said it had all been for kicks, some boys had dared them, and it was easy, a lot of places you could get in a back window or use a shim on a back door. They'd read about that one in some old murder mystery, they said, and it worked just great.

"And you can't do anything to us," said Dorinda triumphantly. "We aren't eighteen yet." How quickly they learned that one; and unfortunately it was true. They'd be put on probation until they turned eighteen, and if and when they got into trouble again they'd get another slap on the wrist, and again: until they got involved in some serious felony, if that happened. Neither of them struck Daisy or Sue as a likely candidate for repentance.

Daisy took them over to jail, and they wouldn't be there long. Sue started trying to call the parents to let them know where their offspring were. "What do you want to bet," she said, "that they're the kind who'll come screaming down to complain that we're picking on their poor mischievous little children?"

Rodriguez said, "Let's just hope to God Busch hasn't left flu germs all over the office."

Brougham and Donaldson were called out at ten o'clock to what looked like a mugging. A squad car man had spotted a body on the sidewalk along Lexington Avenue, and it looked as if he'd been beaten up and robbed—an elderly man in nondescript clothes. There wasn't anything on him but a handkerchief and a book of matches, and he was unconscious, breathing stertorously. They called an ambulance, and the squad went back on tour, and as Brougham put his hand on the car door he stopped as if he'd been shot and said loudly, "B-girls!"

"What?" said Donaldson.

"B-girls—it just came to me, Ken—that mark on that girl's hand. The girls working out of bars, getting the drinks bought for them, they wear some mark like that so the bartender'll know, and not hand out the cold tea with a maraschino cherry to a regular customer."

"My God, sure," said Donaldson. "It ought to have come to both of us before. Leave a note for the day watch."

At twelve-fifty on Wednesday, Patrolman Percy Everard was cruising down La Brea, and as he caught the light at a corner he was reaching for the mike. There was a fair-to-middling coffee shop in the next block. The parking lot to one side and in back of it was fairly full, but he found a slot in the rear, activated the mike, and called in a Code Seven, so they wouldn't try to get him for anything while he had lunch.

He walked around to the double doors at the entrance, pushed them open, and came face to face with Gary Lewis standing at the cashier's desk collecting his change.

Everard thought his mind had never moved so fast in his life. Lewis had looked up as the door opened, and he had seen the uniform. Everard hadn't any idea whether his expression had betrayed recognition of Lewis, but he didn't think so—it had happened too fast. So his mind moved, and he let his gaze pass uninterestedly beyond Lewis to the counter and stools, and he reached into his side pocket, stopped and said to himself, "Hell, I forgot my cigarettes—" and he turned and went out unhurriedly.

He hoped it would work. In thirty seconds he could be back at the squad and on the mike. But there were windows down most of the side of the building, and Lewis could be watching him, if he were suspicious. Everard sauntered casually from the double doors around the side of the building. When he passed the last window he broke into a run, and dived for the squad on the passenger side, looking back the way he had come as he groped for the mike, in case Lewis had suspected—

A man and a woman and three children came out the double doors and started across the parking lot toward a car at the side.

Suddenly Lewis was there, with them between him and Everard. He knew where to look for Everard; he'd been watching the window. He had a gun in his right hand.

The kids were laughing and skipping around the two adults.

It was dinned into you at the Academy—*Think of the citizens first*— Everard plunged out of the squad and ran. He ran deliberately, knowing that Lewis' gun would follow him, away from the unaware citizens. He drew the .38 Police Positive, and the first bullet spanged past his shoulder and hit a car. There was a big dumpster for refuse at the back of the coffee shop, cover of a sort, and he dived for it.

He felt the slug bite into his back and was knocked sprawling by the side of the dumpster, but he rolled around and got to his knees. He had never fired a gun at a human target; he'd never had to draw it on the job; but you had to keep up a score on the range.

Lewis was coming, mouthing meaningless obscenities, the gun jerked in his hand and Everard felt that slug slam him right in mid-chest but he had already aimed and the .38 had a light pull— The last thing he saw was Lewis's contorted grimace as he started to go down.

When Gonzales and Cassidy got there, with red light and siren, five minutes later, there were just two dead men in the bright sunlight on the dirty cement of the parking lot, and a crowd standing silent at a little distance.

The press didn't have much to say about that, of course. There were three nice paragraphs in the *Herald,* and a couple of lines on a back page of the *Times.* Everard was no superstar, and Lewis only a common criminal with an ordinary pedigree.

There was the usual turnout for the funeral on the following Friday, with the motorcycle squads riding escort, and the chief there, and a lot of uniforms showing in the crowd at the church, and the flag on the coffin. There would be another name in gold leaf on the Honor Roll in the lobby at Parker Center.

Young Mrs. Everard was pretty obviously expecting a baby. There were two older couples with her, probably their parents. When the chief handed her the folded flag she put her head down on it and began to cry again.

But the world was still there to be coped with, and the job to do, and the Hollywood men went back to their endless routine on the thankless job because somebody had to do it.

June came in as usual with a respite of the first heat, and it was overcast and hazy on Thursday morning. Maddox added cream to his coffee and said to Sue, "You're taking the day off. It's all right, I told the office yesterday."

"Oh, you did. Why?"

"We're going someplace to get a dog." He grinned at her. "Now don't get your back up at me. I don't very often come the lord and master over you, do I?"

"Well, no," said Sue. "You're quite reasonable as a rule, for a man. But if you've gone behind our backs— What have you been up to? I didn't know you had any opinions about dogs."

"I've acquired one. I'll tell you both about it on the way."

"The man seems to have made up his mind about something," said Margaret, amused.

"Come on, come on, finish your breakfast and get ready. We're all going," said Maddox. "To pick up the dog and bring him home."

"You've already bought— Ivor, for heaven's sake! You know what it is," said Sue to her mother. "He's worried about burglars, and after us weeping at each other the other night, he's afraid we'll never take the initiative, so he's bullying us into it. All right." She looked at Maddox apprehensively. "Break the news. I guess we can take it. You've bought a Dobe."

"No," said Maddox. "They're not fierce enough." Sue just shut her eyes.

"I'm afraid to hear any more. Can I ask what you paid for it?"

"I haven't paid for it yet, but we're getting a five-hundred-dollar dog for seventy-five bucks."

"Oh no, please," said Sue faintly. "One of these fly-by-night back-yard breeders has been conning him. Ivor, you don't know anything about dogs. Really, you'd better let Mother and me—"

"Too late, we're going out to Norwalk to pick up this one."

He had spent some time on the phone yesterday with a Mrs. Murray, of that Akita Rescue League. They seemed to be pretty damned fussy about letting people adopt their dogs, and she'd asked all sorts of questions. He'd had to tell her about their life styles, and the size of the yard, and their attitude to dogs in general. She had seemed impressed that he and Sue were LAPD officers, and relieved that Sue and Margaret had always had dogs and knew about feeding them and shots and so on. She'd approved of the big back yard too, and when she asked him how he'd heard about them and got interested, he told her about Kaji, and thought she'd never stop laughing.

But he thought the girls had better be forewarned, and told them all about it on the way. The boarding kennel was on a green half acre with some old trees, and Mrs. Murray turned out to be young and rather pretty. She took them into a little office and introduced them to a tall raw-boned woman, Miss Dale. "We've decided to let you have a very special dog, Sergeant Maddox. You know, we try to be very careful about getting the best homes possible, and after all you told me I think—and so does Jane—we're going to let you have Tama. Now remember, it's conditional—if you don't get along with the dog, or there's any problem, or for any reason you can't keep him, we want him back. But I really think you might give him just the right home."

"Beautiful temperament," said Miss Dale gruffly. "You be good to'm. Never a cross word before."

"He's not one of our abandoned ones, you see. He belonged to Miss Blaine—she was one of our faithful supporters. She hadn't any relatives, and it was a shock to all of us when she had the heart attack, she was only fifty-three. But he's a young dog, just a year old, and he should settle down. I do so hope you'll all take to each other. His name means jewel, you know."

"Well, let's have a look," said Maddox briskly.

"Bring him out side yard," mumbled Miss Dale. They all went outside.

When Miss Dale came out the back door with the dog on a lead, Maddox was interested to see—Joan Reeves had told him they came all colors—that this one was, you could only call it tortoise-shell colored: a dark brindle with red-gold stripes. He had one very small white spot on his chest, and he was about as big as Kaji, with the same massive head.

"My good heavens," said Sue. The dog gave her his sinister oriental stare. She had been warned, but she looked startled. "I do see what you mean." She put out a hesitant hand and the dog sniffed, gave it a casual lick, and moved his brush of tail, and smiled up at her.

"Another actor," said Maddox. Tama smelled him carefully, allowed his ears to be scratched with a more emphatic wag of appreciation.

"Good heavens, he *is* big," said Margaret. Tama lifted his head at once and moved over to her. He put his wet black nose against her skirt and sniffed. The other people were all right, said his tail, but here was Somebody Important. He uttered a long satisfied bass *wurf* and stood up on his hind legs and put his paws on her shoulders. She clutched him around the middle to keep her balance, and Tama began to wash her face enthusiastically.

The Maddoxes burst out laughing. "Well, you have made a hit, darling," said Sue. "Good Lord, Ivor, he is a monster—"

"Our own private monster," said Maddox.

"Now if you have any questions or difficulties, don't hesitate to call us, and do let us know how he settles down, and remember—"

"I have a hunch," said Maddox, "that we're all going to settle down together just fine."

Tama evidently thought so too. He sprawled on the back seat with his head in Margaret's lap, and snored gently all the way home.

The body of the B-girl was never identified, and presently the city buried her. They had two homicides and the heists, and the Warden murder was slowly edging toward the Pending file; it was still officially open but to all intents and purposes dead. The press was still asking questions occasionally, but Jan Warden would probably, thought Maddox, have been astonished and furious to know how quickly she'd been forgotten.

One homicide got solved and one never would be. They dropped on one heister out of ten; and another body showed up on a Tuesday night in the middle of June. Maddox was reading Brougham's initial report on it the next day when unexpectedly the little director Jerry Ross invaded the office, beard and incipient paunch waggling, and Maddox looked at him in surprise.

"Well, what can we do for you, Mr. Ross?"

"Listen," said Ross urgently, "did you abscond with all Jan's scripts? I've been hunting high and low for the damned things, they've got to be somewhere, and I thought she'd taken them home with her. I got the lawyer to let me in there, but they're nowhere. And that fat housekeeper said the police took away some of her stuff—I don't know what the hell the fuzz would want with marked scripts, but—"

"No scripts, Mr. Ross. Sorry."

"Hell, hell, hell," said Ross without emphasis. "This is *the* worst damned mishmash—everything going wrong. Everything."

"The scripts of the new TV series. Marked?"

"Oh, for God's sake, marked for her part—cues and action and— Never mind. Take six typists a week," said Ross, "but I'm not paying the bill, thank God."

"It's going back in production?"

"Which is crazy," said Ross. "June. *June.* We'll be lucky to get twelve episodes canned by September. Well, it's probably going to bomb in mid-season anyway, but if it doesn't— Expect us to go on shooting ahead of episodes getting aired! My God. The only thing is, this is a good little girl, got a lot of potential, and she's smarter than Jan. I'd like to give her a good send-off, she's only had supporting parts and vignettes. But damn it, we'll never meet schedule— June!"

"So you got a replacement for Jan Warden."

"A good girl—takes direction fine—Andrea Forcell. Not a big name yet but the P.R. men are working on it, with our Ringo egging 'em on."

"Another of Mr. Wells's clients."

"Yep. Even if this thing does bomb, they'll get her built up, get her ready for top place in something next season. Si Kleinert's got a script idea under his hat I'd like a hand in—but, God, I don't know if Ringo'd let her do anything that offbeat. And he's got a nose, all right—an instinct. Like he's got an instinct for picking the one gorgeous lovely out of a hundred who's got something enough different to build the image on. Even if he's one of our gay boys."

Maddox laid down the report. "Wells?" You could never tell on looks, of course.

"Oh, gay all the way, friend. So you don't know anything about those scripts? What the hell the damned girl did with— Well, that's that. Just one more disaster." He bounced out, and Maddox swiveled around and looked at Rodriguez.

"And isn't that interesting," said Rodriguez, smoothing his mustache. "Don't tell me that thing's going to come to life again."

"What do you think?"

"I think we have a little session with Ringo Wells. To ask about—"

"Yes, that's just what," said Maddox.

He sat behind the eight-foot desk with the wall of window behind him, and for a moment as they came in he didn't move, and then gave them his jolly smile.

"I'm just a little occupied today, Sergeant, but I can make a few minutes for you."

"That may be all it'll take," said Maddox, and sat down in one of the Danish chairs. Rodriguez took the other one. "You told us before, Mr. Wells, that the night Jan Warden was killed you took Miss Sheri Wynn home and spent the night with her. That was a lie, wasn't it? Because you don't seem to be interested in the females that way."

Wells sat immobile for a moment, and he looked at them speculatively with his cold agate-colored eyes, which were such an incongruous contrast with the perpetual jolly smile, and then he uttered a short laugh. "So you finally caught up, did you? One has to do one's best for one's clients—and at the time she was a client, still with a little something to sell. If she was slipping. But I'd got her that contract with Maxim, and if she'd behaved that might have opened the door to a few more things before she was definitely through and useless. But forget it —she's on the way out, she's out now. Next year, who ever heard of her? She's been nothing but trouble the last couple of years, thinks she can get away with anything, and it's no never mind if you're a little name or a big name, you don't get away forever with coming to work when you feel like it, and blowing lines and cues and picking fights with everybody on the set. Producers take so much, and bingo. Maxim's had enough, he's kicked her out of the picture—and I don't blame him, it's worth it to him to pay out the rest of her contract and get her out of his hair. And that is the end—because reputations get around, and she's poison, she'll never get another contract. I'd have kept quiet—what's in it either way for little Ringo?—but, the fuzz starting to catch up, so I'll throw her to the wolves. I knew she was the one took Jan off. She was really mad at her that night, it was the first time she'd seen Jan since the big break, and she'd been brooding over that ever since. 'Newcomers' was the best part she'd ever had, and she knew it wasn't likely she'd ever get another chance like that. When she started screaming at Jan that night, she kept yelling, I'd like to cut up your face so nobody'd want to look at you again. So when you tell me Jan's been cut up, I knew. But at the time she was worth a little something to me."

"I see," said Maddox gently. "You do have your own point of view, Mr. Wells."

"She's hitting the bottle these days, and I wouldn't doubt the dope bit too. She knows she's had whatever she'll ever have in this game. And right now she's ten per cent of nothing to me. If you ask her the right way," said Wells, "she might even decide to tell you about it."

They left him reaching for the contract he'd laid down when they came in.

"It might be awfully good publicity," said Sheri Wynn. "There's something about a girl on trial, the judge and jury and all. I could wear black all the time and maybe just one string of pearls." Her shallow little heart-shaped face wore a thoughtful look.

Maddox exchanged a glance with Rodriguez. She hadn't taken in a quarter of what he'd said, about the probable lab evidence still to be found (there'd have been blood carried into her car, and Jan Warden's was an unusual type, AB, the clothes she had worn, those unknown prints which might turn out to be hers), or the evidence to be had from the people who had heard her that night.

She was older, seen close up, than they had thought, beginning to look a little raddled. Hitting the bottle, said Wells, and she looked it; she was sober at the moment, but her clawlike little hands with the pointed red nails trembled as she lit a cigarette. Her kind of surface prettiness was the sort which faded early, and there was no force of character to take its place, not even that elusive thing, charm.

This was an expensive apartment in Bel Air, and this room at least was in the wildest disorder, women's magazines scattered all over furniture and floor, dirty plates and glasses on the big color TV and coffee table, and in the door to the kitchen past a tiny dining area, a bottle of wine smashed on the floor and the stain like blood on the carpet.

"I didn't mean to kill her, you know. I was surprised when Ringo said she was dead. I just wanted to scratch her eyes out, cut up that face of hers—her so damned smug—didn't care who she kicked in the teeth—"

"We'd be interested to hear about it, Miss Wynn," said Rodriguez.

"Oh, well. If you know it was me—and it might be pretty good publicity, I don't care what Ringo said. I never meant to kill her, I don't know how I did. It was just a little knife I took from the kitchen, not very big."

"Did you have much to drink at the restaurant?"

"No, Ringo wouldn't let me, and I was all nervous and uptight—seeing her again. When he left me off here, I had a couple of drinks, and I kept getting madder and madder, thinking about her. Her! I wanted to cut up her face good—and I went out and got my car and went up there—"

"How," asked Maddox, "did you get into the house?"

"Oh, that," said Sheri Wynn, and laughed. "That was why I thought about it at all. Nobody knew about it, but I had a key to that. house. Greg Ryan gave me a key when we had a little thing going about five years ago. I had to hunt for it, but I finally found it in a bag I hadn't carried in years. I don't throw things away much. And I changed my clothes, put on slacks and flats to get up there quiet from the road. I guess it was about one-thirty when I got up there, and I knew where her bedroom was. She was asleep— I just looked at her awhile, it was dark but I could *see* her face, that bitch, everybody slobbering over her and it was just smart publicity and Ringo's fast talk that put her where she was, she was a nothing, but she could stab me in the back and walk away laughing— I was going to cut up her face for her." She stopped. She said, "I got to have a drink," and went out to the kitchen, came back with a bottle of vodka and a glass, and poured it straight.

"Miss Wynn—" said Rodriguez. Maddox shrugged at him. She was going to get a charge of involuntary manslaughter anyway and it wouldn't make much difference if the defense attorney brought it out that she'd been drinking when detectives questioned her. Rodriguez shrugged back eloquently, and his dark eyes were cynical.

"*All that blood!*" she said. "All of a sudden! Oh, my God, it was—it was like a fountain or something—" She gulped vodka. "I don't know how I got home, I was shaking all over—" She poured more vodka into her glass. "I never meant to kill her. When I stabbed her first she jumped up in bed and knocked against the headboard, she didn't try to fight me or anything, but the next I knew there was all that blood—"

She didn't seem to remember what she'd done with her clothes. They didn't know if there was maid service here, or about trash collection; there were a lot of things they'd be asking about, and looking for. But the lab should be able to turn some concrete evidence.

Maddox told her she'd have to come with them; she was under arrest. She said, a little slurred, "It might be good publicity. I got to see what Ringo thinks before I decide—but I forgot, he said—not a client anymore—"

Maddox got home a little late that night. It had been Sue's day off. He left the Maserati in the front driveway and went through the chain-link driveway gate. Margaret's car and Sue's were parked in the double garage.

There was one short bass utterance from the house to acknowledge his arrival. He went in by the service porch. Margaret was in the kitchen, supervising something on the stove. Tama came to him, tail moving pleasedly, to welcome the rest of the family home. He gave Maddox's hand a casual swipe of the tongue and went back to his usual place when Margaret was in the kitchen, under the table. His usual places were about five feet from wherever Margaret happened to be, though he was fond of Sue and approved her special way of massaging his stomach which did get itchy in warm weather. But as far as Tama was concerned, Margaret was the head of the household.

Maddox ripped off his tie and unbuttoned his shirt, going down to the living room. Sue would be interested to hear that they had, unexpectedly, closed out the Warden thing. The press would be around again, damn it. There was another new homicide to work, and doubtless there'd be something new down tomorrow. But for the moment, he could relax at home with his family and forget the thankless job.